CHAPTER 1

TRISTAN

"N O, YOU'RE BEING too subtle," Jessie told Aurora, Alpha Austin Steele's niece.

They all sat in the front room of Ivy House, empty coffee cups in hand, having a conversation about Edgar's new attack flowers. The vampire was on version four or five or—Tristan had lost count after flower versions Y and T. No one was quite sure if Edgar realized the alphabet and number systems were different, or if he knew the alphabet at all.

Aurora angled her head a bit more, her meaning plain. *I just don't get it.*

Jessie's face scrunched up, and everything tensed. *What the hell is she trying to tell me???*

Tristan hid a grin. Well, the meaning was plain *to him.*

Aurora was in charge of helping Jessie learn body language in anticipation of meeting shifter packs, headed up by stoic alphas that took every subtle body tic as a complete sentence. Being Austin's mate and the co-leader of this territory, Jessie would need to sit in on the meetings and help bring these new packs into the convocation, a merging of various species and groups of magical people that could hopefully push back against the corrupt Mages Guild and their biggest ally, Momar.

These alphas wouldn't be as lenient with Jessie as Alpha Steele was, or as patient as Alpha Kingsley Baraza, Austin's brother. Many likely wouldn't be as reasonable as the alpha they'd met in Los Angeles, either. These would be shifters at the top of the power scale who wouldn't want their rule and command overshadowed by a new, made-up faction, regardless of the aid they'd provided Kingsley. Or so the alpha rumor mill claimed.

Jessie would have to show that even though she was a past Jane—a non-magical person—and now a gar-goyle, she still understood and respected shifter culture. Which wouldn't usually be hard for her…except for the body language aspect. That was…tough going, it seemed.

A smile budded on Aurora's lips. *It's funny when you get annoyed.*

Jessie's brow crumpled. *Smiling isn't allowed.*

"You're still advertising your every thought," Auro-

Magical Midlife
Rescue

ALSO BY K.F. BREENE

MAGICAL MIDLIFE RESCUE

BY K.F. BREENE

ra told her patiently. "Literally, every single one. Even if you don't know what I'm saying with my body, you need to keep your thoughts and emotions buttoned up. It's like poker. Remember when you taught me poker?"

Jessie sighed and leaned back. *Defeated.* "I do, yes. As I recall, you took all my money."

Aurora laughed, very free and expressive with Jessie—for a shifter, at least. She never showed this side of herself to anyone else, not even her uncle. Jessie had a way of thawing even the hardest, most severely trained people.

Not for the first time, Tristan wondered if Jessie shouldn't just stay a free spirit. Respecting shifter culture was one thing, but she shouldn't have to bow to it. She was looser than even a gargoyle cairn leader with her crew, and that worked. She managed a *lot* of power with a distinct style of leadership. Changing who she was…*minimized* how well her style worked. Conformity wasn't her strong suit—in Tristan's opinion, anyway.

Then again, shifters were a rule-based, prickly breed. This was Alpha Steele's show. He'd know what might work best to get other packs on his side.

"I think the answer is Xanax," Jessie said, and leaned forward to put her mug on the coffee table. She paused when she didn't see a coaster.

"Here." Tristan dug into his jeans pocket and pulled

out a scrunched, oblong doily. Edgar had grown worlds better at making flowers but somehow worse at the doilies. He really needed to find a new hobby for the quiet hours of the night. "Use this," he said, and tossed it onto the coffee table in front of her.

She hesitated as she stared down at the craft item, her gaze tracing the large hole in the design and the loose strands of fabric making up the other side. *Bewildered. Resigned.*

Aurora started laughing again.

"When Mr. Tom berates me for this"—she set her mug on top of it and glanced at Tristan—"I'm blaming you."

"Blame Niamh," he replied, leaning away and throwing an arm over the back of the couch. He made sure to bend his elbow to keep his hand from resting behind Jessie's person. If he didn't, in shifter culture it would hint at a claim, despite how far apart they were sitting. He was practicing shifter rules as well, and a faux pas like *that* wouldn't be easily forgiven.

Aurora looked over at him with a delicately curved eyebrow. *Questioning.*

He still wasn't great at nuances. Brochan, Austin's shifter beta, probably would've read a novel within her posture.

"Right, *why* do you have Edgar's doilies in your

pocket?" Jessie asked.

"Yay!" Aurora clapped at her. "You got it!"

"I mean...you were being pretty obvious about it," Jessie replied, back to sagging against the couch.

Tristan moved his hand a little further away from Jessie. "Not all *that* obvious."

"Not at all obvious," Aurora said supportively. She might have Alpha Steele's wild streak and fire, but she had her dad's patient and levelheaded way when in a teaching role. She'd be one *hell* of an alpha someday, especially since she watched everything Alpha Steele and Brochan did. She was eager to learn and quick to apply. "I'm now challenging Tristan's grasp of body mechanics. I'm just as expressive with him as I am with most shifters."

Tristan preened, shaking his shoulders and ruffling the ends of his wings where they draped over the edge of the couch.

A tiny crease at the corners of Aurora's mouth and a slight relaxing of her shoulders were the only indications she gave of thinking that was cute or funny. And then she shook her head and bent to put her mug down as well.

He threw out another doily.

"If Mr. Tom doesn't want doilies around the house, he shouldn't keep moving the coasters," she mused before sitting back and looking Tristan's way. Her eyes kindled with cunning intelligence as she tried to piece something together. She did that a lot with gargoyles, trying as she was to learn his culture as they tried to learn hers. "Would you preen with anyone, or just because it's Jessie and her family?"

A soft glow of warmth radiated from Jessie to accentuate her pleased smile. She loved the addition of Alpha's Steele's family into her circle. It was clearly an extension of the incredible love she had for the man himself.

The same glow immediately infused Aurora. She seemed to feel the same, cherishing her uncle being back in her life after a difficult separation and loving Jessie like a sister. It was very cute, the two of them.

Actually, Tristan mused, the whole dynamic of this house and its inhabitants was cute—but with bonds as strong as the roots of an oak, and just as deep. The residents would die for each other, and they'd proven it. Their odd little family was a better core of an army than he'd ever seen. If they could continue to grow the convocation, the corrupt mages wouldn't stand a chance.

If.

Aurora quirked her eyebrow at him in a different way. *I asked you a question...*

She might as well have been tapping her foot.

"Oh, sorry, I was waiting for the family love-fest to subside," Tristan said with a grin. "I'd show pride—"

"You preened," she interrupted. "You basically flicked your hair and batted your eyelashes."

He laughed. "I'd *show pride* with most people, and *preen* with other gargoyles and certain ladies…"

"I'm one of those ladies?" Her eyes shuttered, and her body tightened with unease. He didn't miss her slight flush, though. The unease wasn't because of his notice, but because of her response to his notice.

Aurora was a lady who needed to get out more. Who needed to sow her wild oats and break a few hearts.

He made a mental note to talk with Jasper and Ulric about it. They'd help her carve out more time for play. She worked too much.

"…and gentlemen," he finished with a smirk. "And yes, you are one of those ladies. As is Jessie. As is Niamh. It's not in any way sexual. It's not flirting, it's just…" He struggled for how to explain it. "It's adding a little silliness when showing pride. I was paying you respect by being tickled that you should praise me. Like a dog wagging its tail."

Her stare was utterly expressionless. "Your confidence, even when essentially calling yourself a happy dog, is inspiring. Why only *some* people?"

"Most ladies enjoy when a man acts silly. Guys are a harder sell, especially shifters. They're too wrapped up in being"—he did bunny ears with his fingers—"macho. A lot of gargoyles aren't worried about that, though. We're expressive. We enjoy using our bodies." His eyes darkened. "In all things…"

Her flush increased, and she looked away. He laughed as Jessie rolled her eyes.

"Don't mind him." Jessie waved him away. "He doesn't have Nessa here to tease all the time, so he's spreading it around to everyone else."

Tristan tried to stop his thoughts from skittering away to Nessa—that beautiful deathwatch angel mage—and his worry over her mental well-being. His worry at what she was resigning herself to do without help. She'd cut them all off and disappeared into the shadows, always a step ahead of him and Niamh. For the past month, he hadn't been able to track her down. His growing concern that there was a problem was haunting his dreams.

Aurora's gaze found him again, her eyes piercing and direct. Reading him.

He let her. He had many things to hide, but his affection for that broken, radiant, intelligent woman wasn't one of them. She might never give in to him, but if she could be safe and secure, happy, he'd consider it a win. She deserved that. *At least* that.

Aurora switched gears, for which he was grateful. He needed the distraction.

"So, you wouldn't preen with most shifters, then?" she said. "Because of the cultural differences?"

Jessie leaned forward, eyes narrowed, watching them both closely. She was still trying to read the cues.

"Most gargoyles would preen," he said, "because they don't care about the cultural differences. That's why there has been such a problem acclimating the two groups within this territory. Lots of aggression and challenges. But me in particular…" He shrugged. "It's complicated."

Aurora's huff was barely noticeable. He was frustrating her.

"There's no point in trying to hide your smile— you're showing it in your body," Jessie told Tristan, smirking.

"Pretty obviously, yes," Aurora grumbled.

He laughed, checking his watch. "Basically, if it would incite a challenge, I wouldn't do it unless I could dominate the other party."

"So, you wouldn't preen with Uncle Auzzie?"

He hesitated. "Okay, yes, in certain situations when he's relaxed, I would. He'd find it funny. He understands and enjoys gargoyle culture better than any other shifter I've met—even you, with all your questions."

Her slightly narrowed eyes made his grin spread. As an alpha's daughter, she wasn't used to teasing.

"What about Brochan, then?" she asked.

Tristan pulled his lips to the side in thought. "Not ever, I don't think. He wouldn't challenge me, for many reasons, but he wouldn't appreciate the expressiveness. It would make him uncomfortable, and that guy is far too uncomfortable with his life as it is. I try to stay respectful with him as much as possible and adhere to the rules he understands."

Jessie smiled and reached up to rub his forearm, pleased. She liked when people showed kindness to each other and rewarded it with unspoken praise. It was effective and welcomed, but the touch went against shifter protocol. Too buttoned up, that culture. They were missing the finer things in life.

He casually altered his position so that he wasn't within reaching distance. Practice.

Aurora's slight inclination of her head said she respected his move. Or maybe his answer? It was hard to tell.

"How did Uncle Auzzie manage to learn gargoyle culture in such a short time?" she asked as Naomi, her great-grandma, strode in. Shifters, like gargoyles, had longer life spans than their non-magical or mage counterparts.

"Ah, Jessie, there you are." Naomi stopped a short distance away. Her posture was perfect, her movements brusque and no-nonsense, and no emotion was on display. Talk about buttoned up. She had no intention of relaxing, *ever*. "I came across a purchase order, we'll call it, that isn't mine."

The last word was clipped as her gaze darted to first one doily, then the other. Her disapproval was plain.

"It was Niamh," Jessie said automatically, her eyes slightly rounded and her eyebrows raised. She looked like a kid who'd gotten her hand stuck in a cookie jar.

Naomi's eyes flickered to Tristan, the glance barely noticeable. She handed a slip of paper to Jessie, then pointed at the document. "For that salary, he'd need to work miracles."

Jessie's brow furrowed as she looked at the paper. "What is this? Or...*who* is this, I guess."

Tristan leaned closer to see. What appeared to be half a résumé was copied onto a page with some sort of police report. At the bottom of the mishmash was a yellow sticky note with a very large dollar amount.

"A...computer expert?" Tristan asked, unable to see the details.

"A hacker, I think," Naomi said. "With a criminal

record. Well, I'll just let you—"

"Oh, my, no. No! What—" Mr. Tom bustled into the room, tsking as he did so. He'd spied the doilies. "Miss, now, I'm surprised at you. What on earth could've possessed you to put such a crafting monstrosity under that stylish coffee cup Naomi painstakingly curated for your enjoyment? No. Who brought those god-awful things in here?"

"Niamh did it," Jessie blurted, her face turning red. She was really bad at lying.

"That horrible woman has no appreciation for the fine work done to this house." Mr. Tom grabbed two coasters from another table and switched them out for the doilies. "I swear, if Edgar knew what a practical joke was, I'd think he were playing one on us. Would you like another cup of coffee? We haven't reached the critical hour where it will keep you awake at bedtime. After your efforts with Austin Steele last night, you'll certainly need to catch up on sleep tonight."

Jessie's face turned redder. "No, I'm fine."

"Fantastic. Aurora?" He paused with Jessie's empty cup in hand. "Ah, yes, how wonderful. The infamous blank stare. It's quite rude in mixed company, if you ask me, but of course, no one ever does. Alas, you will actually have to use your words this time. I don't have an inclination to read into the many nuances of an eye twitch."

"The twitch means you've overstayed your welcome in any given conversation," Naomi murmured as she headed for the door.

Mr. Tom pretended not to hear.

"No, thank you," Aurora answered.

"There. You see? Words. The way of the world." Mr. Tom took up her mug as well. "Tristan? I sure hope you won't let me down. It's been a while since you were able to stump me."

Tristan thought for a moment. "How about a mocha Frappuccino, decaf—so that I won't stay up too late—with oat milk, double blended, extra whipped cream, one pump of white mocha, one pump of hazelnut syrup, and topped with cookie crumbles and a light dusting of cinnamon powder."

Mr. Tom studied him, his gaze going far away. "Oat milk…hmm. I'm not sure I have that. And why would I? Regular milk will do you just fine."

He spun on his heel and bustled away.

"Is fussiness another trait of gargoyles?" Aurora asked with a straight face.

Tristan felt his smile grow. "Careful there, Madam Alpha's Daughter. People might catch on that you have a sense of humor hidden away in that straitlaced personality."

Her lips quirked, and she looked away. Maybe she

13

didn't mind teasing after all.

But Jessie hadn't been paying attention to their banter. "Who's trying to hire this person?" she asked on a release of breath, studying the paper Naomi had delivered. "If given half the chance, he'd rob Ivy House blind…"

CHAPTER 2

NIAMH

HER CHRISTMAS PRESENT from Nessa and Sebastian, a basket of rocks the perfect size and shape for throwing at people, sat on Niamh's lap. She slowly rocked, sitting on her porch and enjoying the day. With fewer Dicks and Janes living in the area now, and it being winter, the street was blessedly free of gawking tourists intent on getting a gander at Niamh's neighbor, the hulking form of Ivy House.

Unfortunately, that cursed golem trapped in Betty's basement down the street was making an awful racket. Let the poor wee bugger out once in a while, why didn't she? It could use the Ivy House wood to run around in, chasing or being chased by the basajaunak. Give that animated clay some exercise.

The door to Ivy House opened, and a large shape filled the frame—Tristan, taking a break from shadowing Jessie. That great lummox wasn't filling the late

Nathanial's old role at all. When Tristan predicted she'd tilt left, she went right. He had one helluva flight plan, and he was an exceptional leader for those stubborn-arse gargoyles, but he just couldn't *anticipate* Jessie. On a regular basis, she blew his organization all to hell. It was funny to watch him try to control his frustration with himself.

Niamh had to hand it to him, though—he hadn't given up, and he hadn't slacked off. He continually tried to evolve, to change himself to fit what Jessie needed. It was commendable. Niamh hadn't thought he had it in him to try.

Oh, aye, he'd say it was because he was too stubborn to give up, or he hated to fail, or he didn't want to prove Niamh right that he was too narcissistic for the post, but she'd got his number at this stage. She knew how he ticked. All of those things certainly played a role, but his underlying desire to succeed was because he wanted to help Jessie, plain and simple. He loved her like they all did. He wanted to be an asset to her, to protect her, and to help her achieve greatness. Because of her rarity and her past, she was a misfit in gargoyle culture, as was he. He saw himself in her struggles. He saw her as family, and with each passing day, he was thawing in his mistrust of people in general. He was starting to let Jessie in, and by extension, all of them. That *oul* gargoyle-monster had a heart cloaked in shadows, and it was beating in time to the Ivy House team. As well it should.

It was time he got a wee shove in the right direction, so it was. He'd proven himself. There definitely wasn't anyone as strong and cunning in the air, and it was time for him to finally find his place on their team.

Tristan's gaze zipped directly to her, as though she were his target. He carried a to-go coffee cup as he crossed the grass, heading in her direction. He wasn't a guy who cared about the etiquette of taking the walkway and saving the lawn. Not that she blamed him.

Based on his speed and direct gait, he meant business.

She didn't slow in her rocking as she slipped her hand into the basket. Great throwing rocks, these. Sebastian and Nessa had got it right. After she threw them, she often went and collected them anew. It was better than scouting for others. Work smarter, not harder.

Tristan stepped off the curb and kept coming. She waited until he closed the distance before she gripped a rock, turned in her chair, and let it fly. Her aim was true, but the power of the throw wasn't great. Standing would've helped, but surprise would win the day.

He flinched when the rock was nearly to him, and

his hand darted up, but he was too late. It hit him square on the chest, nearly at his throat. He jerked backward before catching himself and stopped.

Most people would've rubbed the offending spot, but Niamh knew he wouldn't give her the satisfaction. He stared at her menacingly, his arms flared, his wings fluttering dangerously.

She started chuckling while reaching for another rock, an idle threat. He'd react too quickly for her to hit him a second time, and then she'd have to retrieve another rock. Best to bluff this time around.

He picked up the offending rock while taking something out of his jeans pocket. He kept it concealed in his big hand, disappearing the rock into his fist as well. His free hand dipped into the inside of his stylish bomber jacket and grabbed something out of a pocket. After he started walking again, he fiddled with whatever he'd retrieved before lobbing the whole lot back to her.

"What in the…" She snatched it out of the air.

One of Edgar's worst doily efforts was wrapped around her rock and secured with tape.

"Ye've lost the plot now, boy," she said as Tristan walked into her yard and stalled at the bottom step of her porch. "It's bad enough that Edgar makes these things, but now ye walk around with them?"

He smirked. "I figured handing these out as gifts

would darken everyone's day."

"Is this ye crying out for help, then?" She held up the concoction. "Ye haven't got to lead battles or torture mages, so ye go around with these horrible excuses for arts and crafts?"

"Maybe." He shrugged. "Or maybe I'm a giving sort of person."

"Giving sort of person, me arse," she grumbled. "C'mere, what of yer latest efforts to find the mages?"

That knocked him down a peg. He sighed and leaned against the banister, looking out at the bright street in the crisp late morning. "I'm still coming up empty. I enjoy playing in the shadows—"

"Clearly," she muttered, unwrapping the rock and slipping it back into her basket.

"—but I can't hold a candle to Natasha's technology prowess."

"Same as that. What about the essences or energy or yer cosmic connection or whatever la-la ye're always on about?"

His eyes took on a distant look. "I can't properly get in tune with that if I don't have contact. Everything is echoes. Sometimes, I can connect through dreams if the other party reaches halfway. She isn't reaching, though. She doesn't know how—or even of the possibility, probably. I have more books to send her, but I can't find her to send them. I'm reaching from my side, and the dreams…" One of his hands balled into a fist. "They're dark. Full of turmoil. It feels like she's hurting worse than ever. They're both hurting. Emotionally, I mean. Internally." He shook his head. "But honestly…I can't tell if that's her, or if it's my anxiety about her well-being. The emotions feel too…enormous, somehow. I can't get an accurate reading. I need contact with her to sort it all out."

"*Jaysus.* Forget the doilies—ye need to be givin' out crystals and salt lamps."

"I tried that. People seemed too happy about it. I had to stack them all in weird designs in the graveyard to freak them out again."

She huffed out a laugh. "No wonder ye've taken such an interest in those doilies. Ye're following that vampire around the bend. Ye've gone pure fruit loops."

"Yeah. Edgar stole all my marbles."

"Janey Mack," she breathed, grinning. Niamh could get under most people's skin, and she'd made a lifelong art of manipulation, but this gargoyle-monster seemed impervious to her "charms." He purposely muddled the banter so that she couldn't get a toehold to control it. He definitely needed to be at Jessie's side. Jessie was much too gullible. She needed people who couldn't be manipulated to help steer her.

"But seriously, I don't know how she's doing," Tristan said. "How either of them are. I catch traces of acts they might have done, or rumors of where they might be, but nothing comes of it. I thought I was good with technology, but she's far better. And smarter."

Niamh resumed her rocking, feeling the breeze ruffle her hair. Letting her mind drift as it had been. "Aye. She is both of those things." Not even that computer clown they'd hired downtown could keep up with her. Niamh needed someone better.

"The deeds they've claimed—the deaths and whatever—have gotten the right people nervous, did you see that?" he asked. "She's good at working the underbelly, and Sebastian is good at knowing the right pressure points to push at any given time. They're a damn good team."

Niamh didn't slow in rocking. Didn't focus her vision. *Did* shake her head.

"She is great, I'll give her that. But he's a child in that role. He hasn't been at that job—or even on this earth—long enough to *properly* understand motivations. He understands the human condition to a point, but only as it concerns mages. He's blind to most of the magical world and all of the Dick world. Ye can't get a clear picture unless ye're looking at the whole landscape. He's barely fit to be an apprentice; don't even talk to me about being a master. And subtlety? He hasn't a hope of understanding that one! Subtlety is nothing but a tool in the toolbox. Ye need to know when to use it, o'course ye do." She held up a finger. "More importantly, ye need to know when *not* to."

His head swung around, and his eyes glowed brightly. He surveyed her for a long moment before pushing forward up the stairs, and then he sat in the seldom-used second chair. He didn't speak, perhaps having realized he should listen.

"He's implicated us in another one," she said. "Another murder."

Finding out they'd been framed for that first murder had been somewhat of a shock, Niamh had to admit. They'd all known Nessa and Sebastian were trying to play the puppet masters in the mage community, and that they'd do some off-color deeds, but dragging in the convocation like that? Without their knowledge or consent? Jessie had reacted as though slapped. Austin Steele had vibrated with anger. But the bonds of friendship were strong. The services Nessa and Sebastian had rendered the convocation in Kingsley's territory were too great to lose faith in the mages so quickly. It had been left to Niamh to analyze the situation and find a reason the mages might've set them up.

And analyze she had.

The cobwebs from many decades of inactivity were well and truly dusted away. She *did* understand motivations and excelled in viewing the whole landscape before drilling down to each minute detail. She enjoyed finding the one precise straw that would crack the camel's back and made an art of throwing it on. A body couldn't deal in the sort of shady behavior a puca usually got up to without extreme knowledge and appreciation for manipulation, and she was one of the very best. It was why she was still alive after all this time. Most of her family had been caught during one underhanded affair or other and killed in short order.

Nessa and Sebastian were playing a game, and they didn't trust Jessie and Austin Steele's team to be adequate participants. The mages were trying to maneuver on Ivy House's behalf.

Well. That would never do, especially since they weren't doing it right.

"Still no clue why they're framing us?" Tristan asked.

"Don't be daft. I know exactly why they're trying to frame us. Two semi-powerful mages, in prominent roles in the Guild, who were instrumental in planning the attack on Kingsley's?"

She dropped the rock she held into the basket and

took out another. Information flashed through her mind. *Thank you, Ivy House, for once again making me sharp between the ears.* Memory was a blessed thing.

She'd thought she'd waved goodbye to memory at about two hundred years old. Well, three hundred had rolled around, and she'd found herself in the kitchen, no idea why, wondering if she'd brushed her teeth earlier. Four hundred? Feck off. If she didn't write a thought down, it was gone for good. She'd had a million things put away in "safe places" with no idea where those places were. But with Ivy House's magic, she was back to her prime—thinking-wise, at least. All systems were firing.

"They're showing off our power to the Guild while simultaneously saying we hold a grudge against Momar," said Niamh. "We didn't just thwart Momar and that was that. No, no. We're hunting those who wronged us. It has some people nervous—those we wouldn't want to ally with Jessie anyway—and the *right* people curious. There's a great many powerful people in the Guild that weren't asked to play on Momar's team. They're on the outside. That used to put them on the losing team, but now, with Jessie, they have a chance to be on the winning team. That's a powerful motivator. Sebastian and Nessa are making it so the left-out mages will want to connect with us."

Tristan rocked slowly. "Which is good news. It sets us up nicely, even if they did make us look like messy animals."

Niamh chuckled softly. "Don't like that, do ya? Looking like a messy animal?"

His jaw clenched slightly. He was too distracted by the mages' activities to hide the tell. Whoopsie. He'd just given her a button to push.

She filed that away.

"It's good they did," she went on. "Perfect, in fact. That is Austin Steele's play: look like what they expect. *Act* like what they expect. Keep the mages in the dark about what we really are. It'll give us an edge for a while. The problem is, Sebastian and Nessa extracted the information like a powerful mage would. Like Elliot Graves and the Captain."

Tristan's head whipped around.

"Did ye see the pictures?" she asked.

His eyes glowed as he thought back. He grunted in acknowledgment.

She nodded. "Claw marks around the house, things knocked over...and a meticulous murder scene. Are ye *jokin*'?"

"The Guild hasn't mentioned that in any of the reports, unless it's in the files we couldn't access."

"It probably isn't. They don't seem overly bright,

the Guild. Anyone with reasonable intelligence who wants an organization to work in has moved on to Momar. Even before that, the Guild as a whole seemed mostly ineffective. It's no wonder Elliot Graves found it so easy to come out on top. Momar, however…" Her thumb stroked the rock slowly, and her thoughts continued to drift. "Momar is very intelligent," she murmured. "Cunning, calculated, a great planner…"

"Do you think he'll catch on?"

"I don't know. I know next to nothing about him, his people, or his organization. Their systems are shut down tight. Their lips are sealed. They seem to have loyalty, and I don't know if that's induced by fear or something else. I'd guess fear, but I don't like guessing. Guessing gets people dead. I need to get deeper into all this, and for that, I need tech."

"Your proposed applicant ended up in Naomi's pile."

"Of course it did, ya donkey. What do ye think, I'm going to go right out and ask Jessie to hire a criminal? As a past Jane, she'll have *thoughts* about doing that. No, ye gotta massage the situation a bit. Let her ask Mr. Tom about it. Let her ask Naomi. Austin Steele. All people who won't give a fiddler's fart if this Dick got into a bit of Dick trouble. Did he kill anyone? No. Did he torture someone for information? No. Compared to the lot of us, he's clean, like. Jessie needs time to see that. I'll go bug her in a day or so."

Tristan shook his head. "Don't you find all this manipulation exhausting? You never strike me as a person with a lot of patience."

"I don't have patience for *eejits*. But massaging a situation just right to get what ye want? Now, that's a game. That's fun." She dropped her rock into the basket. "Look up my magical breed, boyo. This is what we do. We're good on the battlefield, oh, aye, but our true talent is the art of manipulation."

He nodded slowly as he rocked, taking that in. He really had no idea. Back in the day, she could bribe a king's royal staff, then travel from tavern to brothel, from bard to kitchen maid, collecting information. Each little scrap was pieced into the whole until she had the complete picture—or near enough. She could always follow the informational trail, albeit literally, as she went from place to place and physically heard things from mouths or read them in print.

Now? Ones and zeroes. Numbers and code. Cloud storage, firewalls, aliases, and anonymous message forums. It was a *nightmare*, like. Even if she did go on the road to meet with people—and she did need to get Jessie invited to a whole lot of mage dinners to do just that—she didn't know where to find the buggers, and equally didn't know how or even where to send them a secret message to arrange it all.

Ivy House might've made her sharp between the ears, but this new technology made her feel every year of her age.

When in doubt, hire out.

In the meantime, she had enough to keep her busy and things swimming along.

"Sebastian has done right by us so far, even with his slips," Niamh mused, jiggling her rocks around. "The slips are a problem for him, but as far as our outfit is concerned, we're in good shape. They're making a bollocks of their own situation, though. Given their situation eventually needs to merge with ours, he's making bags of things."

"How do you mean?" asked Tristan. "The message boards are all lit up with fear and speculation about where he might strike next. They think he's climbing back to the top."

She shook her head and picked up another rock. Her mind went to the random threads waving at her to notice, needing her to connect them. People, jobs, and those caught up in the middle of things, forced to bow to authorities they wanted no part of. Some of those people would make great allies. Some of those would have to be killed. Others would need to be exploited.

That was what he should be focusing on. She said as much.

"He's being showy with deaths that no one really cares about," she said. "He's playing in the shadow depths when Momar has brought dirty deeds into the mainstream. He's waging battle the way *we* need to be waging battle instead of the way a person with his clout and social standing should. He's stuck in yesteryear. And sure, maybe he'd eventually get somewhere. He's smart. But he's moving too slowly."

"What do you propose?"

She grinned and dropped her rock into the basket, then set the basket on the ground. "War. They framed us, and now we'll frame them. Time for the two of us to do a little traveling."

CHAPTER 3
NESSA

"**D**O YOU WANT a grilled cheese?" Sebastian asked as Nessa walked through the tiny kitchen in their latest residence.

Her stomach growled. "No, thanks."

Sebastian's grilled cheeses made her wonder what he had against cheese and butter—they never had enough of either. She missed their cooks in the tunnels. Or Mr. Tom. It took a load off her always having to make food. Or, hell, she missed Austin. That guy was a wizard in the kitchen. She missed their friendly but cutthroat competitions to make the best dish.

She smiled through the pain, remembering Jessie and Niamh and Brochan and even Tristan—

Heat suddenly unfurled in her belly at that last name. Shivers raised goosebumps along her skin. Memories assaulted her of his body pressed against hers, his strength as he held her firmly and whispered threats in her ear…

She ripped her mind away from the gorgeous gargoyle-monster that dogged her steps.

"You know…" She paused at the edge of the hallway beside the kitchen. "No one ever found us in those caves. Maybe we should establish a permanent residence again. Then we can employ some staff and actually *use* all this money we've accumulated."

Sebastian layered one measly slice of cheese onto a piece of unbuttered bread. Did he not have any taste buds?

"We'd stepped away by that point," he said, not looking up. "Only the Guild was really looking for us, and they were woefully ineffective. You said it yourself—Momar's people have been asking a lot of questions. They're cunning in the way the Guild isn't. Momar wants us brought in, and if he can't have that, he wants us dead. Moving around is the only way to keep him guessing."

Nessa twisted her lips to the side, knowing he was right. "Okay, well…I need to do a little work."

The hollowness of the house pressed on her as she continued down the hall. The weight of loneliness put a lump in her throat. She hadn't ever felt this…solitary before. She had Sebastian, but he didn't feel like enough anymore. She'd gotten used to the Ivy House crew. To the small but growing town of O'Briens. To having people around all the time, laughing and joking and being okay in their weirdness. She'd thought the homesickness would fade, that she'd once again get used to life on the go, but instead, the loneliness kept worsening. The work was more dismal, the misdeeds more incriminating.

She sighed and pushed her way into the tiny office in the corner of the house. She shouldn't have let the Ivy House crew in. She shouldn't have gotten so familiar with them, so dependent on them. She'd tried to protect herself from the pitfalls of her upbringing, not allowing people close so that it wouldn't hurt when they abandoned her or turned on her, but this time, she'd been the one to do the abandoning, the one to walk away, and it somehow hurt just as much. The heartache was a tough thing to bear.

Curse this life. Curse this road she was forced to tread.

Feeling sorry for herself, which wasn't like her, she glanced at the encrypted phone perched on its charger in a prominent location on the desk. She didn't dare turn it on. Tristan would surely be paying attention at this time of day. He had a very strict lunchtime relaxation policy and always took his breaks.

Then again, it had been over two months now of no

contact between them, and he was incredibly desirable among the ladies. He'd probably moved on by now. He probably didn't check the phone all that often or think of her. Or dream…

"That's not helping your heartache, Nessa," she murmured, running her thumb across the blank screen as she sat down at the desk.

It was then that she noticed the line of notifications flashing across the computer monitor.

"What the hell?" she whispered.

She clicked to check them out. Her entire network was abuzz, everyone discussing Elliot Graves's latest move.

Frowning, because there shouldn't be anything newsworthy for another couple weeks, she clicked play on the video everyone was talking about. A camera mounted up high showed a large warehouse in the distance. The structure stood alone at the corner of the block. Abandoned cars littered the curb, many sprayed with colorful graffiti. Cracks marred the dirty street and what she could see of the sidewalk. It looked like a rough part of town, run-down and forgotten. Which town? She had no idea.

As she watched, several figures ran from around the back of the structure, and then one man strode after them. His gait was long and his shoulders back, utterly confident. His pristine suit said he was a man with means, something catching and throwing the light on his wrist suggested an expensive watch—which denoted his status as a player in the mage game—and his slicked-back hair and thin frame was uncomfortably recognizable. His face was obscured, likely by magic.

He'd barely exited the screen when several explosions made her jump. Glass blew out of the windows, and then large patches of the walls went tumbling away. Fire shot up over the roof. The camera shook on its base. More explosions, these on the roof. Additional explosions went off into the twisting black of the interior.

Two people from inside tried to run out, but cracks from what sounded like gunfire dropped them to the ground. Someone jogged along the front, and then two people. One tossed something into the smoking inferno—grenades, Nessa realized, as the new explosions sent a body flying through one of the holes.

"Sebastian," she called as she yanked her keyboard closer and went to work, trying to figure out what she was looking at.

In a moment, she had it. Momar's storage facility.

He had a few such strongholds for the bulk of his decently powerful potions. They were all said to be heavily protected with spells and guards; the spells covered the doors and windows, while the guards were rumored to prowl the interior and look after the workers and their creations. Mages would want to get into the building to steal the goods. *Normal* mages wouldn't want to destroy all that bounty.

But Elliot Graves wasn't a normal mage. He was as powerful as they came, and his spells were much more effective than anything in that warehouse.

And he'd just walked away from the scene of the crime.

"Sebastian!" she yelled as she replayed the video and paused it on the figure.

That wasn't Sebastian, of course. Too thin, too tall. But damn it, from a distance, it might as well have been.

"*Sebastian!*"

"What?" He raced into the room with wide eyes. "What is it?"

She started the video over as she worked on the other monitor.

When it got to the person leaving the scene, he shoved forward. "That kinda looks like me."

"Yes, it does," she said as the explosions went off.

He jerked, startled. "What is that building?"

She told him, and then the conclusions the magical world had already come to. It was all over the message boards on the magical dark web.

"I don't understand," he whispered, needing to watch it again. He stopped on the image of the person, just like she had. "No one has come forward to claim this?"

"Someone definitely has."

She clicked into one of the forums. The Elliot Graves account.

The message had been typed for them. Posted on their behalf from *their* account.

> I do love watching the world burn. This time, I had to set the fire myself. Sorry for your loss, Momar. Maybe beef up that security a little more, hmm?

"Did you do this?" Sebastian asked her.

"Of course I didn't do this!" She clicked into the account setup and saw that a few details had been changed. Under account holder, now it said, "Mommy Monster."

Nessa's eyes flicked over to the encrypted phone. She snatched it up and turned it on. She didn't care if they found her and Sabby's location. It was time to move, anyway.

"Who has the knowhow to hack into our account?" Sebastian asked, taking over the mouse and going back to all their posts. Only one was from someone else. The rest were untouched.

"Any decent hacker can get into an account on this platform. I've hacked into many."

Jessie's team had that hacker in O'Briens. He was plenty good enough to do this. She had no idea who had been playing Elliot Graves in that video, but it wouldn't be challenging. Neither would hiring people to set off those blasts, assuming they had the money.

Ivy House definitely had the money.

A new message waited on the phone.

Ye think ye're a monster, do ya? Ye ain't got nothing on me, girl. Thanks for the help thus far. I'll take things from here.

"Niamh," she murmured.

She stared at the message dumbly before holding the phone out for Sebastian to take. Next, she stared at the frozen image on the computer. Her mind churned. Niamh obviously knew about the deaths Sebastian and Nessa had framed them for. On behalf of Ivy House, was she taking revenge?

"She doesn't seem mad." Sebastian put the phone on the desk. "Is she getting even?"

"I don't know," Nessa said, drumming her fingers on the desk. "That act pushed our strategies into an entirely new direction, though. Remember when we were hashing out the plans for the visiting gargoyles, and she showed us that she's really good at connecting dots?"

"Yes. And good at knowing how to push buttons. Remember that torture session with the mage that one time? When the mage went half mad?"

"She has something up her sleeve." Nessa chewed her lip. "Why is she being so flashy about it? We're not flashy people. We don't blow up buildings like that. We don't show ourselves. Hitting Momar like that..." She leaned back. "I have to think about this. He'll want to retaliate."

"But...so?" Sebastian leaned against the desk. "He already wants us taken in. Or dead. This isn't going to put any more urgency on the situation. And after this action, the whole magical world will know we stand against him. That we're openly defying him." He crossed his arms over his chest. "That might've been a good move, actually. Bold, but...good."

She continued to chew her lip. She wasn't so sure. She had to think about the implications, how it would alter her current plans.

"Why would Niamh retaliate?" she muttered, her gut tightening. "Maybe she didn't sound mad, but you know her. She's not one to take out her anger on someone. She just slowly makes your life a living hell instead. Do you think maybe Jessie is pissed and Niamh is handling it?"

Ye ain't got nothing on me, girl.

"Do you think they're turning on us because they think we turned on them?" Nessa asked in a small voice.

"I don't think Jessie is capable of turning on someone. She'd want to save us, not hurt us."

"Jessie will protect her people at all costs. We're no longer her people. If she thinks we're against them now…"

Sabby put his hand on her shoulder. "Even if they did, they can't find us. We can hide from them as easily as we can hide from Momar."

Her stomach churned now.

She didn't want to hide from them. She didn't want to create enemies of her friends.

But in the end, it was inevitable, wasn't it? She was helping Sabby drag them into danger yet again. First, they'd pushed Jessie to take the magic, and now they were making her a bigger target. Enemy Number Two, right behind Elliot Graves and the Captain. How could Nessa expect forgiveness for that? How could she expect them *not* to turn into enemies?

When all was said and done, Sebastian and Nessa had never believed they'd get to keep the Ivy House crew in their lives. What did it matter if their parting happened sooner rather than later? The result would be the same.

"It'll get easier," Sebastian said, hugging her.

The tears streaked down her cheeks. "I know," she lied.

Because it wouldn't. It wouldn't ever get easier. She knew that now. She also had no choice in the matter. She'd made a vow to protect Sebastian and his sister years ago, and after Jala died, it was just Sabby she'd made herself responsible for. He was all that had ever counted, repercussions be damned. He'd chosen an end goal, and she'd vowed to help him see it through.

"Okay." She took a deep breath. "I have a new wrinkle to iron out, thanks to Niamh. Time to get to work."

CHAPTER 4

JESSIE

T HE SUN DANCED across the windowsill as the leaves outside wiggled and spun in the late winter breeze. I lay curled up against Austin's side, his arms wrapped around me tightly, even in sleep, and his hard chest rising and falling. I stroked my thumb across his pec, letting my mind wander.

It wasn't often I woke before he did. He'd been going hard these last couple of months, preparing his people to meet the alphas from across the country. We'd be leaving soon on our grand tour, and he was feeling the pressure.

I really should be, too. I was the weakest link in all of this. A rare creature with a bunch of magic she got from a house wasn't the sort of thing shifters understood or wanted as a leader. Austin had impressed upon me time and again that Kingsley wasn't a normal sort of alpha. He was a lot more open-minded and patient than most, a rare example of someone who could be taught new tricks. The rest wouldn't be so open to gargoyles, and definitely not a gargoyle who could do magic like a mage. They wouldn't care that, technically, I was a sorceress.

In fairness, I didn't understand the difference between a mage and sorceress, either.

Even though Austin should have been incredibly frustrated that my people *still* couldn't walk in an organized line, or stand in one, or even get to a line without tripping and falling over their own feet, he wasn't. He didn't seem troubled about my side of things at all. Not even that I couldn't seem to close down my body language, despite my best efforts.

My heart warmed, and I pulled back so that I could see his face. As I moved, so did he, rolling toward me. His arms shifted, but his touch lingered, never wanting to be far away. He rarely admitted it, but he was still freaked out over nearly losing me during and after the battle at Kingsley's.

I got it. While I was still sad over Nathanial's loss, keeping busy was helping. The hard days of training made me feel like I was doing something to prevent losing anyone else. My growing knowledge of spells, sought out in the Ivy House library and all old as dirt, helped further. I might not know how to wow an alpha, but if a mage tried to attack when we were on the road, I had a vastly growing arsenal of horrible ways they would die.

I felt Mr. Tom moving around the kitchen, but our privacy was safe for the moment—he wouldn't come in our room until Austin was up. He was probably making breakfast and thinking about the best ways to force it on Austin before my handsome alpha went about his day.

My heart swelled as I ran my hand up his muscled arm and over his shoulder before lightly trailing my fingertips along the base of his stubbled jaw. We had a hard road ahead of us. Impressing the shifters, dealing with the mages, connecting with more gargoyles, finding other creatures for our convocation, and eventually presenting ourselves to the most influential family of basajaunak in the extended family...but I wouldn't trade this life for any other. Peace would be nice, but if the choice was living here with Austin and Mr. Tom and everyone else, and leaving it all behind for a quieter existence, I'd choose this every time. I'd choose them, even with the danger. I'd choose magic and this house and even the gnomes over my old life.

Maybe not the dolls, though. Some things just crossed the line.

Austin's eyes fluttered open, the cobalt blue so beautiful. He focused in on me for a moment before closing his eyes again and scooting closer. His arms tightened, and he laid his head on my chest, his face against my cream silk nighty.

"Morning, baby," he whispered, and I wrapped my arms around his shoulders.

"I love you," I blurted.

I could barely see his lips tweak up at the corners. "Love you too."

I ran my fingers through his unruly hair before smoothing the pad of my thumb across his forehead.

"I should probably get going," he murmured. He didn't move.

"You haven't had any breaks. You're due a lie-in. Or a lazy Sunday."

"Today isn't Sunday."

"A lazy Wednesday, then."

He laughed softly before rolling away from me. "It's not Wednesday, either."

I let my hand fall on his side of the bed, still feeling the warmth as he sat on the edge and ran his hands down his face. "Aurora is challenging for placement today," he said. "It'll be a tough challenge for her. A vicious fight, most likely. I've let Mr. Tom know to put it on your schedule." He turned back with a weary sigh. Austin definitely needed a day off. "You need to start preparing yourself to watch grisly challenges. You're going to witness them when we meet the other packs."

I sat up, watching him. I didn't voice my concerns, as I knew my misgivings about what he was saying showed in my body language. It wouldn't be random pack members I'd have to watch—it would be Austin. Maybe Broken Sue. Probably Tristan. It would be the cream of our pack that the other alphas or betas would challenge and try to dominate.

That was the issue that had stopped Kingsley's efforts. If he'd had to meet those challenges, there were a few he didn't think he could beat. And if he did, it would be tough going. The hope was that Austin could win those fights, but that hope was anything but a guarantee.

I'd get challenged as well, but only once by each pack, as I would make an absolute spectacle of my challenger. My gargoyle was already spoiling for a battle just thinking of Austin being in danger.

His gaze traveled my body, landing on my hands. He didn't reassure me. It was time I got used to the harsher realities of shifter life.

I took a deep breath, held it for a moment, and then nodded. "It'll be fine," I said, because *someone* had to reassure me. "They'll see the need for a unified front. Only a fool wouldn't after what happened at Kingsley's."

He shook his head and pushed up to standing. "I have a bad reputation among alphas, and my brother has a vested interest in me. We're family. The alpha network assumes he's trying to protect me, which isn't unreasonable. Half the alphas don't believe any of the stories are true, including the extreme danger Kingsley's territory faced."

"What?" My brow furrowed. "But…the entire town can vouch for it."

Austin went to the dresser and took out his daily uniform, jeans and a white T-shirt. "They don't want to hear it. They want to put their heads in the sand and pretend life doesn't have to change. Once dominance is proven, shifters will listen, and then they'll come around—but until then, they'll approach this a lot like the gargoyles did. Remember? They didn't want the new kid on the block to have more status than they've spent their lives building. It'll be the same here. They just won't hold out as long to face reality."

Yeah. The freaking cairn leaders. All but one of them refused to admit my power or grant me status. The lone leader who'd joined the convocation was powerful, but the others *still* ignored me. It was frustrating as hell.

"Well." I pulled the covers away and swung my feet over the edge of the bed. "We'll show those shifters that we can handle them." I hesitated. "*You* will, at any rate. I still can't get Indigo to stop tripping over nothing and bowling down the rest of the Ivy House crew. I'll probably get the first challenge out of the gate."

He grabbed a pair of socks and sat with me on my side of the bed. "Your gargoyles are organized and pristine. Tristan has that down. The Ivy House crew will be ignored or looked down upon—at the start, anyway. Once the packs realize the rumors they've heard are true, they'll come around. We really do have a phoenix, we have the basajaunak, and our thunderbird is awe-inspiring. Once they see the proof for themselves, they'll give you some grace, I have no doubt. No, *I'll* raise the most contention. It's about my past versus my present. The packs view stability like the gargoyles do—they want to make sure I can foster it. They want to make sure I can lead. That I won't drive a pack—or this convocation—into the ground. They don't trust me. I'm going to have to prove that they can and should."

I put my hand on his leg and leaned over to rest my head on his shoulder. "Once they see you now, you'll get just as much grace as we will. Probably ten times more, since your people can actually form a line. Like...it's a *line*! How hard is it to get in a freaking line?"

He huffed out a laugh and put his arm around my

shoulders. "Let's hope so."

"I know so. It'll be fine," I assured us both, or maybe just me again. "We can do it. We've overcome worse."

That had to be true. We'd be sunk if it wasn't.

A knock sounded at the door. "Your link is open," Mr. Tom called. "I presume that means you're merely chatting and not about to launch into time-eating fornication. May I come in, or will it kill the mood that you don't have time to indulge in anyway?"

I sat up straight again. "Since when is Mr. Tom the keeper of my schedule, by the way?"

Austin hesitated in getting up. "Hasn't he always been? That's how he talks."

"You know very well that the jobs he *says* he has aren't actually the jobs people have given him."

His smirk was unapologetic. Apparently, Austin thought I needed to be marshaled so my team's random problems couldn't slow me.

And boy, did my team seem to come up with the most random of problems. Apparently, Cyra was in a full-fledged war with the gnomes. She was a powerful phoenix, and yet she hadn't made much headway. Ivy House had to be put in charge of making sure the resulting fires didn't burn the whole place down. I just didn't have the time to keep on top of it and didn't want to tell her to stop. Edgar wasn't getting rid of the problem, so Cyra was now our only hope.

"Well." I didn't know what else to say.

I pushed off the bed and headed to the table by the window. Austin met me there and slipped his arms around my waist, both of us ignoring Mr. Tom at the door. Austin's lips trailed against my neck.

"Don't worry about me going into these meetings, okay?" he murmured. "And don't react to the things you hear them saying. You're in charge of recruiting the gargoyles. I'll manage the shifters."

He needs room to earn the title of "King of the Shifters," Ivy House said, pride rising in her voice.

"Miss, you are giving me mixed signals," Mr. Tom called. "Am I to keep waiting at the door like some sort of vagabond, or are you decent? At this rate, your coffee will be stone cold."

I sighed as I sagged in Austin's arms. "I really hate you for putting him in charge of my schedule," I told him.

"How dare you," he replied softly, mocking what had come to be Mr. Tom's catchphrase. "And, as I said, I didn't expressly put him in charge. I—"

"Enabled him. Don't try to get out of it. You knew what you were doing."

He kissed me and pulled away. "I do need to get going."

"Apparently, so do I, or didn't you notice the urgency in Mr. Tom's voice?"

I didn't move from the window but did magically open the door.

"No shower?" I asked Austin as Mr. Tom hurried in.

"I took one before bed."

I'd been sound asleep by the time Austin climbed in beside me.

He slipped on his shoes, his expressiveness and good humor giving way to a hard-faced alpha with a stern voice and hostile bearing. It was his way of keeping Mr. Tom from fussing after him in the mornings.

It never worked.

"I have a nice cup of not-so-steaming coffee for you, Austin Steele," Mr. Tom said, holding two mugs and handing mine to me first. "You seem to be running late. I figured I'd strip a little time off your morning. Additionally, I cut up some items for an omelet, but given the late hour, I figured you'd rather an already made breakfast sandwich. How many would you like? One, two? Four? I realize you can be quite hungry these days, what with all the hard work." He paused in the center of the room, his wings fluttering. "What will it be?"

Austin stared at him, a look that would probably

make most people cower. Mr. Tom just waited patiently.

"I'll grab a sandwich on the way out, thanks," Austin said with a tight jaw. He hated when Mr. Tom succeeded in looking after him. But honestly, when a person was in a rush, it was amazing to have someone waiting to make life easier.

"Fabulous," Mr. Tom said, doing a half turn to face me. "What do we think this morning, miss? How about a breakfast sandwich as well? You need to get into the shower posthaste, and then meet with a very insistent garhette." He meant Patty, Ulric's mom and a world-renowned gossip within the gargoyle community. "You can't dally with her because after that, we need to meet Tristan at the practice grounds, and—Oh! There are Edgar's latest flowers to look over. We need to get to those, or he's liable to plant them anywhere he likes. I really think his obsession with surprising and killing hikers needs some attention. We missed the appointment with him yesterday—"

"Okay." I held up my hand. "Okay, okay. Let's…"

I glared at Austin as he made his way out of the room. He winked at me.

"Let's do one thing at a time," I told Mr. Tom. "First, coffee. Then, shower. And so help me, if you start giving me T-minus warnings like Edgar does, we're going to have a problem."

"I wouldn't *dare*," Mr. Tom said, ruffling his wings. "What do you take me for? *I* was not influenced by a woman we will not name." He meant Nessa, and my heart lurched. "I am able to properly keep time, thank you very much, or why did I get the job to—"

I let him rattle on as I headed for the shower. I'd just drink my coffee in there. It would be more relaxing.

CHAPTER 5

JESSIE

"YOU LOOK LOVELY, miss. Very good, indeed," Mr. Tom said as I met him at the base of the stairs. I wore jeans and a baggy T-shirt with my hair pulled up into a ponytail. I had a feeling he hadn't even glanced at me, given he was currently tapping a page in a book that looked like a child's diary. "Now, here we go. Let's just—No, Edgar, it is not your turn."

Edgar waited by the front door with a fedora clutched in his spindly fingers, pulled in tight to his chest. He looked like a character out of *Oliver Twist* asking for more food.

"I hear you loud and clear, Sir Tom, but if I may…" He shuffled farther into the entryway. "It's just that the flowers started singing, and when they do that—"

"No, no." Mr. Tom held up his hand as he tried to marshal me past Edgar. "It is not your turn! We have to keep things orderly or it'll all turn into chaos."

"Yes. I agree," Edgar said, blocking our way now. "But yesterday, you said you would come by, and I waited all day, and into the night, and looked in the windows when they lit up, watching everyone, and into the darkness when they went out, and—"

"Edgar, for the last time," Mr. Tom said, "stop looking in the windows and spying on people. The kids these days call that creepy."

"Everyone calls that creepy," I said with a grimace. "After the meeting with Patty, I can—"

"Oh no! No, no." Mr. Tom shook his head adamantly as he put out his arm. He shielded me like I was a celebrity and he my bodyguard, trying to shove past Edgar. "No. Alpha Steele put me in charge of your schedule, and I mean to uphold that prestigious and somewhat impossible duty."

"He didn't actually put you in charge—"

"You are penciled in later, Edgar," Mr. Tom said. "After Aurora's challenge and lunch. The miss is very busy. She has many things to get to, and she doesn't need to be skipping meals so that your flowers can sing to her. Now—"

"But…" Edgar lifted one finger, still clutching the hat.

"No buts! Make way. Her mate has made her late for the first meeting of the day. If you keep us here any longer, I'll have to—"

"Oh, Jessie!" Patty stuck her head out of the sitting room doorway. "Fantastic, you're here. Just wait until you hear what I have for you today!" She noticed Edgar. "Yes, hello, Edgar. Fine morning, isn't it? I heard you have some trouble with your flowers. What a pity. You've been working so hard. But never mind that now—we'll get to it just as soon as we can, okay?"

Edgar lifted his eyebrows at Patty as Mr. Tom continued his attempt to shepherd me past.

"No, you're going about this all wrong." Patty shouldered Edgar back to make room for herself. I was too stunned to comment. "That's not how to manage a schedule. Is this your first time? I know it's difficult when someone is as busy as Jessie, what with her demands and her appointments—no, this is something I'm probably better equipped to handle."

"No, that's okay." I stuck out my hand as she took over trying to move me past Edgar. "Honestly, Austin wasn't aware of the setup. I think I'm fine to—"

"Unhand her, woman," Mr. Tom said, charging back into the fray. "I have it all written down right here in her diary." He held up the little book. The edge gleamed with a metal clasp that would fit a tiny key. "Along with her daily activities and various thoughts she probably had when doing those activities."

"Wait…what?" I asked, perplexed. "You're keeping an actual diary for me? Like…a real diary?"

"Of course he isn't," Patty reassured me. "That would be bonkers. He's touched, but he's not as bad as the vampire, are you, Mr. Tom? No offense, Edgar, but I think we're all on the same page here, aren't we?"

"I think maybe," Edgar hazarded.

"I'll have you know—" Mr. Tom started in.

"*Enough.*" The voice was deep, full of power, and the command shocked through those gathered.

Tristan walked down the hall, just finishing off a breakfast sandwich. He crumpled the foil in his hand as his glowing gaze traced over Patty and then Mr. Tom. "*I* will handle Jessie's schedule," he finally said. "Mr. Tom, you already have plenty of very important tasks as it concerns the miss. If all your time is spent managing a diary, we'll have to bring in someone else to see to her day-to-day, like cooking and laundering and cleaning. Someone else will need to handle her."

Mr. Tom pulled his hand away from shoving Patty and brought himself up to his full height. "There is no need to go into such hysterics, Tristan. We all know that I am the most capable person in this house when it comes to looking after the miss."

"Exactly," Tristan said without skipping a beat. "We wouldn't want to have to replace you." He stopped at my side, darkness swirling around him. His glowing gaze bored into Edgar. "You're already on the schedule for today. Give that hat back to the person you have stashed in your cottage, free them, and make sure your flowers are seen to until Jessie can visit you."

"Yes, sire. Of course, sire." Edgar bowed, dropped the hat, and spun toward the door…only, it didn't open when he got there. Nor did he lift his hand to open it himself. He slammed into the hard surface, bounced back, and shrieked. A glance over his shoulder told him Tristan and his glowing eyes were still pointed his way, and so he spun again and then raced down the hallway toward the back door.

"Kind of extreme," I murmured.

An image of a woman holding her stomach and laughing magically appeared in the wood on the landing.

Not funny, I told Ivy House.

Her wheeze of laughter was the reply.

Tristan barely spared the dropped hat or dashing vampire a glance. He held his hand out for Mr. Tom. "I'll take the diary, if you please."

"It seems like you understand what's important here. Unlike that meddling woman loitering in the doorway of the sitting room." Mr. Tom put his nose in the air and surrendered the diary.

"I'd like a coffee made in the French press, please, Mr. Tom," Tristan said. "And one for Jessie."

"Coming right up!" Mr. Tom strode down the hall without another glance at Patty.

Tristan's stern demeanor melted into a smile and sparkling eyes. "Patty, lovely to see you." His charm was off the charts. "If you wouldn't mind stepping into the sitting room for another moment, I need to look over the day's events and confer with Jessie. We're already behind schedule and need to come up with a plan of attack."

Patty blushed. "I would be glad to. Good for you for helping her! And just let me say, you've been a wonderful addition to this team. Everything runs so smoothly with you here!"

"Thank you so much, Patty." He spared her a moment of attention before turning to me. "Now, Jessie, let's just step into this other sitting room, shall we?"

I watched as Patty disappeared through the doorway before following him across the hall.

"Privacy, please," he murmured.

I wrapped us in a soundproof spell, looking at him like I'd never seen him before.

He noticed and grinned. "I've had a lot of experience with hardheaded gargoyles and garhettes. Sorry about taking over in there, but it seemed like you needed a helping hand."

"No, don't apologize. You handled that much better than I could've. You got Mr. Tom off my back without hurting his feelings and Edgar out of here without him asking to be retired. Where have you been until now?"

His mood darkened. "Mistaking where you needed me most."

Our training wasn't going well. He couldn't seem to get in tune with me, and I didn't know enough about his flight plans to figure out where I should be and when.

I put my hand on his arm in support. "We'll get it—"

He brought that hand up to cough, just once, before shifting his weight and looking down at the diary. He'd effectively removed my touch.

I clasped my hands in front of me. "Sorry."

"I'm not worried about the touch, and neither is Alpha Steele," he said, turning a page. "I prefer it, actually. Gargoyles in general do. But you and I both need to practice shifter rules if we want to seem natural in the moment. The packs will notice."

"Right. Definitely."

He flicked another page. "Mr. Tom wrote down your heart's desires."

"*What?*" I inched forward to see, putting my hands behind my back.

He chuckled. "That's not really advertising *natural*."

I pushed my hands to my sides. "None of this is exactly natural for me."

"Yes, I've realized that." He flipped to the most recent page, and his finger traced down the lines before he snapped the diary closed and handed it over to me. "One of your heart's desires is a house in a meadow with a white picket fence and a window box with an apple pie sitting on it."

I looked down at the diary in bewilderment. "A window box has plants and flowers in it."

"Usually."

"White picket fence?" I whispered. "Where did he get that?" I shook my head and handed the diary back to him. Trying to figure it out would make me dizzy. "Not my problem. This is *your* problem now. You took the job."

"Um…" He hesitated before closing his fingers around the diary, his expression confused. "I…must've gotten it wrong? It seemed like you didn't actually want Mr. Tom taking over your schedule…"

"I didn't."

"Nor Patty."

"Correct."

He narrowed his eyes slightly, trying to read me, and then sagged in defeat. "I don't understand."

I laughed. "Yes, I caught that." I took a deep breath. "I thought I was doing fine managing my schedule, but there's a reason Austin told Mr. Tom to help me. He passed it off as a joke, but clearly, I'm not being as punctual as I probably should be. Practice, remember? He was probably trying to protect my feelings, but shifters tend to be incredibly punctual, and I allow meetings and trainings and whatever to run long. I always feel bad cutting someone off, whether it be Edgar explaining his flowers or Mr. Tom trying to give me one more cup of coffee in the morning to improve my mood, or lengthening training when someone is right on the cusp of getting a maneuver."

"You don't like being the bad guy," he surmised, his eyes glowing brighter.

"I really don't. I've gotten better, but…" I shrugged. "You're clearly very good at handling people, as I've just seen. And you're always hanging around, anyway, watching. Well…now you get to take an active role. Maybe if you can get me through a day, then you can get me through a battle."

He huffed. "You're reaching."

"Yeah, I am, but I do think I need help with this, and I really don't want that help from Mr. Tom or Patty. Aurora is busy, Nessa is gone—and besides…" I put my hands in my pockets. It was a sign of trust—for shifters, anyway. Practice. "You're my flight commander. My beta. It makes sense for you to give commands for me and organize the day-to-day."

He nodded slowly. "I did something similar as the lead enforcer for my old cairn, Gimerel, but only as it pertained to the guardians within the cairn. I didn't manage Nelson's personal life."

"Yeah, well, Nelson probably *had* a personal life. I am the job. It'll be fine." I pulled down the spell and started walking toward Patty. "It'd *better* be fine, because I cannot have Mr. Tom insulting every person who tries to meet with me. That'll be a nightmare with the shifters."

I heard his dark chuckle. Tristan probably wanted to see that.

Patty looked up from a magazine when I entered the room. She beamed at me and then Tristan. "All caught up?" She didn't wait for an answer. "Fantastic. Listen to this, Jessie. Tristan." She barely paused for a breath, putting down her magazine and leaning forward. "Nelson isn't faring well after certain events came to light regarding his mishandling of his production cairns. The cairn's finances are down nearly twenty-five percent, which is no small number. Then there's the issue of him making people disappear…"

Austin and I had acquired a couple of Gimerel's

production cairns after Nelson's mishandling came to light—sussed out by Sebastian and Nessa and "leaked" by Patty. They were the factions that made Gimerel, the cairn Nelson headed up, money. Without those production cairns, he'd be limping financially, which was what Patty was saying.

Making people who didn't agree with his methods or who stood in his way disappear, though…

I barely kept from glancing at Tristan. He'd been the one to carry out those directives, a secret Austin had realized and then told me. Then Niamh. That was as far as the information had gone. We didn't want Tristan implicated in Nelson's affairs.

"I can see you grimacing out of the corner of my eye," Tristan murmured.

Dang it! I tried even harder for a straight face.

We hadn't told him that we knew. Cat was out of the bag on that one.

"Yes, dirty business, that," Patty said without blinking. "But great for us! If the cairn was financially healthy, most people would ignore the transgressions if they didn't happen again. And they won't. Nelson realizes he's being watched. He wants to hold on to his leadership role. But with the cairn struggling…well…" She lifted her penciled eyebrows, her eyes glittering. "There is unrest. A *lot* of unrest. Nelson is holding it together—he's so charming and good at public speaking—but only by a thread. He's sitting atop a card house. All that's needed is a stiff breeze, and it'll topple over. And that breeze would want to come quickly, because he's already acquired two new production cairns that he's saying will more than make up the difference." She shrugged. "They might—he's good at business. They need to get up and running, though, and that takes money and time. There's a small window for *timber…*"

Tristan gracefully sat on the couch facing Patty. She'd launched into her chat so quickly, and with such gusto, that neither of us had thought to break the string of words by sitting. She hadn't seemed to mind or maybe even notice.

I took my seat next to Tristan as Mr. Tom reentered the room.

"We could destroy their operating production cairns," Tristan said while Mr. Tom set down the mugs.

"There you are—"

"Maybe just one," Patty said, cutting Mr. Tom off. "A larger one. We'd reduce their income that much more and squeeze the cairn. The desire for new leadership—leadership that might better protect them—would increase. It would prompt Nelson's critics to get even louder."

"I know which one to hit," Tristan replied. "If we do a thorough job, it'd take years to rebuild. It would also show our battle prowess. We—"

"No." I tried to keep the distasteful expression from my face. "I will not make people suffer for my own gain. Besides, there's no guarantee a new leader would be any more interested in joining our convocation or even giving Austin and me the time of day. There has to be another way to show our power, something to make the people in that cairn sit up and take notice. To want change."

Tristan was looking at me steadily now. No expression showed on his face or through his body. He'd gotten too good at that shifter body language training.

"Yes, hmm." Patty tapped her chin and looked up at Mr. Tom, who was still standing there. "Did you need something, Mr. Tom?"

"If I did, I don't imagine you'd stay quiet long enough to hear it." He sniffed. "Miss, did you need anything else? Earplugs, maybe? A timer?"

"No, thank you, Mr. Tom, that's great." I smiled at him.

He spun on his heel and left the room.

"Let's table Gimerel for now," Patty said. Tristan was still looking at me.

I was about to ask him, "What?" but Patty was away again.

"Now, how about this!" Her smile stretched. "Remember that little spot of trouble Withor got into? The surrogate for his heir that his mate didn't know about? His mistress, in other words. He'd promised that poor woman the world, thinking his mate would die from her sickness. Well, the baby was born…and the mate didn't die!"

"Nikken cairn. I remember." I'd sent word, asking that she be sent to my territory. We would look after her so she didn't have an "accident." Gimerel wasn't the only cairn that made people disappear. So far, we'd gotten no reply. It was time to force the issue. I'd asked Patty to get more information before we created a plan.

"Well…" She leaned forward and then away again. The woman was entrancing with her gossip. "The young woman's second cousin got wind of all this. He's a guardian in a cairn in the Rocky Mountains. He'd been angling to take the cairn over and make something of it—it's a medium-sized cairn—but decided instead to travel to Nikken and protect his family's honor."

"He saw an opportunity," Tristan murmured.

"Yes, he did." Patty nodded adamantly. "He did, indeed. That's how these things go. He called down Withor, talked about the failing finances and the problems with the production cairns and the instability of the cairn, not to mention the lack of an heir, all while demanding justice. He demanded something be done for the poor woman. Well, Withor's mate was appalled. *Appalled!* Out came the stories of how horrible Withor had been to her on her deathbed, yelling at her about not being able to produce an heir, and all sorts of filthy things. Nail in the coffin."

"She saw the writing on the wall," Tristan said. "She knew Withor's time was over. If she helped facilitate the new leader, he'd be inclined to look after her."

"Exactly that!" Patty beamed at him. "Only fifteen years in a cairn and you're well versed on all the politics. With her supporting the new guy, and Withor having plenty of naysayers *without* knowing about the mistress, and the mistress—well, he was basically flung out. Exiled. The new guy tried to offer him a place, as is decent, but the people of the cairn would not hear of it—"

"That's pretty common with a downfall like that," Tristan murmured to me. "He'll find a cairn to take him in. He has his riches to offer, not to mention experience. Someone will be glad of his company."

"Not that he deserves it," I grumbled.

Tristan's head snapped my way. This time, confusion poked through his expression. This gargoyle just didn't get me.

I laughed and so did Patty, though I wasn't sure

what she was laughing at.

"Yes, so that is Withor off his stoop," she said, clapping. "And do you know what else?" She pursed her lips and lifted her eyebrows before springing up and walking around the couch.

Tristan checked his watch, a Cartier Tank Must, with its iconic rectangular shape and minimalistic aesthetic. He was going for refined simplicity without sacrificing style, a good choice for an everyday watch.

I knew way too much about watches now, but I didn't like what the mages had chosen for me in L.A. Their pick just didn't seem like *me*. Neither did that ridiculous dress and those stupid gloves. They had a vision for what I should be in their world, but I wasn't a part of that world. I wasn't a mage, just like I wasn't a shifter. I was even having a hard time fitting in with the gargoyles, which I was supposed to be.

If I were forced to stand apart, I'd do it *my* way. I'd choose my own dress code, I'd choose my own watch, and, now that I'd learned mages were starting to care about cars, I'd choose my own transportation, too. This new life was supposed to be about my fresh start, and I wouldn't trade that because extreme weirdness creeped mages out. Honestly, I could "weird" in my sleep. My crew greatly helped with that. I didn't need a stupid dress to prove it.

Patty held up a large box with a reinforced bottom and corners. She wove around the furniture to deposit it on the coffee table. Her expression was delighted and expectant.

I threaded my fingers together, looking at it. "A...connection req—"

"*A connection request,*" she practically yelled at me, bouncing up and down.

Tristan sat forward, bracing his elbows on his knees. "That's good news."

"That is *very* good news," Patty said. "Open it up— let's see if he has good taste."

The lid of the box came away to reveal a heavily wrapped object inside. Wood secured it, and Styrofoam kept it from bumping into its supports. Tristan stood to help as Patty pulled out an envelope. She handed it over with barely contained excitement.

"I've looked into him," she said as I opened it. "Top guardian in his cairn, of *course*, but also noted to be kind and generous. He worked up to lead enforcer quickly and protected the cairn against several raids. I have his stats here, somewhere, let me see…"

Dear Miss Ironheart,

My name is Evan, the new leader of the Nikken cairn. I believe you met my predecessor, Withor.

I wanted to personally thank you for bringing to light the treatment of my cousin. More importantly, I wanted to express my utmost gratitude for trying to help her in her time of need. She informed me that several other people knew about her situation, inside the cairn and out, but no one raised the red flag or, when the situation became clear to her, tried to step in. You alone did that, even though it would hurt your standing with this cairn and within the community to do so.

I've seen all of your correspondence, including your most recent threat. If not for you, I might not have had the courage to take on someone of Withor's stature. My cousin and I owe you a debt of gratitude.

Please accept this formal connection request as the gift I mean it to be. It is a production cairn newly established and recently acquired. Their work speaks for itself. I asked them to create something fit for a female gargoyle. I think it is their best work yet.

Warm regards,
Evan Smithenson
Controller for Nikken Cairn

"That's sweet," I said as Patty passed off a piece of paper to Tristan.

She then reached for the letter I held. I gave it to her before standing to see the wrapped gift. It had been taken from the box and set on its own. I pulled the wrapping away, then sucked in a breath.

"Oh, it's beautiful," I sighed.

The object was a stunning, handcrafted glass sculpture shaped like a large bowl but with parts of the sides pulled up artistically. The form was dynamic and fluid, with a wavy shape that gave it a sense of movement. The glass itself showed multicolored, vibrant swirls with hues of amber, gold, purple, pink, and blue. It created a captivating, iridescent effect when it caught the light. It was delicate yet bold, stunning and sophisticated, with an almost luminous quality that did remind me of my gargoyle form. I didn't care what Naomi said—this was absolutely going to be shown off in Ivy House.

"Oh, Jessie, *look*," Patty said in awe, her eyes wide as she took it in.

"Very classy," Tristan noted, putting the piece of paper Patty had handed him on the coffee table. "If nothing else, we'll want to establish trade with them. Oh, and there's another envelope," he said, pointing to a plain white one beside the box. "It was at the bottom of the package."

Patty scooped it up and looked at the front. "Not addressed to Jessie." She started to open it. Finders keepers, apparently.

Tristan grunted before setting down the letter. "He's certainly new to the post. That letter is too ass-kissy for a cairn leader of Withor's stature, but it seems genuine. He's going about this the right way, and not just because Jessie will respond well to his touching sentiments. I wonder if he knew that, or if his personality will match up well with hers..."

Patty held up what looked like documents with an *I told you so* expression. Tristan took them without a word.

"What is that?" I asked, leaning over his arm to look. He didn't move away, which meant he was thinking like a gargoyle right now, not a shifter.

"He's rescinded all the grievances that Withor filed against you." Tristan put the documents on top of the letter and leaned back. "That's his way of saying he wants to start fresh."

"He surely knows all he can about Jessie," Patty said, busying herself with cleaning up the box and packaging. "And he might've gone with the *touching* angle, as you said, because of that. But his letter *was* genuine, you can tell. He wants to thank her, he wants to meet her, and he'll have an open mind about her and the things she has to say."

"I agree," Tristan said. "His newness will work for us. He won't be as inclined to dig in his heels. He also has a grace period within his new post. His status and that of the cairn will be frozen for a time so that he can make adjustments and settle in. It would be best to meet him within that window—that way, he won't feel so much pressure. He could ally with us on a temporary basis to see how it benefits him without fear that it'll tank his status."

"How much time do we have?" I asked.

"A couple months. It'll make things tough because of the shifter situation, but getting another big cairn to ally with us would be a *huge* boost to your status. He must know that Khaavalor has joined with us, and that they participated in a battle that the whole community is intrigued about. We *are* a battle species, after all, and gargoyles want blood and victory. We thrive on it. They all want a piece of the action, but the politics involved are scaring away most of the midsized and smaller cairns. Gimerel is obviously still against us. Solgid has gone silent about it, but they haven't pulled their grievances against you. That's them saying they'll side with Gimerel...for now. If we can get Nikken, and get Gimerel out of the way, then we could turn the tide."

"And if we can turn the tide, we can open up trading with all of them." I tapped my knee.

Our production cairns were producing at incredible rates, thanks to the money Austin and Ivy House jointly put into them, working out of warehouses and anywhere else we could put them. Their occupants were living all over the place while we bought land and started on plans and permits to build more housing, but it didn't stop their hard work. We had storage facilities filled with top-quality products and storefronts going up within the territory and online. Once sales from that came in, we would expand.

Setting up trade with the other cairns wasn't our top priority. We were eager to tap into the Dick and Jane markets, which encompassed mages and shifters and anyone with a foot in the mundane world, but eventually, we wanted to bring the cairns into the twenty-first century with us. We'd first establish trade with them, and either they would sell to Dicks and Janes, or we'd treat them as wholesalers and resell their items accordingly. We'd all profit, and everyone would benefit.

When Austin did something, he didn't do it by halves. The sky was the limit. *Fuck* I loved that man. The alpha network were idiots if they didn't see his incredible value.

Good status within the gargoyle community would accomplish so much. We did need to meet that new leader.

We also had a bunch of other stuff going on and not enough time to do it all.

"Okay." I stood, ready for the next thing. Tristan checked his watch as he stood with me. "Let's send a thank-you note for the gift. Let's not call it a connection request. Is that possible?"

Tristan and Patty both looked at me in confusion.

"We don't have time to wait for them to come here, and we certainly don't have time to entertain them. We need to get on the road. I don't want to advertise the fact that we'll be gone, though, or they might send someone to attack us, or the mages might, or who knows anymore. So, let's thank them and send a connection request of our own. Something…" I paused. "No, I shouldn't be the one picking it out. Damn it, I really need Sebastian. He's perfect at picking out gifts." I looked around for the encrypted phone, as though it followed me from room to room. "Tristan," I said, "make a note…in the diary, I guess, to send Sebastian a message. We'll ask them to look into this new dude and come up with something he'll love. Something that will fit his new post within the cairn. Something thoughtful but, like…*chic*. I don't know. I'm not good at this stuff."

"I can ask," he said dubiously, and I knew what he was hinting at. Most of my messages went unanswered. Almost all, as a matter of fact. It was like speaking into the void. I still tried occasionally, hoping to remind Sebastian and Nessa that we were here for them, and there was no reason to brave the darkness alone, but I didn't think I was getting through.

I nodded and thanked Patty for her good work before I exited the room.

"Look at that," Tristan said, following me. "A hair early. You don't need a schedule keeper at all."

"That's only because you scared Edgar away. Otherwise, he'd be waiting at the front door for me. I do need to go over the latest flowers, though I can't fathom why he keeps creating different ones. There's hardly a difference between versions X and…eight, or whatever we're up to."

Fire seared the grounds way out in the wood, hot and spreading fast.

I sighed. "Cyra is going to be late to practice."

CHAPTER 6

JESSIE

I STOPPED AT Mimi's desk at the back of the house. Only blood-related family were allowed to call Naomi the nickname. I was given a special privilege. Noticing my presence, she glanced up from a paper she'd been studying.

"We got a gift from a cairn," I told her. "It's a lovely blown-glass bowl. I left it in the front sitting room, but I'd like to put it on display somewhere. It's really pretty."

She studied me for a brief moment before nodding and turning back to her work. She wasn't one for chitchat.

"Have you been able to find them?" I asked Tristan as we grabbed muumuus, changed into them, and headed out the back door.

He didn't need me to elaborate. "No. Nessa is better at the tech side of things than we are. More experienced.

She's way ahead of us."

"Even with that computer guy in town?"

"Yes. He was plenty good for the gargoyles, but he's not even remotely good enough for the more powerful mages. He doesn't hold a candle to Momar's setup."

I blew out a breath as we walked through the flowers. Edgar was there tending them. When he saw us, he sank into a crouch, lowering his head, as though that would render him invisible when the flowers only reached his shins.

I pretended not to see him. I'd make sure to meet with him sometime today. Other than that...I just wasn't able to cope with his oddity.

The fire in the woods continued to spread.

You do have a handle on that, yes? I asked Ivy House.

Mind your business, and I will mind mine. That mage needs to help you with magic. Keep your focus where it will do the most good.

Gracious, she was surly today.

You're barely staying alive through all your skirmishes, she went on, probably having heard my thought. Sometimes, I broadcast them. *You can read spells out of a book, but Sebastian could make them better. He could find the best ones to focus on. He's a genius with magic. You need him. Find him, kidnap him, and chain him in the crystal room. If he won't help you of his own free will, he will need other motivations, like starvation.*

"Good Lord," I muttered.

"What?" Tristan asked.

"Ivy House. She's…cutthroat."

One of us has to be, she told me.

I changed the subject, knowing I wasn't going to win that argument. She'd just call me a watery Jane with no spine, and it would be a whole thing.

"That other hacker guy," I said to Tristan. "The one who was in Mimi's pile?"

"Yes?"

"Did you look at his résumé and rap sheet?"

"Yes…"

"Someone put that sheet together, but no one has approached me about it. You seemed interested in it, so it isn't you recommending that person, and it wasn't Austin. That leaves Niamh or one of the mages."

"One of the mages?" He frowned at me, genuinely shocked that I should make that connection.

That meant it was Niamh, then.

"I didn't know if they might have…sent the recommendation to help us out," I said.

I'd hoped they had, and that they were still on our team, however distantly. I didn't like hearing that Sebastian and Nessa were trying to set us up or frame us, pushing us toward danger without an explanation. We needed a conversation. I needed to be in on this leg of the journey…or I needed to pull away. I couldn't live in the dark, not knowing if they planned to betray us— if they thought that betrayal was necessary, like at that mage dinner in L.A.

Like with those deaths.

I hated even thinking about it.

"Anyway…" I brushed the thought aside, my heart hurting. "That guy is obviously good, but not so good that he didn't get caught."

"It looked like he got caught when he was younger. Went to juvenile hall. He's thirty-six now and hasn't stopped stealing, but he hasn't gotten caught since."

I paused to face him. "There's a warrant out for his arrest."

He grabbed my arm and tugged to keep me moving. "Exactly. Which proves he's evaded the law."

"But, like…he's wanted by the cops. He *steals*. We can't hire a person like that!"

Tristan didn't reply for a moment. "How'd you know it was me who disappeared people for Nelson? Did Alpha Steele figure it out, or do you believe the rumors Nelson is spreading about me?"

"Austin told me. I haven't heard any rumors—that's Patty's department, and she hasn't said anything."

"You never mentioned knowing."

I shrugged. "Why would I?"

"Because I killed people and buried them in an unmarked grave. That's alarming behavior."

I grimaced this time. "I did those things, too. It was in self-defense, but still. You're in a precarious position with your ancestry, Nelson is an ass, and you're not worried about taking the moral high ground. I figured you didn't much care, and given Niamh would do worse…" I rolled my eyes. "Yeah, fine. I see the absurdity in my argument about stealing. It's just that…the hacker's a Dick. They have different rules. Their society isn't loose about stuff like that. He knew it was wrong, and he stole from people anyway."

"Firstly, you're back to thinking like a Jane. In our world, his transgressions are so incredibly mild, they aren't worth thinking about. Stealing? Gargoyles steal all the time and destroy production cairns so they can get ahead. We have a whole set of rules that make stealing and destroying okay. Shifters are saints where that stuff is concerned, but then they'll kill you if you flirt with their woman. That's extreme behavior in a different way."

We pushed through the trees as the fire raged on. I wasn't sure if Ivy House was intentionally trying to make me sweat or if Cyra was having an effect on those gnome nests. I hoped it was the latter, even though currently, it was the former. My muumuu was uncomfortably damp.

"Second, he steals from large corporations with insurance, the kind of conglomerations that come by their money on the backs of their underpaid workers. And then he distributes more than half of those funds to charities and people in need. Sure, he's getting rich as well, but he's taking all the risk and only hurting organizations. He isn't hurting Mom and Pop trying to make a living. Even in the Dick world, that doesn't seem so bad."

No, it didn't.

"It's a big salary," I said, my last holdout.

We stopped in a small clearing. We'd rise into the sky here and practice summoning everyone for training. They obviously knew it was time, but we needed to work on all facets of battle, not just flight.

"Five hundred grand a year is definitely a lot of money," Tristan concurred. "We'd also have to harbor a fugitive, though I'm assuming we can alter his identity and make him disappear. Not like N-Nelson would," he hastily added, "but the guy needs to disappear from the Dick and Jane world, you know. Just, like…change his records so the cops can't trace him, I mean." He cleared his throat.

I'd never heard him stammer like that. Maybe he *hadn't* been so morally ambiguous about some of the stuff he'd done, which made me hate Nelson even more.

"I want to rub Nelson's face in it," I said through my teeth as I pulled off the muumuu. "Make an utter fool of him. I want him to regret how he treated me and how he's currently treating you. With the rumors, I mean. I want to shut him up. If he's good for that cairn and the people he rules, fine, but I want to knock him down several pegs and then...taunt him. I don't know. Give him a smug look or *something.*"

Tristan huffed out a laugh. "I hear you. I'll figure it out. And about the salary... I mean, Jessie, you have a closet full of gold bars and an attic full of precious gems so big, they should probably be in a museum or something. Assuming they weren't stolen and...well, who knows with this house." He bent to be on my eye level, his gaze dulled and solemn. "How much is too much when someone can help us save our friends from themselves?"

He was right. I'd pay anything to drag Nessa and Sebastian off the dark road they seemed to be traveling. The two thought they were an island, but they weren't—not anymore. Sooner or later, Momar was going to figure out they were the ones helping me. If he was good enough to plan that incredible attack on Kingsley, one we'd almost succumbed to, then he'd figure out my secret partner. There could only be a handful of mages powerful enough, and Momar held most of them within his employ. He could also check on those mages in the Guild. If he was half as good as he seemed, he'd piece it together. Maybe he already had and was looking for Nessa and Sebastian now.

I didn't need to pull away from them, but rather to find them and force them to see reason.

Told you so, Ivy House said smugly, and the fire extinguished.

I said "see reason," not chain them up and starve them until they help me.

I fail to see the difference...

I rolled my eyes and resumed my focus on Tristan. "Tell Niamh to invite her hacker in. I want a sit-down with him before I invite him into our world. If he's safe, then we can create some bonus-based incentives to ensure we get the best work out of him. We need to bring our people home."

I shifted and took to the sky, probably a little late but nearly on time. Probably.

Crap, I was starting to sound like Edgar.

✧ ✧ ✧

TRISTAN

HE CUT THROUGH the air on autopilot, his interactions with Jessie during the last hour swirling within his mind. It was no surprise to anyone that he wasn't filling Nathanial's role. Everyone thought he was too self-centered, too headstrong, and too used to doing things his own way to be the wingman Jessie desperately needed. But he wanted to surprise them, damn it. He wanted people here to know that he was more than what he seemed—much more. He also wanted to repay Jessie's faith in him by being her shield, being her power and endurance when she needed it. He didn't want to shine—he wanted to help *her* shine.

And he didn't freaking know how!

At every turn, she surprised him. She went left when he assumed she'd go right. She balked when he talked about financially hurting a cairn, but then wanted the leader tossed out on his ass. She was fine with him killing people because his leader told him to but not okay with a guy stealing. It didn't make any sense.

What *did* make sense was how he felt when he'd stepped in to help her earlier that morning.

Tristan had heard the voices when he was walking down the hall and realized what was going on pretty quickly, but it wasn't until he noticed Jessie's tightened frame that he'd intervened without thinking. Sending Ivy House people on their way was child's play. Dealing with guardians had been so much harder.

His goal had been to afford Jessie some breathing room. He hadn't expected to be handed control of her schedule, and certainly not her professional well-being. Was Tristan now Jessie's work-life Mr. Tom? Was this the point at which he needed to randomly create a new name for himself? Call him Weatherby. Mr. Weatherby, if you please.

It did have a certain ring to it…

Before now, he'd resigned himself to failure. He'd devoted hours to watching her, tailing her, analyzing her thought processes, to no avail. Delaying finding her a solid wingman was putting her in danger. He already had five guardians that might do a better job picked out. They weren't as fast or strong as some of the others, but they anticipated her better than the rest. Better than he did.

But interceding today had felt…different. More his speed. And now, he understood why.

Nathanial had been great at observation, holding back until the moment Jessie faltered. Only then would he step in. But Tristan didn't work like that. He didn't wait for things to happen—he *made* them happen. He liked control. He liked to orchestrate what went on around him, and that failing, he thought on the go. He couldn't do things Nathanial's way, and it had been stupid of him to try.

Then there were Jessie's motivations…

You don't like being the bad guy.

I really don't. I've gotten better, but…

He watched the ethereal female gargoyle dive, putting herself in the way of a guardian as though he were an attacking mage. She was ready to take a blast. To protect her own.

And while that would have been a good move if her opponent had been a mage, it wasn't smart with a guardian. Not without backup. She was fighting as if she were solo…probably because she was used to being the only one doing magic. Even with Sebastian, she'd had to play defense when he attacked.

She had to protect her people.

Hundreds of dots connected in a flash, and Tristan felt like he'd been blinded.

Jessie was a caretaker by nature. She had been in her Jane life, and then she came here and was handed the house and a staff, and then an army. Her duty was to take care of them all.

More than that, though, she was a female gargoyle. A battle species, yes, but not like him. Not like the other guardians. Not even like the garhettes. She didn't rush into battle, club people over the head, and shout her victory. Instead, she united her people, connected them, and made it her duty to protect them. That was why she'd sacrificed herself at Kingsley's and why she hadn't taken the honor for doing so. She hadn't viewed her actions as heroic, but as a necessity. And after...as a failure. She was supposed to protect her people, and one of hers—someone dear to her heart—had died.

Stupid, he berated himself.

Why hadn't he thought of that before?

And their differences in battle tactics? Simple: Jessie didn't know what the hell she was doing. He'd trained all his guardians, even ones who'd come to him with impeccable previous instruction. They'd had to learn how to work with his setup. He hadn't trained her, though. Instead, he'd followed her lead, not sure how the magical aspect of things worked.

Now that he did know, he saw the truth: she had virtually no experience in aerial combat. She was the newest among them, lacking the basics and relying solely on survival instincts. She couldn't tell when to maneuver or hold her ground, struggled to maintain the guardians' formation while dodging and diving, and had no idea how to build a unified defense. She needed structure.

It hadn't been lost on Tristan that Nathanial had gotten to see her in her flying infancy. He'd helped shape her reactions. And Sebastian had trained her how to counter mage attacks. They'd worked together seamlessly, having forged that connection in the same way.

Hopefully, as Tristan refined Jessie's training, he could gain the insight that had made Nathanial so effective. Maybe down the road, Tristan could honor Nathanial's memory by continuing his outstanding teamwork.

Dare to dream.

He'd give himself one more month. One month to do things *his* way. He'd confront problems with her and Ivy House in the same way he'd confronted problems in his former cairn. At the end of that month, if he wasn't a helluva lot closer to being what she needed, he'd start trying out other guardians.

He had to figure this out, not just for her, but also because he really didn't need Niamh heckling him with an *I told you so.*

CHAPTER 7
JESSIE

THE CROWD FOR Aurora's challenge consisted of about two dozen people in a field, all standing around chatting. They weren't in a line or a circle, and there didn't seem to be much expectation or heightened energy surrounding the event. In fact, it wasn't an event at all, not like the time I'd been challenged.

Aurora stood within one of the clusters of people like this was no big deal. I couldn't tell from those gathered whom she'd challenged.

Austin stood with Broken Sue off to one side, removed from the others. Neither of them seemed tense.

Tristan pulled my door open, then stepped back so as not to hurry me.

"Thanks," I murmured, pushing myself out of the car. "Have you seen one of these before?"

"Many, yes. I try to see all the major challenges in the pack. They're people I need to work with."

"Right, right." I shut the door. "And this one? Would you have come out for this one?"

"Yes, but only because I'm curious about Aurora. People are in awe about how quickly she's rising in this pack. She still has a ways to go."

I nodded as I walked on the brittle grasses of the field, the vegetation broken and dead from winter. "This setup isn't anything like when I was challenged."

"Oh yeah?" He checked his watch.

"On time?"

"Ten minutes early. You can continue to drag your feet if you want."

I huffed. "Is it that obvious I don't want to be here?"

"Yes. Why is that? You're worried about Aurora getting hurt?"

"Yeah, and fear of what I'll do if that happens. Sometimes, my gargoyle sweeps me away, and I get really violent without meaning to. That happened during my challenge, but it was okay because it was *my* challenge. I can't mess this up for her or Austin."

"She'll probably get hurt, and I'm sure she'll get bloody, but Alpha Steele or Brochan will step in if it gets dangerous. They're very experienced," Tristan assured me. "They've had to step in multiple times during challenges. She'll be okay."

I took a deep breath, held it, and let it go slowly. I

knew that—it had been explained to me—but knowing didn't negate the fact that I would have to witness family get ripped up.

"How the hell am I going to handle this when Austin fights?" I murmured.

"How'd you handle him fighting the phoenix?"

I thought back as I neared the others. Aurora leaned around someone, catching sight of me. Her mouth moved, but I was too far away to hear her. The people she stood with looked around and spied me approaching.

"Watch your body language," Tristan murmured. "You're advertising how nervous and uncomfortable you are."

I tried to rein in my emotions. "The phoenix thing was different. It was attacking, and Ivy House was after a blood oath, and Kingsley was in my way, and Sebastian was freaking out… It wasn't like standing on the sideline and watching two people tear into each other."

"Have you watched boxing? UFC?"

It was annoying how much sense he was making, and far more annoying when he laughed at me. Clearly, I'd relayed that in my body language, too.

"No one will die," Tristan said, peeling away as I neared Austin.

Austin stopped talking and turned, his stern shifter

persona melting into a grin. "Hey, babe." He checked his naked wrist for the time. "Mr. Tom is keeping you on schedule, I see."

I furrowed my brow. "We're fighting about that."

"Right now?"

"Yes, right now, we're in a fight."

His smile was a thing of beauty as he let his arms fall around me. "We can't bang it out here, I'm afraid. Time constraints and all."

It was hard to keep a straight face. I angled for a kiss, and he complied eagerly, his lips soft. Afterward, I glowered. It was important to keep up pretenses.

"You could've just told me you wanted me to get better about watching the time instead of throwing me to the wolves," I groused.

He smoothed his hands down my back, holding me close. "I'd intended to. This was Niamh's idea, actually. Not just to corral you and your crew, but to help Tristan step into a more active role. Where it concerns you, he's languishing. She thinks he needs a kick in the arse, as she put it."

I pulled back so I could get a better look at him. "How did she know his managing my schedule, of all things—or even that he would end up managing my schedule—would be that kick in the ass?"

His eyebrows rose. "Was it?"

I told him about Mr. Tom and Patty arguing about managing me, and Edgar pushing for a meeting, and Tristan handling it all. "And then, on the way here, he's suddenly talking about better aerial training and how to work as a team in the air, even when mages are present. Which…" I ran my hands down his chest to his flat stomach, thinking about it. "It's a good idea. I'm like a hot potato with those guardians, a wild card that they basically improvise with. I always mess up their organization. It's not like with my crew, where we've all learned to kinda figure it out and work off each other. With them, it's more disruptive, which is dangerous in battle. I can't just get out of the way like Cyra and Hollace do because I'm not strong or fast enough."

He nodded thoughtfully. "Tristan's right. You've never had any sort of proper training, not in a larger framework. If nothing else, it'll help you to at least understand their structure. It certainly couldn't hurt. If you're to lead an army, you have to understand that army."

"Yeah. True. Something we probably all should've clued into before now."

Austin shrugged. "You're a unique case. Your position in the army isn't the same as everyone else's, and you have different talents. It's been working so far, but with all these new people, and with the size we are now, the system we've got going might become increasingly difficult to maintain." He shook his head, baffled. "But how did a fight over a schedule get us here? Niamh…" He laughed softly. "She said she was feeling like her old self again and mentioned how happily meddlesome pucas were in olden times—I have a feeling we haven't seen her real power yet."

Not even close, Ivy House said. *There is a reason she held a high position in that circle. I'd worried she wouldn't reclaim her former glory. Looks like she just needed higher stakes. The mages pushed her. Their leaving was a blessing in disguise. She'll rise again.*

A feeling like Ivy House rubbing her hands together, as though she were some sort of villain, infused me. That couldn't be good.

"Ignorance is bliss," I mumbled. At least for a little longer.

A crease formed in Austin's brow—he couldn't hear Ivy House and had no clue how dark she could be—before he gradually pulled away. "Time to get to it. Are you ready?"

"She's in no real danger, right?" I asked as he took my hand and led me toward the cluster of shifters. They fell silent as we drew near.

"No," he murmured. "Less so than normal, I'd wager."

I didn't get a chance to ask why as the group fanned out into a haphazard line. Aurora stepped forward…along with a big dude stacked with muscle and sporting a hardcore resting dick face. He had tree-trunk arms and topped out at probably six foot three. There was not an ounce of fat padding his frame.

"She's going to fight *him*?" I accidentally said, my face probably showing my intense unease.

Aurora's eyes glittered in that way that said she was laughing at me. I had zero idea why. He was a monster compared to her.

"She wants the position he holds," Austin said. "This is how she gets it. Now, Jess, as co-alpha, you will be monitoring the challenge. You've heard—"

"Wait, what?" I blurted.

He slowed his words. "You will be monitoring the challenge. I'll help you. It's important that you get practice on when to intercede and when to let it go. When it's me being challenged, my well-being will fall solely in your hands, as will my status as alpha. Stop the fight too early, and you risk people thinking you have no faith in me. Too late, and…curtains. You've had experience being challenged and experience when someone—me—cuts your challenge short."

My thoughts flashed to my fight with Sebastian.

"You've seen me battle a phoenix when victory was

anything but decided, and you didn't intercede," Austin continued. "This is just like that."

He failed to mention that I *couldn't* have interceded in his battle with Cyra. I hadn't been strong enough to take her, or even to help him.

"You can also heal," he said. "So, you have a better idea than most about how close a fight can get."

"Is this another one of Niamh's ideas?" I asked as quietly as I could, trying not to move my mouth. "Toss me into the fire?"

"No. This is training. There might be times when a challenge for me comes out of the blue. Maybe not even a challenge, but just an attack. You'll be thrown into it just like you are now. The rules will still apply."

Maybe I was biased, but I liked the gargoyle way of doing things much more than the shifter way. None of this felt natural. Leadership shouldn't rely solely on strength and power. A good leader could still lead when they were older, as *some* gargoyles had proven. Hell, Mimi hadn't been the strongest or most powerful, but the pack had helped her keep her placement anyway because she was excellent for their well-being. This just seemed barbaric.

But I nodded, because it wasn't up to me to change this culture. That was up to Austin. He'd already loosened the pack mentality and blended much better with the gargoyles. Hopefully, he'd come to see that experience, intelligence, and logic went a lot further in a leadership role than strength and brawn.

"Right. Fine," I said, doing a really good job of hiding my annoyance. Hopefully.

"Okay."

Austin faced the others, who fanned out a little more, giving the challengers space. Aurora and the mammoth stripped off their clothes. Someone came forward to take them, and then the challengers nodded respectfully at each other. That was nice, at least. There was no animosity.

When they shifted, Aurora's flash of light and heat was significantly brighter and hotter than the other's.

"Wouldn't males have an advantage over females with this system?" I couldn't help but ask as Aurora morphed into a Siberian tiger like her dad. The other guy changed into a massive wolf, but his form wasn't as large as hers. "And the type of animal? Wouldn't this system pass up someone who's extraordinary at organizing and leading and managing a pack because they turned into a...a deer, or something? Or even a smaller wolf than this guy?"

The wolf's head lowered as he sized up Aurora, slinking around her as wolves so often did.

"Sometimes yes, and definitely yes," Austin replied.

"It's something I've thought about because a situation like that has cropped up. Most packs are small, and the members of the hierarchy are mostly peacekeepers and enforcers. They're extensions of the alpha, who needs to protect the pack against people trying to take it over. They hold power like a policeman might. The rest of the town is essentially just a town, part of a pack but not needing to challenge for the protective, peacekeeping role. As you saw with Kingsley's pack, there are a great many more townspeople minding their own business than enforcers. Our setup here…is quite a bit different, especially concerning the various species we have cohabiting," he continued with a faint shrug. "We need to stop thinking like a pack and a cairn and Ivy House, but rather as one big unit. For that, we'll need a governing body. That body will have a different skill set than the peacekeepers and will need to elevate themselves in a different way." He paused. "I just haven't figured out how that's going to work yet. I want us to talk to my brother about it, and maybe a couple of the other more levelheaded alphas too. I also want us to talk to some of the cairn leaders, if we can, to ask how their setup works. Tristan is very knowledgeable, but he didn't hold the position. There's a lot he doesn't know. I want to ask the lead basajaunak…"

He trailed off.

"I've thought about it," he finally said as Aurora started to circle the other shifter. "It's reassuring that you have, too."

I mean...I hadn't until right this moment. I hadn't had the time to really delve into and understand pack mechanics. I was trying to learn about it through Aurora, but there were only so many questions I'd thought to ask. She, growing up in the culture, often didn't know what to cover other than the basics. She also didn't ponder why they did certain things, and if those practices were the best way. If some things were even necessary.

I needed to better understand cairn life, too. I trained with the guardians, but I didn't even know half of their names. I didn't know how Tristan worked them into shape, what they did outside of training, what an entire *cairn* did outside of training...

Then there was the complex and dirty world of mages. Well, not all mages were dirty, just some, except you didn't really know which because they all tried to blend together so no one got caught in the crossfire.

There just wasn't enough time. I couldn't fit a lifetime of knowledge about three different factions and the magical world as a whole into a few months of training and instruction. When I tried, I felt like I was drowning, like the mountains of information were tumbling down on top of me and burying me alive.

That was why I hadn't thought about better aerial combat training, or why I couldn't seem to maintain a schedule, something I'd been great at as a Jane. Or why I couldn't feel too bad about Edgar peering in the windows at night, hoping I'd come out and talk to him about flowers, something that really shouldn't have been as important as he was making it out to be. I was hanging on for dear life here.

Austin's hand closed gently over my shoulder, and he stepped a little closer. "You okay?"

"Yeah." I pushed everything but this moment away and took a deep breath. "Yeah, sorry."

"We'll talk about it."

He didn't even know what was wrong, but he was being supportive. He was such an amazing leader.

Then again, he'd been thrown into the deep end too. He didn't show his feelings because of his training, but he was probably struggling with the same issues.

I nodded and shook it out. Sometimes, it helped to know someone was in the trenches with you.

It was then I noticed the furtive glances from the gathered shifters, all of whom were trying to watch me on the sly. Broken Sue and Tristan had wandered closer and pushed in around me.

"Sorry, did I send out a pulse of magic?" I asked,

trying to relax my bearing and offer a smile. I could do that here—they knew better than to challenge me.

"No," Austin murmured, his hand still on my shoulder. "But you're advertising your turmoil. Everyone knows what we're up against, Jess. That you, above all, are a target. Mages are after you, cairn leaders are talking negatively about you, and soon, shifters from other packs will be against you as a figurehead. Our pack is protective of you because they know you're protective of them. As a whole, they're worried about you."

I jerked my head to Austin, but he wasn't looking my way. "Really?" Tears unexpectedly filled my eyes. "That's sweet of them."

I swallowed the lump in my throat. When I was frustrated and overwhelmed, I often relieved stress through tears. Too much wine, a tragic love story, and ugly crying did wonders to vent. But this wasn't the time for my personal hysteria. I was making people nervous.

"It's fine." I gave everyone a thumbs-up. "I'm good. I don't care about the shifters being dicks, and I care even less about the cairn leaders. I'll give them better than I've gotten, just you wait. The mages...well...I guess I'll just have to blow up their world. I don't know. But I'm good. Don't worry about me. I'm expressive. It's a Jane thing. I'm working on it."

Austin squeezed my shoulder before pulling away. It couldn't be easy for him with a co-leader like me. I blasted normality all to hell on a regular basis, something I didn't notice when I was with the Ivy House crew. They were weirder than me, so it was easy to forget I always used to be the oddest one in the room.

The wolf suddenly lunged for Aurora, and I jerked in surprise.

"Here we go," Austin said.

CHAPTER 8

AUSTIN

AURORA MET CARLOS'S lunge with a calm and fluid dodge before she twisted. He chomped into her rear, and Jess gasped. He scratched at Aurora's flank, opening up minor gashes. Wolves were better as pack animals, working together to take down an adversary. They couldn't latch on with their claws like a tiger could.

Aurora knew that. An alpha's daughter, she'd trained for this her whole life, and she'd been taught by one of the best. This would be a tough fight for her because of Carlos's size and strength, but she was smart enough to compensate. Besides, she had size and strength of her own. She might've been smaller in her human form, but her animal was one of the biggest around, and she had more power and dexterity. Frankly, the odds were tipped in Aurora's favor.

But Jess didn't know any of that, and Austin wanted

to see how she'd react to a loved one in a bloody fight.

Aurora spun and launched herself at Carlos, landing on his back and digging her claws into the sides of his neck. Her big-cat power kept him from throwing her off as she bit and released, bit and released, fighting to stay balanced and work her jaw closer to his jugular.

He was too smart, experienced, and powerful to let her win so easily, however. Carlos dropped and rolled, more flexible than even Aurora was. Her hold loosened, and then he was up, taking advantage of her on the ground and biting the base of her neck. He jerked his head back and forth, ripping her flesh. Blood splattered onto the dead grass.

A pulse of energy cut through Austin's middle, a warning.

"Keep your power contained," he murmured to Jess, leaning closer to brace his arm against hers. "Keep your cool. You can't interrupt the challenge. Aurora has a long way to go before she's in danger."

Jess's hands balled into fists, but the feel of her magic deadened.

"Good," he said. She needed to relax her body, to show she was unaffected even if she wasn't, but for now, they'd just work on her magic. Austin should probably battle Cyra again to give her some practice...but he'd really rather not. Fighting that phoenix hadn't been at all pleasant.

Aurora was up and after Carlos, bleeding but showing no sign of pain. Neither did Carlos. They were both impeccably trained shifters, and they wouldn't show pain until they were almost dying.

He backed off to keep her from jumping on him again, and she stalked toward him. He tried to circle, but she cut him off. Tried to circle back, and she cut him off there, too. She was on the attack. He'd riled her up, and she was about to fully unleash her beast and let the darkness consume her. It was a trait she'd gotten from her grandfather—one she shared with Austin.

In a blink, she was all action and big-cat power. Wrapping her forearms around the wolf, Aurora wrestled him, crashing her heavier body into his. He struggled to stay on his feet, fighting against her grip, then faltered. She was at his throat in a moment, but she didn't just grab and hold on, cutting off his air. Instead, she tore at it, ripping left to right, essentially chewing his throat open to do maximum damage.

Blood gushed, and Carlos struggled weakly.

Aurora wasn't in control of herself anymore. She settled on top of him, still ripping. It looked like she was trying to kill him, and equally like she would succeed. This hadn't been much of a fight at all, just like every challenge before. When Aurora lost herself to the darkness, as when Austin did, she boosted her power—her effectiveness, her unbridled viciousness—in spades.

Unlike Austin, she'd never been afraid of the darkness. He wasn't sure that was a good thing.

But Brochan, tensing at Austin's side, realized the danger. It was time to stop this.

Austin nearly turned to Jess, but she held up her hand as she stepped forward. "Enough, Aurora," she said calmly, and a pulse of magic hit them all. It felt...almost peaceful, tranquil, but was a command nonetheless. "It's over."

Ignoring her, Aurora kept at it. Carlos barely moved. He'd thrown in the towel and needed the challenge to end before it turned fatal. They were in the red zone, almost to the limit...

Austin stepped forward this time. "Jess—"

She shook her hand a little, and another shock of magic cut through him. Peace...with an edge. A warning to calm down. It wasn't for him—it was still directed at Aurora—but everyone felt it. Jess was being transparent in her leadership. "Aurora, enough. It's *over*," Jess said, violence ringing in her voice.

The magic changed, a countdown now, hard and stinging.

Aurora tensed but didn't relent. Fights went this far, especially when someone lost themselves to their beast, often had to be forcibly ended. If the shifter had a lot of power, people could get hurt in the process. This was why Austin wanted Jess to get used to this—he needed her at his side in case the worst should happen. He needed her to protect others if he should lose himself and not be able to come back, just as they were witnessing with Aurora.

"Je—" he started, ready to handle it himself.

Aurora yelped, then flew, rolling through the air. She slammed into the ground ten feet away, nearly hitting a spectator. The great tiger righted herself with a snarl, then lunged forward, aiming for Jess.

Austin tried to intervene, but he bounced off a wall of magic that gleamed around the challenge area.

Calm as could be, Jess gracefully stepped over the prone wolf in a protective posture. "It's over, Aurora. You need to claw your way out of the darkness. Come back to me."

He realized she was talking to Aurora like he had once spoken to Jess when her gargoyle weighed her down. She was trying to guide Aurora as he had once guided her.

Aurora bunched and lunged, but Jess thrust her hand forward, magically batting her away. The tiger flew again, this time to the right.

"Climb out of the darkness, Aurora," Jess said in

that calming tone, this time with a command worming through it. "Your beast does not rule you—it helps you. *You* control *it*, not the other way around. Fight your way back to the surface."

"I'll be damned," Tristan whispered. Austin would have to ask him later what he was responding to.

Carlos's throat began to mend, and his bleeding slowed. Jess was healing him as she worked with Aurora, a protector and a teacher at the same time.

Austin's pride swelled. He couldn't have picked a better co-leader or mate. This would get out to the rest of the pack. *This* was why they were all concerned about her well-being.

Aurora lunged once more, but her heart wasn't in it.

"Claw your way to the surface," Jess commanded, and this time, power roared in her words. "Come on, Aurora, you're more than a mere beast. Prove it." She waited a beat. "Austin had to find his balance as well. So did I. You *have* to have balance when you're flirting with the darkness. That side of you is a great asset...until it's a danger. Stability should not come with a warning label."

"That's something a gargoyle would say," Tristan whispered, leaning toward Austin. "Language like that appeals to the cairns."

Good to know.

"She's blossoming as an alpha," Brochan murmured. "Looks like she needs to be in the action to really own that part of herself."

"I agree," Tristan said. "It's something I've learned about myself recently."

Austin kept himself from huffing out a laugh. Tristan had learned that by taking over a schedule, of all things. He needed to buy Niamh a beer, or perhaps a whole vat of basajaunak special brew.

A flare of light preceded Aurora's rising to stand in her human form, her gaze acutely focused on Jess. She didn't speak or step forward. She didn't posture with the victory or even give a cursory glance to get reactions, something most shifters did.

Jess nodded at her as though there had been a silent exchange. "Good," she said. "Work on it. Eventually, it won't be such a struggle. I should know—I went from a Jane to a violent, dark-dwelling death machine. If I can do it, anyone can."

"Kind of extreme," Tristan muttered, laughter in his tone.

Jess pulled her foot from over Carlos before kneeling at his side and putting a hand on his shoulder. "How do you feel? Better?"

He let his tongue roll out.

"He's good," Austin translated, because Jess would

have no clue what that meant. "He just needs more time to heal."

"I'm letting him feel most of the pain to keep him from shifting or moving too much." Jess rose. "His throat needs to be better stitched together, or it'll tear. Blood loss could still kill him if he's not careful."

The magic winked out from around the challenge area. Aurora lowered her gaze, contemplative, before making her slow way to Carlos. She knelt beside him as someone brought her clothes. Austin couldn't hear what she said, but it was customary to thank the other shifter for the fight.

"Okay." Jess stopped in front of Austin with her hands on her hips. "What's next? Tristan?"

"Give me a minute. I just need to jot down your thoughts and hopes in your diary really quick," he replied.

She rolled her eyes as Austin nearly turned back to see what he was talking about. Jess grimaced at him, though, stealing his attention. "Sorry," she said. "Hopefully, with practice, I'll get better."

He wrapped his arm around her shoulders and led her toward the car. "You did perfectly. I'd never thought to coach Aurora on the darkness. She always seems much more together than I ever was. I didn't realize it was a concern."

She half glanced back. "I'd ask if I overstepped, but I have a connection with her through my gargoyle." She didn't elaborate on what she'd felt. "It probably isn't a concern for your day-to-day shifter stuff. No one else seemed worried about her. They were only worried about the wolf. Those I could feel through connections, anyway. But losing control like that *is* dangerous. We both know it firsthand. I think it should be addressed, that's all. Maybe not for everyone, if you don't think so, but at least for the people…at least family."

For the people she cared about directly—that must've been what she was about to say. But she cared about *all* of her pack directly. Maybe not randomly on the street, but once it became about battle and fighting and danger, she cared. It was her duty, whether personally assigned or assigned by Ivy House. Or, hell, maybe that was what a female gargoyle was. It was why there were so few—it only took one to get the job done.

She needed to attend more challenges. She needed to ingrain herself in the shifter lifestyle every bit as much as that of the gargoyles. Her insight, and her personal touch on the members of the convocation, were clearly important. He wanted to nurture that.

Austin sighed. If only they had years to do all this instead of weeks. They needed to leave soon. Kingsley had organized a meetup with some open-minded alphas before Austin hit the packs that already planned to say no. They'd just have to make do.

"We get lunch now, right?" Jess asked.

Tristan hesitated. "We're ahead of schedule. Do you maybe want to knock out Edgar's thing before we break for lunch?"

Her sigh matched Austin's from a moment ago. "I guess. Maybe you can help me put an end to the constant stream of new flowers."

"Oh." Tristan was quiet for a moment. "Okay, I need to prepare. He twists my mind up when he argues. Let's do lunch now, and then we'll shove him in the slot before you meet the hacker."

Jess spun around. "That's happening *today*? I only decided to meet him a couple hours ago!"

Tristan stopped next to them, a little diary held open by his thumb and a pen in the other hand. Brochan, having walked with him, looked down at the pages with a furrowed brow.

"Yeah," Tristan said. "Apparently he's been staying in a hotel for the last few days, waiting for an interview."

She stared at Tristan for a solid beat, tensing in frustration. "Is that right?" she said slowly, narrowing her eyes. "Was it your job to help bring me around?"

He showed no expression, not in his face or his body. He was damn good at hiding his thoughts when

113

he wanted to.

"To bring you around?" he said. "No. I was honest with you. I try to always be honest with you. But I did know Niamh planted the slip of paper in Naomi's pile. When I saw it, I suspected her, and she confirmed it after the fact. I didn't tell you because she planned to herself. She wanted you to go to your...*advisors* first, and then think about it. You brought it up before she could. I'm not trying to manipulate you, Jessie. I'm trying to learn to work with you. To be someone you can lean on."

Her bearing thawed, and Brochan straightened, no longer peering over the gargoyle's arm to read the diary. He believed Tristan and respected what he'd just said. Austin agreed wholeheartedly.

"Well." A sheen covered Jess's eyes. She was still struggling with losing Nathanial and under a lot of pressure, and she didn't have a tight hold on her emotions. "Thank you. That means a lot to me." She cleared her throat and pointed at the diary. "Bake in a couple minutes for me to punch Niamh in the face for manhandling all of us. I don't care if it's for our own good—I've about had it. It's annoying."

"Manhandling...*all* of us?" Tristan asked, and Brochan's lip twitch and sparkling eyes were the equivalent of another man blurting out a laugh. Tristan wasn't aware that he, too, had been "guided."

Jess turned to Austin, once again stealing his focus. Her beautiful hazel eyes were large and open. "Do you have some time to meet this hacker with me?" she asked. "The one I asked you about the other day."

He inclined his head toward Brochan. Jess wasn't the only one needing help with a schedule of late.

"I can have Kace sit in on the challenge this afternoon," Brochan offered, "and I can take the one you'd planned to attend."

Right, that challenge, another high-level placement. The challenger was from a prominent pack on the East Coast. She'd left without looking back, coming here with no safety net or even a hotel reservation. She'd shown up at the bar when Austin was working, waited until he was finished, and asked to challenge into the team. Not the pack, the team. The convocation.

Usually, Austin started people low and made them earn their placement by working their way up. That was standard shifter protocol. But not this woman. Her experience and her belief in what they were doing had him granting her permission to challenge for placement at any level she chose.

She was going for the top, but not the very top. Not the level she *could* challenge into, if he'd read her correctly. When asked why, she'd said that she still needed to learn the ropes and wasn't ready for a leadership role yet. She'd elevate when she felt she could increase the value of the team.

Perfect answer. Perfect disposition. He hoped she worked out.

That was the only reason he hesitated now. He wanted to see her fight.

"How about we push Niamh to the evening?" Jess said without missing a beat. She winked at Austin. "Look at how good I am at reading body language."

"He was all but screaming at you," Brochan said, and Tristan laughed.

Austin kissed her. "Evening I can do. Good luck with Edgar."

Her world-weary sigh spoke volumes.

CHAPTER 9

JESSIE

"PREPARE THYSELF," EDGAR said with a flourish as the sun sank toward the horizon. We'd gotten delayed with other matters and had to shift him to later in the day.

We stood deep in the wood, where most of Edgar's experiments were held. Flowers of experiments past were either watching us, swaying randomly, or wilting vines with their tops chewed off by the basajaunak. They policed the more dangerous of the creations and ate anything that had gone too far.

The basajaunak stood around us now, presumably hoping Edgar's latest batch would be deemed edible. The almost cognizant flowers tasted better than the run-of-the-mill magical flowers, apparently. To my dismay, they also tended to be worse for flatulence.

Ten thick stalks with large, waxy petals each supported a chrysanthemum-style blossom. Each flower was a different color—fuchsia, sunbeam yellow, lavender, chartreuse—and a dusting of bronze sat at the bloom's center.

"For the flower of the century," Edgar said in a strange, echoing voice.

Indigo stood in the center of the setup. As our resident healer, she didn't have much to do until we had to battle, and so she passed the time helping Edgar with the flowers, hanging out with the nature-loving basajaunak, or running in blind terror from the gnomes.

As Tristan, standing a few paces behind me with his arms crossed, harrumphed at Edgar's act, Indigo winked at us. "This one is really special," she said.

With her words, the flowers started swaying and twisting in unison. After a moment, they broke formation and switched to a series of independent movements that somehow worked together before returning to their choreography. I realized they were essentially dancing.

"This flower has it all," Edgar said, stepping closer to one of his babies. "It has teeth!"

The flower opened a mouth that hadn't been visible before, revealing fangs.

"It has poisonous saliva!"

On cue, a fang dripped.

"Razor-sharp leaves!"

The flower sliced one of its leaves through the air, then the other, like a ninja.

"Projectile killing spores!"

It bent to the ground and shot a stream of small orbs at the dirt.

"They listen like your best friend"—all the flowers turned to him at the same time—"never need to sleep, know friend from foe after just *one* introduction, and have a long striking distance for a quick or torturous death, depending on which they deem worthy. They have different kinds of poisons—all natural, of course. This is a purely organic flower. No chemicals or pre-servatives."

"Besides the original formula to grow them," Indigo added.

"Well, yes, besides the formula I injected into the soil thrice daily," Edgar amended. "All natural."

"Except for the magic," Indigo said.

He nodded. "Yes. Except for that."

I rubbed my temples. "How does a flower decide the speed of death?"

"With its flower brain," Edgar replied.

"It has an actual brain?" I asked incredulously. "Like...a human brain?"

"No, silly. It's a flower. Why would it have a human

brain?" He laughed, and Indigo joined in, but I stood there, feeling uneasy and more than a little perplexed.

"And if it isn't introduced to someone?" I lifted my eyebrows.

"Its instinct is to kill first and ask questions later." Edgar put his hands behind his back and blinked asynchronously. It was like he was *trying* to get weirder.

I should probably thank him for allowing me to feel normal.

"Right," I said on a release of breath, willing patience. "So, the difference between this flower and the last three versions is that it decides how quickly or slowly to kill its foe?"

"Yes."

"You didn't take my notes from the last versions, when I told you that the flowers shouldn't kill unless they were *sure* the person was a foe and not a random stranger?"

"Oh." Edgar tilted his head at me. "Was that a note or a wish?"

I stared at him with an open mouth. "It's the same thing, Edgar. A note is a wish. A wish is a request." My voice rose, out of my control. "A request is a barrier against using this flower until it's safe for strangers. We can't randomly kill wayward hikers, Edgar. It's a huge wood. They get lost from time to time, and they shouldn't be killed for their lack of directional sense. It's bad enough that the basajaunak scare the hell out of them and send them running for their lives. We *cannot* have killer flowers here. I've told you this."

"Ah." Edgar held up one spindly finger. "But these flowers won't go in the wood."

The flowers started swaying and dancing, shaking their leaves and somehow wiggling the petals on their "faces."

"And where will they go?" I asked.

"They will go along the walkway to the house." He smiled as if that solved everything. Indigo nodded, totally fine with this plan.

I turned to Tristan and held up my hands. He didn't so much as step forward to help.

"Right," I said, tired, wanting to slip into the bath, utterly at a loss.

"Great!" Edgar beamed. "I'll just—"

"No. That wasn't acceptance of putting lethal flowers at the front of the house. A wayward hiker is *way* less likely than a stranger delivering a package. Or a Girl Scout selling cookies. Or a new shifter stopping by with a message."

"Oh, well, the shifters should know better. Do we really need packages and cookies?" Edgar asked.

I shouldn't have been surprised that he wasn't joking.

"Yes, Edgar, we need those things. But more importantly, we can't kill innocent people. That's the main takeaway. *We cannot kill innocent people!* Not to mention, the flowers are dancing. There are still Dicks and Janes living in this town. There are *always* Dick and Jane tourists passing through, and they often brave Niamh's rocks to look at Ivy House. We can't have obviously magical flowers in the front yard. That's not how things work. I really feel like you should know that."

Edgar spread out his hands, ready with a rebuttal.

"*No.*" I made a stop motion. "The answer is no. If you can create a flower that isn't lethal to strangers, and that doesn't move all the time, we'll talk. Otherwise, please go back to work on the gnomes."

Before he could argue, I strode away. My patience was starting to fray, I was close to shouting, and I didn't want to be confronted with his desire to be retired. I worried I might actually take him up on it this time, just to get a little peace from the freaking killer flowers.

"Thanks for the help back there, bub," I muttered to Tristan as we worked our way to the house. "I thought you were going to step in at some point and end the madness."

"I'm good at many things, but speaking logic to that vampire is not one of them. I don't even care that I failed you. The less I understand that vampire, the better for my mental health."

"Yeah," I said on a sigh. I couldn't really fault him. "Please tell me that Niamh's hacker is the last meeting of the day, Mr. Tom has prepared an amazing dinner, and Austin will be available to take a very long bubble bath behind a closed, *locked* door."

"Niamh's hacker is the last, no idea about Mr. Tom, but I hope so, because I'm starving, and I'll be taking my own bubble bath, so I won't be concerned about yours. This day has been exhausting, even though I wasn't the one searching for and practicing spells. How have you kept this pace for months?" he demanded. "It's not healthy, Jessie. We probably need to sit down and figure out a better situation."

"It might not be healthy, but it's essential. In a few weeks, we're going to be on the road—Crap, remind me to tell Austin about the latest with the gargoyle cairns. Anyway, we're going to be on the road—Shoot, I need to send a message to the mages about a connection request gift. Or did I tell you to do that? Or can we just show up at their cairn?"

We reached the back door, and he stepped forward to open it for me. "You told me. I think I have it, though—I was looking things up when you were muttering about magical spells. I'll show you after the meeting, while you fill Austin in and Mr. Tom is hopefully serving up something good, and right before we all break for bubble baths."

"Great. But yeah, we'll be on the road. It'll be stressful, but there will be more time to rest. Though…" I bit my lip as I wound through the house. "I guess I should use that downtime to work on body language and subtlety—"

"Jessie." Mimi stopped us in the hall as I felt Austin step onto the property. His stride was slow. Through our bonds, I could feel his exhaustion. "That blown-glass bowl is exquisite. Excellent style and craftsmanship. Did I hear you correctly that you were thinking about procuring that for a production cairn?"

"No, it was a connection request-slash-gift. It's from their cairn's new production cairn."

"Ah. Pity." She passed by.

"If all conversations could be as succinct as that, we would get through the day so much more quickly," Tristan murmured.

"You're telling me."

The front door opened as I reached it. Austin stepped through with a rumpled shirt and sports sweats. He'd obviously had to shift, probably to train. He was doing a ton of that, wanting to show well for the other packs. "Hey, baby," he said wearily, pulling me into a hug. "How was your day?"

"Same as normal. Do you have time for a bubble bath later?"

"Lots of time, yes. What's the story with the flowers?"

I groaned as I leaned against him and felt Niamh coming up the walk. "They're better at thinking now, which doesn't matter because they'll still kill anyone they don't recognize. Edgar just isn't getting the idea. How was your day?"

He stroked my back before pulling away. "Mostly good. The new shifter is a grizzly, highly intelligent, and seems open-minded. I think she'll be a great addition. I messed up on a bar order, though, and had to make a run to get more alcohol." He rubbed his hand down his face. "I need to fast-track hiring a manager, but I don't have time to devote to that right now, or the other businesses." With a quick kiss, he headed for the stairs. "I'll be right back down. Just going to change."

Niamh stopped in the doorway. "Well, Jessie, how's things? Are ye well?"

I pointed to the sitting room. "Would you join me for a moment? Tristan, you can wait out here."

She led the way, settling into a chair and putting her sneakered shoes on the ottoman.

I sat down on the couch. "The manipulation game

has to end," I started without preamble. "I know you're doing your thing, and I have no doubt I'll be glad of it soon enough, but I don't like Austin using those tactics on me, and I don't like you using them on my team. I don't want to feel like I have no control of what happens in this house and in my life. I got out of a controlling relationship, and I will *not* fall into another one, no matter how well meaning. If you want me to hire someone, you bring that person to me directly. If you want to give Tristan a kick in the arse, you tell me first that there's a problem that we can maybe solve. You are not the leader of this team, I am, and I cannot do my job if I'm in the dark about half the things going on."

Her look was placid, and the silence stretched. I let her take all that in.

"I wondered if ye'd push back," she finally said. "Good girl, yerself. There is just one more seed planted, but she isn't actually on yer team, so that doesn't matter."

"Fine." I relaxed into the cushions, a little surprised with myself that I'd been so bold. Then again, I'd hit my limit, and getting that out there was my relief valve. "Tristan, you can come in now," I called.

His glowing gaze was rooted to Niamh. "How did you give me a kick in the arse?"

"I knew full well ye wouldn't tolerate Jessie's frustration over that donkey Mr. Tom smothering her. He's unbearable when he's trying to organize dinner, let alone manage someone with as many demands and interruptions as Jessie has these days. I figured you'd step in to give her some space, and that might remind ye that yer job isn't standing in a corner like some creep. We already have someone doing that, like. The vampire is plenty good at that role, whether we like it or not. No, ye needed a more active role in her professional life. If this didn't work, I had a few other ideas to make ye step up."

He was as quiet now as she'd just been a moment ago, equally taking it all in. "What about your prediction that I was too self-centered for a job like this?"

"Ah, sure, ye might be. But I had a look at the other options, and they aren't good enough. They aren't fast or strong enough. She needs ye, and we need her, so ye'd best cop on so we don't all find ourselves in an early grave."

He grunted and fell into a chair near the back of the room. I knew he wanted to know more about the hacker, but he would clearly let Niamh, Austin, and me handle the interview. For my portion, I really only had one question. Austin would handle the rest. He was the good judge of character, not me.

"I was about to give up," Tristan admitted, getting comfortable and opening the diary. He took out a pen.

"You were going to give—What are you doing?" I asked.

He paused with pen to paper and looked up. "Writing your thoughts and hopes and dreams. Mr. Tom has made it perfectly clear that it's a diary. First, I'm going to pen your absolute love of Edgar's flowers and how you long to put them in a window box…"

"What in the—" Niamh pushed up a little to get a clear look at him. "Ye really have gone around that bend."

"When in Rome," he murmured as I laughed at the absurdity of it all.

Austin descended the stairs but stopped at the bottom. I wondered why until Mr. Tom entered with an air of importance and a freshly pressed tuxedo.

"Ah, yes, fantastic," he said as he noticed Tristan. "It's good to see *someone* takes his job seriously." His withering glance at Niamh made clear whom he was talking about.

"See?" Tristan said to me, continuing to write.

Austin entered the room after Mr. Tom, walked around him, and then settled next to me on the couch. He wore a button-down shirt and nice jeans, professionally casual.

"Should I…" I looked down at my jeans and plain black T-shirt. "Should I put something else on, too?"

"Should ye, me arse," Niamh said. "Ye're grand. Here, Mr. Tom, get me a beer, would ya? I'm dyin' of thirst."

"I most certainly will not," Mr. Tom told her. "You are about to do an interview. At least *try* to look the part."

"I plan on it. Did ye not just hear me ask for a beer?"

He sniffed. "I only have the brand that Austin Steele favors, and he does not need to share. Now, miss, what can I get for you? Water, sweet tea, wine?"

"Just a water would be great, Mr. Tom, thanks. Are you, by chance, making anything for dinner?" I asked.

"Don't be silly—of course I am. Roast beef, your favorite." It wasn't, but I still liked it plenty, so I didn't say anything. "Austin Steele, how about that bottle of suds I spoke of a moment ago? That would be nice and relaxing after a hard day."

"Great, Mr. Tom, thanks," Austin responded as he put his arm around me and hugged me close.

"Fantastic. Tristan?"

"A beer sounds good, if the alpha can spare one."

"I have plenty," said Mr. Tom. "He won't notice if one is missing."

"Let two go missin', then, ye oul goat," Niamh groused.

"I'm fine to share," Austin said.

"You might reconsider, sir." Mr. Tom's wings fluttered. "If she gets started, she'll have them all drunk before you know it."

A stranger walked onto the property, heading for the door. "If Edgar had his way, that person would be just about to die," I murmured.

"If Edgar had his way," Niamh said, "ye would've retired him by now, and we'd all have one less headache."

A moment later, the doorbell echoed through the house. Mr. Tom headed that way, his wings fluttering accordingly.

"Oh, by the way, this person doesn't know we're magical," Niamh said.

I paused, because it hadn't occurred to me to ask. I'd been too worried about the stealing. "Wait," I said, "how is that going to work?"

"It'll be grand," Niamh replied, though a little more detail on *how* might've been nice.

I felt the door swing open. "You rang?" Mr. Tom said. He'd never seen *The Addams Family*, and he wasn't trying to joke.

"Hey," I heard, a rough and scratchy woman's voice.

"Cool cape. How do you get it to move like that?"

"Capes are for superheroes written by mediocre Dicks and Janes with empty existences," Mr. Tom replied primly. "Given your very uninspired disguise, *you* are more apt to wear a cape than I am. State your business."

"That's a lot to unpack right there. I'm Fred. I'm here for the interview. My pronouns are she, her, and they."

"Fabulous. Right this way."

The front door swung shut, and footsteps echoed on the hardwood.

"Wow. This is some house," the woman said. The name on the résumé had given me the wrong idea of her gender. "How big is this place?"

"Big enough." Mr. Tom entered the room, and then stepped aside.

I stood, as did Austin…before freezing in surprise.

CHAPTER 10

JESSIE

THE SLIM WOMAN was a little over five feet and of Asian descent, with short, green-yellow hair sticking up in spikes all over her head. She had slight crow's-feet around her eyes and smooth cheeks—I guessed she was probably mid-thirties, but I couldn't be sure because the rest of her face was covered in a fake gray beard and a long, equally fake mustache that covered her mouth. A fox fur draped around her neck, the old-fashioned kind with the head and paws still attached. Unlike the moth-eaten things I'd seen at the back of vintage shops, though, this fox's mouth open in a grotesque snarl beneath the red marbles of its eyes, while its feet bore red-painted nails and strange bangles like tiny bracelets. Under that, she wore a black shirt with long sleeves and black slacks splattered with fuchsia paint stains.

I glanced at Niamh and raised an eyebrow. *Did you*

put her up to this?

Niamh clearly understood because she shook her head. She seemed just as bewildered as I was, and usually she didn't react to anything.

"Oh, don't worry," the woman said, stopping just inside the room. She pointed at the fur. "It was roadkill."

I wasn't sure that was any better. It was about the same level of horrific and maybe a lot grosser.

"Hi. Fred, is it?" I asked, stepping forward with my hand out.

"Yeah. Hey." She put up her fist, and I changed from a handshake to knuckles. Then she pointed at the fireplace. "Wow. What a mind-bending coincidence."

I followed her gaze to Ivy House's wooden mantel over the fireplace, which currently showed a fox running through a meadow. What a coincidence, indeed. Ivy House loved to mess with the minds of the non-magical. This interview was probably over before it had even begun.

"This is my fiancé, Austin," I said, and turned so that he could step forward to fist-bump her.

"Hey, man. Nice muscles," said Fred. "I thought about working out once. Thought against it, that is. Too much energy, know what I mean?" Her cheeks lifted, and I supposed there was a smile hiding somewhere under that fake facial hair.

I swung my hand to indicate the third member of our group. "And this is Niamh. She's the one who initiated this meeting."

"How're ya?" Niamh asked, not bothering to get up.

"Oh, N*eeeve*." Fred laughed. "Irish. Gotcha. I read the name on the messages and couldn't make sense of it. Hi! Yes, we've been in contact."

"And Tristan."

He had already slipped the pen into the diary to save his spot and now stood with it mostly closed in one of his hands. His eyes were currently dimmed with fatigue, but his long wings fluttered—clearly an attention tactic.

"Another cape wearer, huh?" Fred nodded. "I've seen a ton of them in this town. Are you anti-superhero as well?"

"Only when someone needs saving," he replied, and his eyes glowed a little brighter. He might turn out to be as bad as Ivy House. "I'd rather do it myself."

"Cool contacts. I need to get me a pair of those. I have some green ones, and some blue ones, but I didn't know they made some that glow!"

"And you met Mr. Tom." I pointed back toward the door.

"Yup." Her head bobbed in acknowledgment.

"Please, have a seat," I offered, and gestured toward the couch opposite Austin and me.

"Can I get you a refreshment?" Mr. Tom asked.

"Yeah, that would be great," Fred replied. "Maybe a pop, if you have one? And a little cheese wouldn't hurt. Everyone has cheese, right? It's one of the four major food groups."

"Of course I have it." He turned on his heel and strode through the door.

"What's the wig fer?" Niamh asked. "Or is that part of the ensemble?"

"Oh, this?" Fred peeled the fake beard and mustache off her face. "It's to prevent facial recognition by the eyes in the sky." She pointed upward. "Cameras."

"We don't have cameras posted in this town or in the five surrounding towns," Austin said. "Your indiscretions in the Dick world do not count against you here."

"Right?" Fred said. "The Man!" She gave a thumbs-down and then did a raspberry.

"We have a different set of rules in this town than in…most other places in the country," I said carefully.

"Like the Mafia?" she asked. "No one here dresses like Mafia…"

"Like that but…not as dangerous." I wiggled my hand. "Mostly. Anyway, we'll get to that in a bit. I'm curious about something. Why, when you make millions every year, uh...working for yourself," I said politically, "would you decide to take a job making a fraction of that amount?"

"Well..." She raised a fuzzy eyebrow. "What was your name?"

I flattened a hand to my chest. "Sorry, I'm Jessie. I'm the owner of this house and, along with Austin, Niamh's boss. I'm the one who would actually be paying you."

"Hi, Jessie." She flashed a smile, showing slightly crooked white teeth. "Here's the deal. I'm sliding down that slippery slope toward middle age, and I'm *tired* of all this. I'm tired of hiding. I have to wear scratchy face stuff all the time, dress normally, hunch over when I'm out and about, watch myself in places that have security cameras, keep eyes in the back of my head—I mean, staying out of jail is a *lot* of work. You have no idea. I tried to do nothing for a while because—not to sound boastful—I don't *have* to work anymore. I live frugally, and I've made enough money to live off the interest of my investments. But that's bored me to tears, and I found myself thinking, you know, maybe I could semi-retire. Work for someone else, yeah? I just do what I'm told, have a chat by the water cooler, and keep busy with low stakes."

"Why the high price tag, then?"

Her smile widened. "Someone willing to pay that much has a great need of my services and respects my talent. Given my past, that person's need would outweigh the desire to do the right thing and turn me in."

Made sense.

"And you found Niamh?" I asked.

"She found me, really. I posted on a board that is not totally reputable, we'll say, and she contacted me. She described this place, and how I'd have to follow the rules here or it's dangerous, but that my past wouldn't be a problem. Sounded good. Figured I would check it out. The towns around here are cute, though the people are pretty...serious. The ones without capes, anyway. A *lot* of muscle. Are you guys a bunch of health nuts or something?" She turned her face a little to side-eye me. "This isn't a cult, is it? I don't want to get mixed up in a cult."

"No, it's not a cult"—which was just what a cult leader would say, I mused—"but it's not something you're probably used to. We do have a great need, and we can pay. Now, honestly, I *am* a little concerned about your history of theft. There are a lot of valuable items in this house, and it wouldn't go well for you if you tried to take them."

"Ah, gotcha." She nodded knowingly. "Definitely

like the Mafia, then. No sweat. I only stole from those other places because they were ripping people off. Screw those guys. I figured they'd get to see how it felt. Then it became a game, then a challenge as they got better. But now…yeah. Like I said, I'm worn out, and I'd rather not bother with any of that. Clean slate without going to jail, like Niamh said."

It turned out I had a lot more questions than I'd originally thought. "But you're still okay with a challenge?"

Her face lit up as Mr. Tom came in with drinks. "I *love* a challenge! I love puzzles, and Niamh said you'd have no end of them for me. That I'd be taking on worse than those companies, and people around here didn't go to the cops for stuff." She put her finger to the side of her nose. "Fits me right down to the ground. I love cracking open impenetrable firewalls and peering inside."

I looked at Austin. She sounded fine to me. It probably wouldn't be hard to keep her in line, and Niamh surely thought she could keep the woman busy and entertained. The magical aspect of all this, though…

"Is that normal attire, then?" Niamh asked without expression.

"This?" Fred petted the head of the fox. "Are you kidding? No! This is fun attire. I wouldn't go out like this normally, but—well, you already have my info, and half the town walks around in capes. I figured I had some artistic license."

"And Fred is not your real name," I surmised. "You could be anybody."

"No, my real name is Wilma. Wilma Rebecca Foster. I don't mind my last name, or even my middle name so much, even though it's boring. But *Wilma*? I'm not a Wilma. I could be a Fred, though," she said. "The name Fred has personality. I figure my birth name is for my mom. She likes it, she has terrible taste in names, but she gave me life, so she can call me Wilma. It's not like she could ask for my opinion at the time. But now that I'm older, I should be able to pick my own name, right? So I did."

I didn't know how Rebecca was somehow boring but Fred wasn't. Biting back a *Flintstones* joke, I decided she wasn't any weirder than anyone else in this house, so I left it alone.

As Mr. Tom brought in a cheese plate, I said, "His real name is Earl, but he chose Mr. Tom himself. So you'd be among company."

"I've always wanted to be a Tom," Mr. Tom explained.

"*Right?*" Fred slapped her knee with a huge smile. "Yeah! That's what I'm talking about." She bobbed her head again, and then basically her whole upper body while looking around, tickled. Her gaze stopped on the mantel carving, and then her brow furrowed. "I might've had too much coffee before I came here, but I could have *sworn* the fox was on the other side of that fireplace when I walked in." She blinked quickly and shook her head. "Anyway," she said, reaching for the cheese, "any other questions? Want me to prove my talent?"

I looked at Niamh. "What about the other thing?" I asked her.

"What other thing?" she replied, clearly playing dumb.

I widened my eyes at her, and then pointedly looked at the mantel. "The *other* thing. The"—I whispered— "magical thing."

Austin pushed to standing, taking his beer with him. "Niamh, give Fred the details about this town and us. Mr. Tom, could you bring Jess and me up a plate of food? We're going to our room. Long day." To Fred, he said, "It was nice meeting you. We'll be in contact tomorrow or the next day with an answer for you, assuming you want the job after Niamh fills you in."

"Yeah, sure." She stood and put out her fist. Austin touched his to hers, and I followed suit after I rose. "Thanks for the opportunity. Sounds great so far, so long as it's not a cult. What about you? Do you use your birth name?"

Austin stopped, a smile playing on his lips. "I was born Austin Baraza, but I'm now Austin Steele, even though the name isn't exactly legal. Jess came to this town as Jacinta Evans. She's now Jacinta Ironheart. Tristan won't tell us his real name, and for all we know, the gardener outside doesn't even *remember* his last name. If you're looking for eccentricity, you've found it."

Fred laughed and put up her arms like she'd just won a race. "This is *great*! I've always been called weird, but here, I might fit in."

Boy, would she. Nessa and Sebastian would be tickled.

Thinking about them, I said, "And if you can find our friends, I'll give you a sizable bonus. Niamh will explain the details."

A crease formed between Fred's eyebrows. Before she could ask questions, I turned to leave, only to find Ulric and Jasper ducking their heads in.

"Hey," Ulric said before spying Fred. "Oh, you're busy—"

"Oh, wow, look at that!" Fred pointed at Ulric's hair. "Look at this!" She pointed at her own. "What's your real name?"

"Ulric," he said in confusion.

"What's your *chosen* name?" she pushed.

"…Ulric?"

"Oh, yeah?" She nodded with her upper body again. "I dig it. An original. And more capes! You guys really love those capes, bruh!"

"Good timing, actually." I gestured them in. "Fred is here for a computer tech job or whatever we're calling it, and Niamh needs to explain this town. She's from the Jane world," I murmured.

Jasper pushed Ulric forward so he could get a look. "I heard Niamh mention something about that."

"Yeah, sure, we can help." Ulric walked farther into the room. "Cheese, nice. I'm starving."

Mr. Tom sniffed. "Yes, we are all well aware, given that you are *always* starving."

I slipped out with Austin following. It was time to relax.

"Well?" I asked him once we were safely hidden in our room.

He lay down on the bed and held out his hand for me to join him. I crawled across the mattress and curled into his arms.

"She's genuine. She even seems honest, which is surprising, given how she ended up here. If she can come around to the magical side of things, I don't think we'll have any problems with her. I really don't. And given her, uh…fashion sense and overall love of eccentricity, she might be easier to convince about magic than most."

I hoped so. Sebastian and Nessa were out there somewhere, and if the weird hacker could find them—and didn't run screaming—then I'd pay whatever she asked.

CHAPTER 11

JESSIE

"**W**HAT DID YOU think of training, Jessie?" Hollace, the thunderbird, asked as Ulric and Jasper dropped from the sky. A plethora of gargoyles were still running their flight patterns, but my portion of the training session was over.

Tristan had me on beginner status, and a few of the house crew with me. The crew understood the larger picture and also how to improvise with me. Tristan thought they'd help me learn the ropes and acclimate to the army's strategies.

The *army*.

I had a gargoyle army. Me, Jacinta Evans, the shy and quiet Jane. The thought made me want to cackle.

If someone had told me a year ago that this was possible, I would've shrugged it off. Laughed, as I wanted to do now. I'd never, in my wildest dreams, thought this would—*could*—exist in modern times. But here we were, led by the infallibly confident Tristan, who had to pull double duty managing me and the guardians at the same time. After a few short days' work, he'd begun to anticipate my moves more often, and frankly, I thought he'd grown leaps and bounds—all because he'd stepped in about my schedule.

How had Niamh known?

"Jessie?" Hollace said.

I blinked rapidly at him, trying to corral my mind into the moment.

"Oh. Um…it's complicated," I replied as Cyra streaked fire through the sky, heading toward the corner of the property. She hadn't gotten to set fire to the gnome nest there yet. The crazy thing was, burning the gnomes out didn't seem to be working. They were tenacious little suckers. "It's a lot to remember."

"Yeah." Hollace slipped on a purple muumuu. "Especially when flying is new to you, huh? Once you acclimate to organized flying, though, you'll pick it up quickly."

I headed toward the house in my own purple muumuu, checking a bare wrist for a watch that wasn't there. After I dressed, I planned to head to Austin's bar to meet Aurora and Broken Sue for training of a different sort. The two had agreed to communicate with each other in words and exaggerated body language, and my goal was to decipher their conversation.

Yeah, right. I already knew it would be a hopeless effort. Their version of exaggerated wasn't much more than a twitch and a grunt to express a novel's worth of information. Aurora thought I was intuitive, but I greatly suspected that she was giving me *far* too much credit. I was about to prove it.

"This is all hopeless," I said to no one in particular.

"Seriously, Jessie, you're a fast learner—"

"Not flight," I told Hollace. "That, at least, I think I'll pick up eventually. I've got another session of shifter practice ahead, and honestly, flight feels more natural than noticing a squint and realizing it's meant to be raucous laughter."

"Ah." He nodded as Ulric and Jasper caught up. "Yeah, I'm not great at any of that. It's an entirely different language. Why would they assume you, or any of us, could pick it up in a couple months?"

"Right?" Ulric said as we threaded our way through the flowers. "I tried to learn French a while back. Two months in, and I could say my name and ask for the time. No one could understand me, though. And I couldn't spell the words…"

"Tristan picked up body language really quickly," Jasper pointed out.

"He's unnatural," Ulric replied. "We're just going to

blame it on that."

"I could get behind that…" Hollace's voice trailed off, and everyone slowed.

I'd been looking at the ground, still conscious of my connections in the sky. Now I glanced up to see what everyone was reacting to.

Fred stood a few paces away from the back door. She wore a pink-and-black checkered suit jacket, buttoned at the waist, with no shirt underneath and brown pants. The hand at her left side had apparently just held the closed laptop lying beside her foot, while her right hand had dropped a half-eaten sandwich. Bread stuck out of her lips, and some meat had slid down her chin. She stared at us with wide eyes, her entire bearing tensed.

"*Surprise*," Jasper said with confidence. "She's showing surprise. I'm far enough along in body language to deduce that much."

"And disbelief," Ulric added. "Surprise and disbelief. See? The lessons are paying off."

"*Hey*, Fred," I said, using the soothing voice that had been deployed on me the first time I saw a person turn into a rat. I'd spiraled pretty quickly. "How much did you see?"

"I thought she mostly believed us the other day," Jasper murmured.

"Clearly, you still can't tell when someone is lying to you," Hollace replied.

"Or maybe she was lying to herself," Ulric whispered. "She watched us shift, for criminy's sakes."

"Hey." I approached her slowly, my hands out. You never knew what the brain's reaction might be to something like this. In her shoes, I might try to karate chop, and I had no idea what sort of fighting prowess she had. "So…this is what we were talking about. With the magic. It's jolting, I know. I was non-magical until over a year ago. It's a lot to take in."

Fred hadn't blinked. She stared at me, transfixed…well, at least until Hollace sauntered closer, stuck his hand in front of her face, and snapped.

Her eyes fluttered, and she turned slowly to look at him. "You were a…a…" she stammered.

"A thunderbird, yes," Hollace replied patiently. "And those"—he gestured to the sky—"are gargoyles."

"Remember the other day?" Jasper bent to pick up her laptop. "When we shifted forms?"

She swallowed heavily, and the bread previously caught in her lip fell away. She raised her gaze and flicked her eyes back and forth, clearly watching the fliers. In a moment, she'd re-sighted in on Hollace.

He nodded, as if that were good enough, and walked around her. "Jessie, I'm just going to go change, and I'll go with you. I want to see if I'm any better at reading their body language than you are."

"Do you want to go for a fly?" Ulric asked Fred gently. "I can take you…"

"That other night, I wondered if I'd been high or something," Fred said in a wispy voice. "Like, maybe I took an edible but forgot about it. Or, like, maybe you slipped me something, and I wasn't in my right mind. But I brought the sandwich and bottled water from the hotel this time. I made that sandwich myself. I'm sober. I haven't hit the vape, and I didn't even take an edible to help me sleep the last couple nights. This…" Her gaze went skyward again. "This is…"

"Okay." I gave the guys a thumbs-up. "I'm going to leave this to you. Niamh should be at her house and changed by now. Mr. Tom…is still training for some reason. Not sure why. Maybe you guys can root through the fridge and get Fred another sandwich before Mr. Tom comes down and yells at you for looking after yourselves."

"Yup, yup," Ulric said. "It'll be okay. She just needs to process, and she'll be fine."

I hoped so, because apparently Fred had given Niamh a tiny demonstration of her prowess yesterday in her hotel room, and it had blown Niamh's mind. Fred was a maestro with the computer, her skill set more art than technological expertise, or so Niamh had said. Niamh was champing at the bit to get working.

I changed and found Hollace by the front door. Surprisingly, Ulric and Jasper met us there, still in their muumuus, with a pale-faced Fred in tow.

"She didn't want another sandwich," Jasper said. "She wants weed or alcohol or both, or something harder. Her words."

"I need a minute, that's all," Fred said, her voice shaky and raspier than usual. "I almost want to comb my hair flat right now. My mind is *spinning!*" We all started walking. "I mean...I'd really wanted to believe the towns around here didn't have any cameras and that you were your own law, but I assumed you just owned the police and politicians. That's what the movies always say, right?" She shook her head and looked back over the house. "Oh, wait, the fliers are gone."

"No, that's just a spell Ivy House does to keep people from seeing her property," I told her as we neared Niamh's place.

Niamh gently rocked in a chair on her porch with her basket of stones on her lap. She slowed as we neared, then stopped altogether when she spied Fred. "What's the *craic*?" she asked in greeting. "How's things?"

Fred pointed a shaky hand back the way we'd come.

"You weren't kidding."

"O'course I wasn't kidding, sure. What do ye think, I go around making stuff like that up? I haven't got the imagination. Where are yis goin'?" Niamh put a lid on the basket. "Are yis goin' for a pint?"

"Yeah, doctor's orders," Jasper said.

"Might as well, so." Niamh put her basket on the porch before standing.

"I know we were going to meet up after I checked out the grounds, as you said, but—" Fred started.

"Not at all." Niamh fell in step. "I see ye've got yer computer there. The pub is as good a place as any to get started. Soon as ye have a wee pint to settle yer nerves, that is."

We walked for a moment in silence. Fred looked over her shoulder again at the house and sky above it.

"Just so that we're all on the same page…" Ulric looped his arm through Fred's. "When you twist and move too much in that jacket, you give us a peep show."

Fred looked at him blankly before glancing down at herself. She shrugged absently. "I've never much cared about the construct of nudity. Why should we feel embarrassed in our own skin? And why, please tell me, should women go to extra lengths to hide our breasts when men don't have to? I've seen guys with bigger boobs than mine! But because men have sexualized

K.F. BREENE

them—the instrument with which we feed our young—
we're forced to lock them down with uncomfortable
bras and always cover them up to stop someone from
feeling aroused. How is a man's arousal a woman's
problem? What if I get turned on by a man's boobs?
Should he then shackle them down like society tries to
shackle ours? Nah. I don't want to sled the slippery
slope of logic on that one."

A crooked smile had worked up Jasper's face. "Free
the breasts! I'm in."

Fred nodded once, then took a deep breath. "I'm
used to being thought of as very odd."

"Ye are definitely very odd, make no mistake,"
Niamh said in a drawl. "It's not 'cause of yer thinkin',
though. It's because ye dress like a whacko."

Ulric spat out a laugh, then patted Fred's forearm.
"The good news is some of us, including the vampire,
are also very odd. And dress like whackos. And look,
Niamh tells us you make magic on that computer! So,
really, you fit right in. You're just like us—you just
don't shift or zap people or suck blood."

"When it comes to that last one, be thankful," Jasper
muttered.

"No nudity in the house, please," I said as we
reached the end of the street and turned. "That goes for
men as well as women."

I did have to admit, aside from not being magical, Fred really was a great fit. Loose morals, weird as hell, outgoing, and not overly concerned with skin. If she could get past the magical thing, which still had her whole body tense and the blood drained from her face, we'd be rolling.

At the moment, that was a very big *if*.

We continued to talk about all things magical as we neared the bar. Butterflies filled my stomach. I'd seen Austin just that morning, but it didn't matter how much time had passed—I always looked forward to seeing him again. Everyone said the obsession for each other would fade with time, that once our mating was settled, we wouldn't have this never-ending craving for each other. It hadn't yet. If anything, I felt closer to him than ever and happier than I had a right to be. He wasn't perfect by far, but he was perfect for me.

My "bestie," a guy I called Sasquatch because of his general hairiness, stood just outside the door, sucking on the end of a cigarette. When he saw me, he scowled, as he always did. His cigarette was only halfway finished, though, and he was cheap. He wouldn't finish in a hurry just to crowd in front of me and slow me down. He loved to annoy me, but wasting half a cigarette was too high of a price.

"No life, huh? You're starting to day-drink now?" he

said in a taunting voice. "Lush."

He was purposely trying to goad me—I knew that. He loved to push my buttons. But Lord help me, I just couldn't seem to ignore him.

"Are you kidding me?" I demanded, stopping at the door. "*You* beat me here! What are you even talking about right now?"

He smirked and took a draw from his cigarette.

"Is he one of them?" Fred asked quietly.

"Not one of ours, at any rate," Jasper murmured. "Thank God."

The bar wasn't slammed at this time of day and in the middle of the week, but that didn't mean it wasn't busy. Half the bar was lined with chatting, laughing patrons. The tables were nearly full, and the crack of a pool cue hitting a ball echoed from down the stairs. They only moved the pool table to the side in the evenings to make room for more people. A few people stood around the walls. The middle of the space was mostly clear.

Austin stood behind the bar at the far end, one hand braced against the edge. He'd been speaking to the two people in front of him, but they were forgotten when he noticed me. I claimed his whole focus. His sparkling cobalt eyes entranced me, and I felt like I was walking on air as I approached him.

"Hey, baby," he said, turning to me as I joined him behind the bar and sliding his hands across my hips. "How was training?"

"Complex. Hard." I shrugged. "I think it'll be a really good move in the long run. We'll be a lot more cohesive."

He bent to kiss my lips, and I felt hunger rise, partially from me, partially through the bonds from him. His growl tightened my core. He dug his fingers into my hips and opened my mouth with his before swiping his tongue through.

"Do you have a minute?" he asked. His hardness against my belly made it clear why he was asking.

Anticipation made my stomach dance. "Tristan is busy, so I have no one to monitor my schedule," I said innocently. "It won't be *my* fault if I run a little late."

With a smirk, he grabbed my hand and tugged me after him. He pushed open the office door and pulled me inside before turning and capturing my lips again.

"I need you," he whispered, pushing the door closed with one hand and me against it a moment later.

He needed a release to vent some of the mounting pressure plaguing us. I was only too happy to help.

I pushed up his shirt as he worked at my jeans, yanking the button free of its hole and unzipping. I ran my hands down his washboard abs before following suit, shoving his jeans down and freeing his length. His mouth was hot on mine, his kiss deep and insistent.

My lower half felt cool air before he spun me around, and then my palms hit the solid wood. His fingers ran along my core, and he growled with the wetness he found there. The pads of his finger circled at the top, dizzying me with pleasure. His thrust made light and color dance behind my closed lids.

I dropped my head, pushing back into him. His deep groan matched my own as he started a fast rhythm. Pleasure mounted as his finger continued to circle, as his body plunged deeply into mine. I moved my hips and shoved back as he bore down, slamming against him.

"Yes," I drew out softly, animalistic in my need, working hard to relieve a little stress. "Harder."

The door wiggled against the frame with our effort. He increased the strength behind the thrusts, and my core wound up, tighter and tighter, until the pleasure crested and I blasted apart. I cried out with my release, and he moaned, long and low, shuddering against me.

With a few last strokes, he slowed until he had me wrapped in his arms, tightly held against him. "Hmm," he murmured as he nuzzled into my neck. "That was what I needed." He pulled back and kissed my cheek, his lips lingering. "I wish I had time to clean you up with my tongue."

I was freshly sated, yet a flash of heat stole through me. He *must've* been stressed—he was getting dirty. I turned my head and found his lips, but I knew he was right. Time was a luxury we didn't have.

"Tonight," I replied, hoping we wouldn't be too exhausted by then. I was in too short a supply of energy to do much healing.

He helped put me to rights before opening the door and letting me out first. His hand rested on the swell of my butt, and I could tell he didn't want to let me walk away when we reached the bar.

"They're at the other end," he told me, glancing down to where Broken Sue and Aurora sat.

Yes, they were, and they looked like two statues. They were probably heavily engrossed in conversation.

CHAPTER 12

AURORA

"NORMAL PEOPLE WOULD crack under the pressure they're under," Aurora said as she watched Jessie walk away from Uncle Auzzie. Despite the relief they'd just sought, their shoulders were still tight and bearings tense, as though their territory were under attack.

"Two unders don't make a right," Sue said. He ticked his head forward. *Agree.*

It took her a moment to realize he was talking about using "under" twice in her comment—a "two wrongs don't make a right" kind of thing.

She shook her head, threatening a smile. "That was reaching. Stick to the strong and *silent* type if those are the kinds of jokes you tell."

He blew out through his nose, essentially huffing a laugh.

Jasper, Ulric, and Niamh sat to Aurora's right. In

their midst was a decently attractive woman with hair nearly as wild as Ulric's, wearing strange clothing and no shirt. If it wasn't for all the buckles on her boots and the sturdy belt, Aurora would have assumed she was expecting to shift soon. As it was, the lady looked shell-shocked.

"I'm helping the alphas every way I can think of," Sue said, following Aurora's gaze. "That's Niamh's tech hire."

Ah, Aurora said through her body. *I know of her.*

She'd been the computer thief Jessie wasn't sure about. A Jane with a tame criminal record.

Seeing her in the flesh, Aurora was certain that lady couldn't hurt a fly. She wasn't subtle in her movements or expressions. If she went to grab something, she'd advertise what it was, where it was, and that she'd just done it. They wouldn't have any trouble from her.

Sue ticked his head forward again. *Agree.* He could read Aurora a little too easily. Only her family was as good, and they'd known her all her life. It was…disconcerting. For her, anyway. Good for Uncle Auzzie and Jessie. No one would get anything past this alpha gorilla.

"Hey." Jessie plopped down into the empty seat next to Sue. "Sorry, I got delayed for a moment."

NOT A PROBLEM, Sue said by way of a pronounced shrug.

Jessie squinted at him, her gaze flowing over his muscular shoulders. Then his face. Then to Aurora.

"Yeah, I don't know." She lifted her hand for a drink. "Let's get a sip of wine and try, try again. Honestly, you'd think this would be the easy part. Nope. What's easy is learning spells that literally blow a head off. This is my life now," she muttered.

"You need to add a third *under* to your assessment," Sue said to Aurora, and because it barely made sense, and because he was building off an already bad joke, Aurora let the humor bubble up. Her grin was minimal and purely for Jessie's benefit.

Jessie missed it, the joke, and Sue's calm patience as she waited for a drink.

"No, no!" The new person waved her hand in front of her face with her eyes squeezed tightly shut. "No! Not yet. I need at least one more whiskey, one more flashback of a huge monster turning into a dude my size"—she blindly pointed at Ulric—"and *then* we can talk about stalking your friends."

"*Stalking* is a harsh term," Ulric told her.

Her eyes opened. "Fine. We can talk about finding your friends who don't want to be found and watching them without their knowing. Honestly, Jessie, my thievery was a concern? This one"—she hooked a thumb Niamh's way—"is waging war on your former housemates. *I'm* the problem here?"

"Not at all," Niamh said. "I'm helping them, like."

The woman's eyes were wide as she looked across everyone to Jessie, who'd just secured a bottle of wine. A new bartender, a male, was working, and apparently he was worried about pouring a drink for the alpha's mate. Jessie didn't seem to mind helping herself.

"She's not waging war, she's..." Jessie bowed in defeat. "None of this is sitting well with me, I'll be honest. The mages overstepped on multiple occasions. They aren't acting like themselves. And then Niamh and Tristan... Yeah."

She shook her head and lifted the glass to her lips. The situation with the mages was bothering her greatly, adding stress to an already stressful existence. Jessie had a bad feeling in her gut, and Aurora was inclined to believe the female gargoyle knew her people were in danger.

"We aren't going to watch them without their knowing," Jessie continued. "We're going to bring them home, for their own safety. We just...have to find them. And convince them." She sagged in fatigue.

Sue's shoulders tensed; he was damn near panicked and radiating helplessness. He couldn't see a way to relieve Jessie's burden. There was just too much to do and no time. Absolutely zero time, especially with how the mages were carrying on, setting them up and dragging them further into trouble.

"Anyway," Jessie said, her focus snapping back to them, "this is Aurora, Austin's niece." Jessie pointed to her. "And Broken Sue."

"Broken—*Broken* Sue, did you say?" the woman asked. Humor and delight peeked through her drawn face. She'd gotten quite a shock earlier, that was clear.

"Just Sue is fine, if you like," he replied.

"Yeah." The woman bobbed her upper body. *TO-TALLY AGREE WITH YOU!!!!!!* "You don't look broken. You look like you do the breaking. Heads, bones—but hey, I'll work with what you give me. Broken Sue, Sue, you just let me know. I'm in. Do you guys actually go to the gym, or are magical people just in good shape? You look like you're ready to crush a skull with your bare hands."

"We don't work out in a gym, but we do work out," Ulric said. "You know, flying and—"

"Never mind. Forget I asked." The woman waved to cut Ulric off. She reached for her newly poured whiskey with a trembling hand. "I'm Fred. Fred Foster. Sounds good, right? Alliteration. Well, Broken Sue, Sue for short, I've had a helluva start to the afternoon, let me tell you."

She blew out a long breath and stared at nothing for a while.

Fireworks of movement exploded all over Sue's body. *Bewildered. Humored. She'll fit here.*

Aurora answered in kind. *Definitely will.*

"I feel like I should create a new name," Aurora murmured, reaching for her bourbon on the rocks with a twist as Jessie clued into them again. The training was officially starting.

"Your dad is already wary about this setup," Sue replied. "He worries about your being in Alpha Steele's territory, given the danger." *This is a passive warning.* "I'd give it a while before you spring any new changes on him."

Jessie shook her head. "No idea."

"But at least you knew he was communicating *something*," Aurora said with an encouraging smile. "That's good!" She glanced at Sue. "Way too subtle." *And I know. You don't have to mother me.*

Apologies, he replied.

"What'd I miss?" Hollace walked over in that unhurried way of his. The world could be falling down around him and he wouldn't pick up the pace. The man made an art of looking stylishly unaffected.

Aurora decided she would try to learn it. That sort of thing would be great for morale and peace of mind in a pack, especially in a volatile one like Uncle Auzzie's.

Jessie blew out a breath and leaned her face against her palm, with her elbow on the bar holding her up. "Not a lot. Broken Sue wiggled a bit, Aurora said a few things before barely twitching, Broken Sue then basically mimed an apology, I think I need a coffee because I've just realized how crazy tired I am, and we might be migrating toward calling him Sue instead of Broken Sue. Did you realize how many people we have around here with made-up names? It's actually quite a lot. What does it say about me that I never noticed?"

"Thunderbird," Fred murmured absently, staring at Hollace, her eyes tight. "Enormous thunderbird…with lightning…"

"Nuthouse." Hollace pulled a chair next to Jessie's. "It keeps things fun."

Tristan entered the bar with a cocky strut that did wonders to hide his exhaustion. All the senior staff were under a lot of pressure and working long hours. He glanced down the bar, sighting Jessie, before checking his watch. He didn't veer her way. If he'd wanted practice deciphering body language, it wouldn't happen now. Instead, he took a seat at the other end, where Uncle Auzzie was talking with two shifters who handled border patrol. They needed to make some adjustments for the people going away.

"Okay, let's do this." Fred downed her drink, pushed it aside, pulled the laptop closer, and braced her fingers against the keys. "I'll rationalize the magic later. Stalking has commenced. Point me in the right direction."

"*Concern!*" Jessie pointed at Sue. "He's concerned." She bit her lip, her gaze shifting to Fred. "We all are. Hopefully, Fred can help."

✧ ✧ ✧

AUSTIN

"Sir, can I have a moment?"

Tristan stood at the bar, waiting. He'd come in earlier to meet about the territory line, then left again with Jessie. He was doing a great job keeping her to task, but the added duties had increased the fatigue that now lined his body.

Austin held in a sigh. He was exhausted, famished, stressed beyond belief, tired of bad news within the alpha and pack rumor mills, and wanted nothing more than to go home to his mate, find a quiet room, and relax. Tristan deserved his time, though.

"Sure." He stopped at the end of the bar.

Brochan, sitting on his own at the other end, rose and started their way. He'd been in and out all day, meeting their people and conferring with Austin. He was another of their number who had been tasked with more than his fair share of duties, but he didn't complain. Actually, Brochan constantly asked what more he could do. Neither of these men had downtime, and neither of them voiced their exhaustion or need for a break.

Tristan eyed Austin. "Beer?" He took a seat and pulled out the barstool next to him. "I'm buying. I'm through practicing being a shifter for today."

Austin allowed himself a smile and gratefully took the seat. The guy on Tristan's other side grabbed his drink and evacuated, taking his friend with him. Brochan waited for them to get out of the way before sitting next to Tristan.

"You buying me a beer wouldn't pose a problem," Austin told Tristan as the bartender, Carla, ignored a customer and headed their way.

"Here? No. In another pack?" Tristan lifted an eyebrow as Brochan settled in. "They wouldn't look down on a beta buying an alpha a beer?"

Austin barely kept from rubbing his eyes, and then did it anyway. He'd been loosening things up in this territory to compromise with the gargoyle culture. While he didn't often relax this far, with his two betas sitting here, he figured it couldn't hurt.

"You're right," Austin admitted.

"Then I'd better get it in while I can." Tristan gave his order to the bartender, followed by Brochan and Austin. "Keep it open," he instructed, and handed his card across.

"What's up?" Austin asked him.

"Jessie tasked me with two things—one was to send a connection request to the new cairn leader of Nikken."

Austin inclined his head. She'd told him.

"Patty will send that out tomorrow, priority mail," Tristan continued. "I know for a fact he'll agree to a meeting—the sooner, the better. I'm sure we can negotiate a date. If we show reasonably well, we have a real shot at an 'in' with him. I know you have a packed travel schedule planned, but we wouldn't want to lose sight of the gargoyles. We need to start putting ourselves out there if we want to have better status. With better status comes more support for the convocation."

"Jess explained about the short window he has to feel us out." Austin inhaled deeply, then let it out slowly. It could never be one thing at a time. For them, everything seemed to always happen at once. Last time, mages had interrupted their plans. This time, it was the gargoyles.

Hopefully, it was *only* the gargoyles.

"Most of my plans aren't set in stone," he admitted. "We can rework the schedule in some places. It'll mean we'll have to alter our travel, but it's doable."

Their drinks landed, and Austin took a greedy sip of beer.

"It's a pain in the ass, I know," Tristan said, and that small acknowledgement went a helluva long way for camaraderie. "The other thing is Gimerel. Jessie doesn't want to destroy his production cairns because she's worried about his people."

"Noble," Brochan said.

It was. Jess had a kind heart, and in this situation, that was damned unfortunate. Hitting Gimerel quick and dirty would get him off their backs and get them moving on to the next thing in an ever-growing list.

"She wants to humiliate Nelson, I know," Austin said. "Assuming we can't just kill him and be done with it, that is. He deserves it."

"Or I do," Tristan murmured. "But no, we can't just kill him. That's not how things work. But we *can* humiliate him, as she requested." His smug grin spoke volumes. "He had no choice but to leave his bracelet here after his cairn's visit. Do you remember?"

Austin's head barely dipped. "The connection gift with all the gems, made by one of their productions cairns, furnished in part by one of their mines."

"Correct. The cairn's pride and joy. The envy of the gargoyle world. It's a symbol of status and elegance and beauty."

"That's a lot of weight for a bracelet," Brochan said. "Especially one without the value one might see in the Dick and Jane world."

"That's exactly what I thought when I first saw it," Austin replied. "But I haven't given it much mind since. Where is it?"

"Mr. Tom has it in his closet, hiding it from Niamh." Tristan laughed. "I was thinking, what if we fashion a matching necklace and earrings out of Ivy House jewels? We'd hire the best jeweler and choose the best stones—larger stones, obviously—to improve upon the design and quality and expense, but still have the pieces complement each other."

Austin furrowed his brow, then sighed when he felt the healing magic curl through him. Jess had clued in to his fatigue and was making it better. He loved that woman.

"And then, what, give it as a gift?" he asked dubiously.

Tristan's smile grew as he shook his head. His glowing eyes glittered. "Not even remotely."

Austin listened with growing respect for this gargoyle. Even Brochan started nodding, his posture full of mirth. The plan was simple, yet the effects would be extravagant if they pulled it off.

"I have a jeweler," Austin said. "We can pick the stones and leave them with him. He'll ship it to us when it's finished. I'll make sure it's a rush order."

"Yes, sir," Tristan said, leaning back with his drink.

Brochan's bearing changed to expectant. Apparently, he had something to discuss as well.

Austin nodded at him to go on.

"Alpha, about Jessie," Brochan started, and worry gnawed at Austin's gut. "She's not getting it."

Austin had glanced down the bar periodically, watching the lesson in progress. Jess's growing frustration had made her more expressive instead of less.

"She's *much* better at reading body language," Brochan continued. "There's hope for her there. But hiding it? No." He leaned forward, bracing his forearms on the bar. "The thing is, she's always one hundred percent genuine. If she can't do something, she's honest about that. When she's uncomfortable, it's usually for a good reason. A *noble* reason. And sir...she's not a shifter. She's *not* one of us." His shoulders tightened, and his head tilted forward before he twitched it to the side. *With respect, we're wasting our time.*

Austin took a sip of his beer, containing his disappointment. He'd feared this would be the case. It would amount to one more problem when meeting the alphas who wanted nothing to do with him. His past seemed to be a hard thing to eradicate in the alpha community. His present would offer them red flags—as far as they were concerned, anyway.

"If I may," said Brochan, "I think it'd be better that she continues as she is. Push her to keep learning body language, but don't ask that she change hers. She's always proven herself to shifters. Even the naysayers in Alpha Kingsley's pack stopped talking once she showed her might. She's different—she should act differently. Show how comfortable she is in her differences. She's honest and caring and wants the best for people, and she'll apply extreme force to keep them safe. Let the other packs see that she can't lie—that she *doesn't* lie— so that when it comes to her anger or power, they'll know she isn't bluffing."

"I agree." Tristan nodded. "Like the meeting with that pack in L.A. She had them worried by being worried herself. They'll have heard what she can do. Let them disbelieve her. Let them push her. She gets volatile when she's pushed."

Austin drank again. Deep down, he'd always known it would turn out this way. He'd known Jess's differences would make things harder for them, just like he'd known his reputation would drive a wedge between him and anyone willing to work with him. There would be no miracle fix for either of them.

"Well, hell, that's terrible news," he said with a release of breath.

Tristan laughed, and Brochan might as well have.

"We're ready," Brochan said. "To meet those other packs, I mean. I'm a strong alpha with trust issues, and I would walk into the fire for you and Jessie. You've earned that loyalty, both of you. No one has left this pack. Not *one*," he stressed. "It's hard work, long days, and barely controlled chaos, but even still, people trust that you and Jessie will keep them safe. That's unheard of. Trust me, you'll see the diamond you've created here when you visit those other packs. Even the strong ones."

"I don't know about the shifters…" Tristan threw back his cognac and put his glass up for another. "But I know our guardians are preening like none I've ever seen. They think they're in the best, most powerful cairn—not one of the best, *the* best. They follow a shifter leader because they respect you, a man who leads by example. Who's powerful enough to best them while urging them to rise to the challenge. You're an example. And Jessie…" His smile was soft. "Jessie is the pillar of our people. The best gargoyles have to offer. She brings us all together and promises us victory. Once we get into those cairns, our guardians will talk us up. They'll spread the word, not with stories, but with their bravado. We'll win them over, Alpha. It might take a second, but we *will* win them over. I know we will."

"This convocation will work." Brochan nodded. "We just have to have faith."

"Did my posture scream *he needs a pep talk* or something?" Austin asked, mystified.

"Yep," Brochan said with an uncustomary grin. Tristan outright laughed.

"That just leaves the mages." Austin asked for one more beer before he wrapped this up and headed home to his mate. "For that, it seems our fate is in the hands of a hacker who looked about as shell-shocked as a person could."

"She's odd as fuck," Tristan murmured. "I mean, even for that house, she's odd. I didn't think the Dick and Jane world could produce that kind of weird."

Austin chuckled. "She is, at that. I think that's a blessing. She'll be able to hang with that house. There aren't many who could. Not even me—for any length of time, I mean."

"Me neither," Tristan said.

"Truth," Brochan agreed. "Fred—" He huffed, then bowed. The grin was back. Normal men would guffaw. "She makes the absurd seem justified, somehow, while also highlighting how absurd it really is. It took her agreeing that I should be called Sue for me to realize it. For Jessie to realize it as well. It's strangely... This is going to sound crazy, but it's strangely comforting."

"Gargoyles have never understood the shifter culture of being assigned a name." Tristan sipped his fresh drink. "When you head up a new cairn, you don't get assigned a new name. You *have* a name. People call you that name." He paused expectantly. "Because it's *your name.*" He grinned. "Her choosing Fred..." He shrugged. "Might as well choose one you like rather than other people choosing one you don't. I didn't bat an eye at that. Or Mr. Tom. Or Steele or Ironheart. Whatever. The fox roadkill, though..."

Brochan looked at Tristan for a long beat, the humor draining away from him. "I was Spencer in my old life. In my old pack."

Tristan jerked in surprise. Austin had known that, having heard the rumor from someone else, but Brochan had never mentioned it.

"Spencer Whitman. I wasn't technically a generational alpha, but my birth father had been revered in his day, and since I challenged into his old pack, I allowed the people to pass his name to me. Whitman. It seemed the best for morale. Fred would think that name was very dull, I imagine."

"As dull as the man," Tristan joked.

"Hmm," Brochan said noncommittally. "It wasn't until...after..." After the attack. After he'd lost everything. "I kept my position long enough to reestablish the survivors in a safe location. To help them pick up the pieces and start over. During that time, they dubbed me Brochan. No last name, no remembrance of the name before it, real or assigned. Just Brochan. It's how we all felt. It fit."

"And Sue?" Tristan asked, his tone light but his eyes solemn.

"Sue was an accident. The *best* accident. I didn't know it at the time, but it was a lifeline. It makes me just as odd as that Ivy House crew."

"It's your membership card," Tristan surmised.

"Must be. One I will always hold on to with a tight grip. Names for alphas result from circumstance, half the time. I don't have much in common with Spencer Whitman anymore. I'm no longer that man. I'm not Brochan anymore, either. That was a name for a different alpha. A directionless, hopeless, futureless alpha. I have plenty in common with Fred, though, as odd as she is. With Jessie Ironheart and Alpha Steele, starting over, come what challenges may. Trying to pick up the pieces and make something of themselves. With Mr. Tom, trying to look after his people. Like that vampire—" He shook his head. "Nah. Step too far."

Tristan blurted out a laugh. "Good catch." He tapped his glass with a finger. "I didn't get a membership card."

Brochan—Sue, now?—lifted an eyebrow. "You are your own membership card. Changing your name would be that step too far. Nice eyes, by the way. Where'd you get them peepers, again?"

Tristan's lips twisted to the side. "Touché," he said quietly, still the dark mystery of the group. Not even Niamh had been able to piece his clues together. Rumors in the gargoyle world came up empty. This gargoyle-monster had done a great job hiding his past.

Austin didn't think he'd be able to hide forever.

Brochan shifted the conversation gracefully. He no longer seemed worried or even interested in Tristan's past. Somewhere along the way, Tristan had shown the untrusting alpha-turned-beta that he was in this genuinely, that he cared about protecting Jessie and the convocation. That he *could* be trusted.

"Regarding Fred—she's in," said Brochan. "She might be shell-shocked for a while until she gets used to all this, but you should've seen her light switch on when she worked with Niamh earlier. Hook, line, and sinker."

"Will she be able to help us infiltrate the mage world?" Austin asked, leaning forward. He could get all the shifters in the convocation, Jess could bring in all the gargoyles, but if they didn't have a way into the mage world, it would be all for nothing.

Brochan met his gaze. "Her light wasn't the only one that came on. Fred opened the door, and Niamh waltzed right through, like it was her own personal theme park. I think we're about to see what that puca can really do, and I don't think the mages know what's coming."

CHAPTER 13

SEBASTIAN

THE LIGHTS IN their little bungalow went out, plunging Sebastian into darkness. He paused where he sat at the kitchen table, papers scattered around him. His mind, however, went in a million directions at once.

Light from the street glowed around the drawn blinds, indicating the neighborhood hadn't lost power, just their house. Nessa was very good about paying the bills on time. It couldn't be that. No storms. No wind. This event was isolated.

Though his heart sped up, he put his pen down slowly. At just after midnight, the house lay quiet. Nessa was in her room, sleeping. If the cameras facing their yard had captured movement, the chimes would've woken her. That meant no random Dick or Jane was prowling around. If someone were out there, it would have to be someone with an invisibility spell.

He rose at a measured pace. There could be another explanation for the lights going off besides an invasion.

At the kitchen, he flicked the light switch off, then on again. Nothing happened. The one in the hallway yielded the same result. The oven clock was out, as was the microwave. Definitely a house-wide power issue.

His footsteps were nearly silent—he'd learned a thing or two from the shifters. At one time, he would've assumed a person with an invisibility spell could still be heard moving around. Now, with Momar employing mages with a crapload of power, he couldn't be so sure. If Sebastian and Jessie could make a potion for both, then they could too.

And if they had that much power, they could disable his wards, no problem.

Controlling his breathing as his thoughts spun, he felt around for a flashlight. He wouldn't use it unless he had to, as light would reveal his location. That procured, he walked through the darkness toward the back rooms. Nessa came first. Once she was safe, he could check the other areas.

At the beginning of the hallway, he peeked out a set of blinds. The streetlights illuminated patches of sidewalk in a buttery glow. Across the street, a porch light gave off a weak yellow beam. Next door to that, a small light at the side of the house was on.

Yes, this was definitely limited to his house.

Please have forgotten to pay the bill, Nessa, he thought. *Please have been so stressed and sad and busy that you've forgotten to pay the bill.*

He ignored the pang of guilt at why she would've forgotten as he trailed his fingers against the wall, feeling his way. A doorframe announced the bathroom, the first door on the right. The next was his room, the smaller of the two. Hers was on the left, at the end.

He backed up to her door, peering into the darkness of his bedroom. A spell revealed the room was empty. No one had come through his window, and if they had, they weren't in there now.

Nessa's door opened with no sound. He sent a spell in there as well while also listening. Her breathing was slow and even, evidence of deep sleep. It was testimony to how tired she was all the time now that his presence didn't rouse her. Her window remained shut, the spell still intact.

His sigh of relief was barely audible as he retreated down the hall. The front door was closed and locked. Spell intact. The door to the garage was as well. Windows were secure. Random peeks out of the blinds revealed no one wandering around. Shooting a spell through a wall to search for bodies wasn't ideal—the accuracy would be greatly reduced, and a good and ingenious magical worker would have invented a potion to mask themselves within such a spell.

Why hadn't he created a spell to mask himself against revealing spells? Shortsighted.

The best option was to go outside and use the spell there. Sadly, he was a coward, though not for his own safety. Only a charging alpha shifter really got his blood pumping these days, or maybe an alpha gargoyle. But if he went out and got himself caught or killed, they'd come for Nessa. She'd have no protection. She didn't have the Ivy House crew shielding her or promising retribution if someone should grab her. She didn't even have Edgar, who, somehow, through no logical explanation, always seemed to know where to be at the exact time he needed to be there.

Even thinking about it made Sebastian's mind spin. He hadn't had that vampire's dose of odd logic in nearly three months.

He settled for using the spell through a window, hunched in the corner and trying not to be seen, just in case.

Nothing.

He tried through several others, working the angles. All of them came up empty.

Maybe it really was the energy bill.

He straightened up and felt his way over to the

kitchen counter, where he'd left his laptop. Its glow made him squint. The Wi-Fi symbol wasn't there.

No power, no Wi-Fi, he thought in annoyance, glancing around for his phone. Normal people would've had it in their hand or pocket, ready to call the cops.

Of course, it wasn't like the cops could help him against his enemies. They didn't even know magical enemies existed. But besides them, there was no one to call. His circle had been reduced to the walls of their house. After his sister had died, it had been enough. Now...

Why did his and Nessa's life always seem to land them in the stink? They must've been cursed.

He didn't bother with the flashlight. The house was tiny, the smallest they'd inhabited since splitting from Ivy House. Actually, it was the smallest they'd been in since he could remember, but they hadn't had many options with such short notice.

His phone waited on the kitchen counter next to his plate with toast crumbs. Whoops. He'd meant to wash that.

Thankfully, he still had cell service.

He worked his way back to the table, sat, and unlocked the home screen. He was about to tap the browser app when a face took over the screen.

Adrenaline coursed through him. His finger froze,

hovering above the image. She had jade-green eyes—the result of contacts, surely—and spiky green hair with black roots. Her lips parted, and he knew this was somehow live, or perhaps filmed and now playing. This wasn't some random social media short he'd accidentally swiped into, if that were even possible. He wasn't like Nessa when it came to technology.

"The computer is a window into your soul." The person's voice was gruff, but the face was soft, mostly free of lines except for around the eyes. He or she smiled—he couldn't tell sex, and he certainly couldn't tell magical type, not with so little to go off. "Just kidding." The smile smoothed out into a serious expression. "But the computer *is* a window into your life. Look at me! I'm like a Peeping Tom over here."

"This…this is my phone," he stammered.

The face leaned closer until one eye took up the whole screen, like a T. Rex in *Jurassic Park*.

"It's a handheld computer, you elitist," the voice said. The face came back into full view. "Get those cameras off the cloud! From now on, you keep a hardwired system or none at all. Back up to a tape like it's 1990, you get me? Bet you didn't know they got cameras *inside* that bish. They do. I've been watching you wander around the house. Invasion of privacy, much? You need to do a sweep before you settle down, bro. Cameras are small now. You've got to be detail-oriented these days. At least they aren't in your bedrooms. I call that an almost win."

"Who…" He didn't know what to say, but he rose slowly, knowing he had to get Nessa.

"Ah-ah-aah." The one eye took up the screen again. "Stay where you are. The Captain will get her own surprise in…like…" She glanced to the side. He caught sight of a smallish ear with a skull-and-crossbones earring. "When I'm damn good and ready, that's when." The face came back, smiling. "You had a few tagalongs in your setup. Someone has been spying, my dude. Besides me, *obviously*. Don't worry about them—I gave them the boot a week or so ago. They're good, but they're not *me* good. To keep up with me, you gotta be me, know what I mean?" She grinned.

He did not know what she meant. Not even a little bit. He didn't know what the hell was going on, and he was too shocked to do anything but stare mutely. This had to be a mage. No one else would call Nessa "the Captain."

A mage this obviously odd, this far on the outskirts of what was considered normal, would be of a level of eccentricity on par with Jessie's crew. It meant an incredibly powerful magic wielder. A confident one. One who had crawled in through Nessa's defenses—

hell, not even her defenses. They'd slid into Sebastian's cell phone, with all its security settings. Into the energy provider's mainframe, or however the power situation worked. This was a level of hacking that Sebastian hadn't seen in the mage world. This type of thing existed in the land of Dicks and Janes, where people broke into the government and went to federal prison for a lifetime.

His brow turned clammy.

The person winked. "I'd start jogging, if I were you. Whoever was tagging along on your systems will know where you are. They can't spy with their fingers, but they can surely spy with their googlies, you get me?" A finger came into the screen to point at her eye. "Changing locations keeps 'em guessing." He heard typing. "Byeee!"

The face vanished, showing his home screen again. The lights flared. Appliances beeped as they came back on, the power restored. An alarm or something sounded from down the hall before he heard a big crash.

"Nessa!" His phone clattered across the floor as he jumped up and raced toward her room. He put out his hands, ready to do magic.

When he barged in, Nessa was picking herself up off the floor, wiping her eyes. She looked at him in confusion as she staggered toward her desk. Her systems were aglow, and they started beeping madly.

"What the hell is going on?" she said in a sleepy voice.

"Are you okay?"

"Yeah. My phone's alarm went off for some reason. I startled awake to turn it off and rolled off the bed. I didn't realize I was so—"

The light from the monitors bathed her horrified expression right before she swore.

Sebastian swung his gaze that way. A map showed the location of the video, which pictured the inside of a small living room. Three masses of human pulp hung from hooks. Crimson stained the cream carpet, splattered the walls, cut across the couches, and dripped from the bodies.

"It looks like they've been pulled inside out," Nessa said in a dismayed hush.

Indeed, it did. The scene was grisly, surely the handiwork of a remorseless killer. The perpetrator had created a scene that was so graphic, hinting at pain so absolute and horrific, that it was a spectacle.

A white sign gracefully spun in midair, like magic. It must've been hung from the ceiling with fishing line, invisible to the camera, or else the video had been modified after the fact to erase it.

It read, *We tried to spy on Elliot Graves and the Captain.*

Nessa's gaze traced every inch of the scene. The breath escaped her as she pulled out the chair to sit.

"Get the light," she murmured.

He did as instructed. "Do you think that was the Ivy House crew?"

She didn't hesitate. "Yes. They're making our retribution more gruesome than we ever have. They're making us look more sinister."

He swallowed thickly. That was saying something. They'd never pulled any punches, or so he'd thought. Seeing that image, though…

"Do you think they hired someone?" he asked.

She issued a soft laugh, studying the map now. "You'd need incredible strength and wickedness to pull that off, and you'd need someone with a certain flair for emotional manipulation. That scene elicits a visceral reaction." She shook her head, the barest hint of a smile touching her lips. "Tristan and Niamh. They're proving to me that there are bigger monsters in the world than I am, and they're two of them."

Sebastian didn't mistake the sheen of tears filming her eyes. The tension in her shoulders released slightly. This was apparently a message that she'd badly needed to hear.

He put his hand on her shoulder in support. She'd always struggled with the things she had to do in this life. She hadn't had the morality tortured out of her like he had. She didn't have the same vendetta against the Guild—not as fervent of one, anyway. She struggled with being a "bad" person, a damaged person. A person she didn't think was deserving of respect.

But she respected Niamh and, even though she wouldn't admit it, Tristan, too. She counted them as friends. For them to do something like this—to go to these extremes—when they didn't have to clearly showed her that bad deeds didn't matter an iota to them. Getting their hands dirty was a job, one they had made into an art. Grisly, hard-to-look-at art.

"Edgar would do something like this, too," Sebastian said, a strange mania making him smile. It was almost surreal, all of this. The grimness, the extremeness of the blood spatter, the flamboyance of violence. Yes, they'd made this scene into a piece of art. An emotional punch you couldn't look away from, horrified and awed at the same time, terrified that the monsters that did this might be on your doorstep. It urged you to run. No one wanted to succumb to a death like that because that much blood meant they'd been alive to spill it. At first, anyway.

"Edgar would probably go a step further, actually," he said. "He'd make it into a shrine."

Her body shook as she chuckled silently and wiped

a tear from her cheek. "Yeah, he would. People would think we were unhinged then, though, since the Ivy House crew are framing us again. They're issuing a pretty clear warning on our behalf."

"The mage world already thinks we're unhinged."

"No, they think we're eccentric, powerful, and dangerous, not unhinged. We have very clear motives and very obvious and strategic plans. We systematically create violence, not randomly. We're not hotheaded in our violence." She studied the map. "I don't know this location. Who do they assume is spying on us? And how?"

Sebastian moved so he could lean against the wall. "I don't know, but Ivy House has eyes on us. They seem to have brought on a new crew member," he said absently, before he shocked her with what that person could do. There would be no hiding now, not unless they completely disentangled themselves from the grid.

CHAPTER 14

NIAMH

"THOSE CRAFTY DEVILS." Fred bent over her computer in glee, sitting beside Niamh on Niamh's porch. The extra chair was getting a lot more action since Fred came to town.

A layer of frost covered the yard, the sun having not been up long enough to burn it all away. At the end of the street, mass preparations were underway at Ivy House. Shifters loaded luggage and supplies into vans. In an hour or so, they'd start loading people. The clock had finally run out for Austin Steele. Ready or not, it was time to start his campaign to win over the shifters.

For the first leg of their trip, they'd head across the country. Kingsley had set up a meeting with the group of people who'd originally tried to unify the shifters. None of them had had enough power and determination to make it happen. Austin would attempt to win them over, and then, with their support, systematically hit other prominent packs.

Niamh's luggage was already over there. Fred's, too, as the Jane had proven invaluable. Forget saying she wasn't magical—she all but pulled a rabbit out of a hat with that computer of hers. Niamh had made Jessie give her a raise, and a bonus besides. Fred had found Sebastian and Nessa, after all, and Jessie had promised the moon to do that. Now they had eyes on the mages. When the time was right—or when they had some time at all, rather—they could show up at will and force those meddlers home.

"Who?" Niamh asked her as she toyed with a rock. Every once in a while, a shifter wasn't paying attention, and she was able to startle him with a rock to the head.

"Your mages. They don't have the know-how to keep me out of their lives. Do you know what they did? Those little cave dwellers went off-grid." Fred shook her head, grinning. The woman loved a challenge, and Niamh had handed her a basketful of them. "Smart buggers, they are."

She also randomly affected an Irish accent.

"How can they go off-grid?" Niamh looked over at Fred's computer.

Fred pulled her hands from the keys and leaned back as she laughed. "They ditched their setup. They even ditched their phones! Who ditches their phones?

Like...what if they need to get delivery?"

As Niamh watched the proceedings, Tristan's large form slipped through the hustle and bustle of the shifters on the grass. It was a testament to how stressed Austin Steele was that he was only using his shifters and not any of the gargoyles for travel prep. He was leaving nothing to chance.

Too bad Jessie's crew would blow it all to hell the moment they showed up at the meetings. There was no controlling them, or even understanding them. Their chaos was a strong asset that Austin Steele didn't yet appreciate. He would, in time. The moment that chaos was unleashed on the mages, they all would—Niamh was sure of it.

Tristan held the handle of what looked like a horribly beat-up metal box.

"So, get this." Fred leaned on the arm of her chair, and though there was mirth in her eyes, Niamh could see respect, too. "I love these two! We gave them a scare the other week, right? Got into their system, put out that video—" She suddenly slammed her laptop shut and turned to Niamh. "Do you know what occurred to me last night? Jessie was worried about bringing me on because I was a thief, right? Fine. But then she shrugs off you guys creating some circus-like corpses out of people you don't even know and putting them on display. *Then* framing your friends for them! Like...really?" She tilted her head at Niamh accusingly. "*Really?* Stealing is an issue, but you're cool with all *that*?"

Fred had a *shocking* tolerance for the types of things Tristan and Niamh got up to. Even Jasper and Ulric had blanched at that setup with the enemy spies. Niamh had really put her all into that one, as had Tristan. Fred's tolerance probably had to do with her still acclimating to magic in general. She didn't have the ability to reason any of this out, not yet. Niamh was keeping her too busy. It would help her in the long run. Magic wasn't a place for strict morals.

They hadn't shown Jessie, though. Everyone had agreed it was best not to. She would've felt guilty, even though those mages were not only in bed with Momar but had helped orchestrate the attack on Kingsley and had large body counts themselves. It was best to stay vague. Jessie knew the sorts of things Niamh and most of her crew were capable of. They could just leave it at that.

But Fred? She'd been more concerned with how to break into various systems to post the video so everyone would be sure to see it. Then to create bots to share it...or comment...or some such thing, helping a ripple of fear and uncertainty spread throughout the mage community. It had been sensational, the reactions. Very effective. Better than anything Niamh could've hoped for. Her plans had grown ten times larger in scope. Now they were playing with fire—the only way to go!

"That's why Jessie came around, like," Niamh told her as Tristan stopped beside the porch. "She's rational when ye explain things to her. What do ye got there?" she asked Tristan.

He held out the box—a 1970s cooler, on closer inspection. It had a metal top with scuffs and scrapes and a yellowish stain. The metal sides were dinged to all hell with black patches, as though someone had burned away the mustard-yellow paint. The brand name, Coleman, had what looked like a key mark through it, and the cooler itself bore plenty of dirt smears.

"Mr. Tom destroyed all your coolers," Tristan said.

"I know. I bought new ones."

"I saw. But your new ones are clean and pleasant looking." He set the cooler on the porch. "This one is not."

Fred grinned. "That's one ugly and incredibly groovy cooler. If she doesn't want it, I definitely do."

Tristan put down the picnic-basket–style metal handles, one on each side, and pulled off the lid. "I've got a few beers in there, but it's mostly basajaun brew I got off Phil, and some honey-flavored moonshine I got off an Irishman at the pub in the next town. I tried some. It's awful."

"The Irish have moonshine?" Fred's eyes lit up.

"*Poitín*," Niamh said.

"Bless you," Fred replied.

"No, that's what it's called…" Niamh shook her head. "Never mind." To Tristan, she said, "What do ye want fer it?"

Tristan looked out over the street, subtly shaking his head. "Nothing. It all just kinda…fell into my lap. I commented on the cooler, and the lady who owned it traded me for it."

"What she'd trade you?" Fred asked. "I hope it was something good."

He glanced at her. "Orgasms."

"Like…multiple?"

"Always."

Fred made a *huh* expression. "They must've been good ones. I wouldn't let that cooler go for any price."

"As I said, always."

His confidence knew no bounds. Then again, Niamh reckoned, it was probably earned. He had a reputation, and with gargoyles, who celebrated their time in the sheets, that must've been hard won.

"You went and filled it out of the graciousness of your heart, then?" she asked.

He rested an elbow on the banister. "The beer was left in my fridge. Phil traded the brew for the privilege of watching Mr. Tom's face when he first saw you with that cooler. He's now standing close to the house, waiting for you to walk over. And the moonshine…" He shrugged.

"You gave him multiple orgasms, too?" Fred surmised.

"No. I dodged a headbutt, knocked him out, and stole his stash. Seemed fitting for the lip he was giving me."

"Ye must've been giving it back if he tried to headbutt ya." Niamh reached down and put away her rock. Tristan was in the way.

"Oh, yeah, I definitely started it. This way, it's his fault that I stole it. He reacted first. Fair and square."

Fred opened her laptop again, shaking her head. "I don't get the logic of this place. Don't get me wrong, I like it, but I don't *get* it."

"Ye don't want anything in return?" Niamh narrowed her eyes at Tristan.

He grinned. "Don't mention I gave it to you."

"Well, obviously. What do ye think I am, like? A snitch? Fell into yer lap, me arse. Since when are ye all hearts and flowers?"

"Since never. Take it or don't. I got a few doilies if

you want those instead. Whatever."

But he couldn't hide the true reason. It sparked and glowed in his eyes, sang in his grateful lean toward her and in his newly relaxed shoulders. It had shown in how he'd brutally handled those mage spies. They'd tracked down Nessa, ended the threat to her and Sebastian (for now), and could keep tabs on them. He was thanking her for making this possible, and his relief was plain.

He cared a great deal for that gal pal of Sebastian's. Niamh was seeing a whole new side of this gargoyle-monster—a side he was applying to Jessie now, taking greater care of her and putting her ahead of himself. It was like he was letting the door into his mushy interior open and showing everyone parts of himself he usually kept hidden.

Or maybe it had always been there, and she was just now seeing it with her true magic. She felt like a kid again, watching the world of mages unfold before her eyes. Making connections, coming up with plans, ideas, horrible pranks that would end in bloodshed. What a time to be alive! Imagine wanting to retire from all of this. The world was so much more complex now. More intricate. More challenging. She could barely contain her newfound excitement.

"Hello?" Fred was leaning way over, her face only inches from Niamh's. "What's going on in there?"

"Would ye feck off? Janey Mack, do ye need to get so close? Yer weird might rub off."

Tristan barked a laugh.

"Well?" Fred demanded. "You disappeared there for a minute. Do you want to know their new setup or what?"

"Our mages have gone off-grid," Niamh told Tristan.

He became alert really quickly.

"Right." Fred braced a hand on the top of her computer. "So, we caught them. We tracked them. They tried to kick me out but couldn't, which the Captain realized, even though she couldn't actively find my presence. That lady is smart, bro. If she'd had the right training, she could've been a helluva programmer, I'm tellin' ya. So, they move their setup to, like, a shack or something out in the woods. They operate at weird times, but that doesn't matter, because I'm tracking their keystrokes and sites and everything they're doing. I record all that. They save their files to an external hard drive, but again, that doesn't matter. I've got them on lock. I don't think they know what's actually possible. Phones are left there. All work remains there. When they leave, everything goes quiet. They aren't doing work from anywhere else. Not on those accounts, anyway. I'm combing the magical dark web—which I didn't even know *existed*—for any sign that might be them, but so far, nothing. It's like they…unplugged."

Her obvious perplexity was hilarious. She clearly couldn't imagine a world that wasn't electronically dialed in. Niamh's past, before electricity and gas ovens, would have floored her.

"They still show up to do their work," Niamh said, unbothered. "We know their home base. All we need to do is show up, wait, and grab them."

"Well, yeah." Fred pounded on the keyboard. She did not type lightly. "Anyone good enough could, too. I'm running interference, but there's only so much I can do without direct access. I created a spy hole, and someone else could use it when I'm not looking."

Urgency came through the Ivy House link: Mr. Tom. Jessie must've been ready to go, and he was stressed out that everyone else wasn't there and waiting.

Niamh pushed herself to her feet. "Don't worry about them for now," she said, and waited for Fred to close her laptop and stand. "We know where their intel is. That's enough. Now we need more in-depth information concerning their enemies. I want to know who's pulling the strings. They don't seem directly connected to Momar. Working for him, sure, but way down in the trenches. Something doesn't seem right about that. Momar has a greater interest in Elliot Graves than that.

We're missing a connection there. And then…we need to peel back each layer of Momar's setup. We haven't even scratched the surface, girl. It's time to get to work."

She could hear the excitement in her own voice, matched by Fred's sparkling eyes.

"Oh!" Niamh snapped as they made their way to Ivy House, she carrying her "new" cooler. "We'll be needing a list of possible allies. I'll assemble that. It's time we stopped standing solo with a bunch of animals."

Tristan tensed, and Niamh stifled a laugh.

"Is that fresh dirt on this cooler?" She looked down at it, bumping it off Tristan's leg as she did so.

He veered a little farther away. "Yeah. Fresh dings, too. It looked too nice when I acquired it. I figured I'd rough it up a little for you."

Now Niamh did laugh. She knew how to push Tristan's one button (she was still looking for more), and Tristan knew how to get at Mr. Tom. What a circus.

A damn fine time to get alive.

"What in the holy terror is that?" Mr. Tom yelled when he saw Niamh step onto the grass. He straightened indignantly. "That's going too far! You'll disgrace the whole convocation. Have you no respect—"

His words were drowned out by Phil bending over, guffawing.

CHAPTER 15

JESSIE

I RAN MY palm across Austin's shoulder and then down to his hand before threading my fingers through his. His hand tightened around mine as he stood on a curb surrounding a swatch of grass in a large parking lot. The resort we were staying at spread out all around us, a collection of buildings separated by walkways and paths and patches of grass. A ways behind us, jets of water arced through the air in the late afternoon sun and landed in a fountain basin.

The rear doors on the rental vans were open, and people were grabbing their things and all of our supplies. I could feel Austin's nerves through our bonds. He stood stoically, though, not letting any of it show.

We'd have dinner with his brother later this evening, and tomorrow would be the first meeting to push forward the idea of our convocation. Tomorrow, we'd all have to show well. I knew he would, but I wasn't sure about the Ivy House crew.

"Now, miss." Mr. Tom held out a basket when he reached me. "How about some refreshments? I noticed you partook of the lovely assortment of snacks and drinks I had on the plane, but as soon as it landed, the alpha whisked you away without a to-go bag. It's as if he has no fear of your being hangry. Not to worry, I've packed some snacks here, and I'll outfit your room with all the best options. What would you like? Chocolate truffle? Roasted peanuts?"

He paused with raised eyebrows.

"Do you want anything?" I asked Austin, leaning into him. He was the one who needed to be pampered, not me.

He squeezed my hand. "No, I'm fine."

"Sir, I do happen to have scotch. It's right over there in my emergency pack, which is being rifled through by that miserable old woman who has tired of the alcoholic provisions within that eyesore of a cooler. I can run over there and wrestle her for it. It's never wise to take alcohol from a puca, but if the situation calls for it, I will brave her wrath. You just say the word."

"I'm good," Austin said with a clenched jaw.

"Word to the wise, sir, I'd take that cooler off her as quickly as possible. You don't want her banging that thing around when we meet the other alphas. We'll be laughingstocks!"

Austin ignored him, but I could feel his annoyance rising.

"It's okay, Mr. Tom." I smiled at him. "We're good for now. Maybe just put the snack basket and a bottle of wine in our room when it's ready."

"Very good, miss. I'll just run and get that room sorted now. Broken Sue said he was handling it, but you know him. He'd probably answer a question by flaring an obscure muscle in his left thigh and giving that hard stare, and nothing will ever get done. I'll go use my *words*."

He turned and bustled away, handing off the basket to Edgar as he strode by. Edgar looked down at it in confusion, then hugged it to his chest. He walked over to the closest shifter, stood much too closely, and whispered, "I have the snacks. You let me know if you're hungry, and I'll break the rules for you."

The shifter couldn't stop a deep crease between his eyebrows. His body screamed *wariness*.

Edgar nodded, as if that had been the divine plan, and strolled over to the next person. He whispered, "I have the snacks. I hear they're delicious. I wouldn't know; I drink out of a vein. If you want to trade, we can. Or if you just want to reach into my basket, that'd be okay, too."

This shifter edged away slowly, as if he were afraid to turn his back on a hungry vampire, which was probably the right way to play it.

"That vampire…" Austin murmured to himself, looking off into the distance.

I waited with him patiently, letting the shifters grab my things and prepare to move them to our room. Austin surveyed the proceedings like he was the captain of the ship and didn't trust them to properly swab the deck. It was all for show. If anyone was watching—and they probably were, since all the packs attending the meeting would stay at this resort—they'd know he was alpha.

I guess they'd also know I was his mate, or maybe the co-ruler, but that wasn't why I was by his side. His nerves were worrying me. For the first time I could remember, it felt like he was doubting himself. He had what it took to do this, we all knew that, but from what I understood, his reputation might be the thing to sink him. They might not even give him a chance, all because of his actions when he was young.

Which was crap, obviously. The real problem wasn't his reputation. It was fear. They were afraid of trusting a new setup, or maybe of being a target of Momar. Hell, maybe they were afraid of losing the status of "most powerful shifter in the room." Austin, with his wild past, was a scapegoat. In time, they'd see that. And if they didn't? We'd force them to.

Austin bumped my shoulder with his and looked at me. "You're confident enough for the both of us, huh?" He must've felt my assurance and determination through the bonds.

I smiled up at him. "It *is* my turn, after all. You were my rock with the gargoyles, and then in Elliot Graves's caves. And actually, with the basajaunak, too. It's my turn to be the tough guy."

He leaned down to kiss me. "Too true." Taking a deep breath, he straightened. "I didn't, in my wildest dreams, imagine myself being this nervous."

"Then why are you?"

Austin started forward, pulling me along with him. As we set off, Broken Sue emerged from a hallway, clutching something. He gave off a distinct aura of annoyance, and I had a feeling that was due to Mr. Tom pushing him around.

"A lot is riding on this," Austin said. "Some of these shifters are prickly. They don't give second chances—hell, they barely give first chances. If we can't get these bigger packs on board, I worry we won't have enough might to bring it all together. We don't have a lot of gargoyles, we won't have the shifters, we have *zero* mages who want to work with us right now..." He sighed. "This venture is off to a rocky start, so we don't have a strong case with these people. We can't fail—our safety depends upon this working—but our odds aren't nearly as good as I'd prefer."

"Okay, yes, the venture is off to a rocky start, but we *do* have one of the bigger cairns on board, and we have interest from another. We have the basajaunak, which is huge. We have a phoenix and a thunderbird. And a warning: come together, or next time, the large pack Momar is targeting will fall, and the rest of the shifters with it."

"Yes," he murmured.

I knew him well enough to know that he needed a pep talk, and later, he'd need a distraction. I was ready to provide both, and I'd be thorough. He'd done the same for me a few times over. "Look at it this way. The gargoyles were never in any danger. They didn't know me or anything about me, but they still joined up. So did the basajaunak, even though they didn't want to leave their cozy refuge in the trees. They didn't have any reason or need to, but they joined our cause. But the shifters? The shifters have a *lot* to lose. They're targets. Their families are on the line, their packs. They need help, and we're offering them that help. They'd be idiots to ignore what we have to say."

He stopped in front of Broken Sue.

"Mr. Tom is preparing your suite, alphas," Broken Sue said. "He wrestled your key away from me." He held out a plastic card. "This is the ghost key, if you will. It works for every room in this building—well, for our collection of rooms. Everyone else will get their specific room key."

Austin nodded, took the key card from Broken Sue, and waited to hear our room number before starting forward again.

"And honestly, we don't need them," I told Austin. "The shifters, I mean. We were able to fight Momar off with what we have. Niamh is confident we can gather more mages, and I'm inclined to believe her. We'll be enough without these people—it'd be a bonus to have them, sure, but we can stand without them if they turn out to be fools."

He didn't wait for the elevator, pulling me toward the staircase instead. The resort was a sprawling complex of two-story buildings.

"I stayed in O'Briens all those years ago to give people a refuge," he said. "To give them a safe haven. I became alpha to provide that safety for you. This convocation is to protect the vulnerable. The masses. I *cannot* allow them to be idiots, not when it might mean their lives. Momar will try again, I *feel* it. We nearly lost the last time, and he knows that. Next time, he'll be better armed. Without a larger force, we won't be. We might not even know it's coming, not if we aren't connected with the packs. I need to make these alphas see reason to ensure shifters as a whole aren't taken down bit by bit."

And there it was. Austin wasn't confident he could make them see reason, and while I would just shrug, he wouldn't accept that outcome. In his head, he was already king of the shifters, the alpha of alphas. But he didn't want to force them to agree. He wanted them to come to him of their own free will, and he knew it would be an uphill battle. He knew he'd keep trying anyway.

My heart swelled.

"We'll convince them," I said softly. "We will, I promise. We'll fight, barter, and plead if we have to, but we'll do it."

He scanned the numbers as we passed and stopped at our room. Before he opened the door, he pulled me into a hug. "Good cop, bad cop," he murmured into my hair. "Usually, you're the good cop. I have a feeling you won't be this time."

"Why is that?"

"Good cops don't usually call people idiots, and I see that in your future."

I laughed and pulled away, then he scanned us in.

The suite was gorgeous. In the more public area was a small kitchenette, a sitting room, and a dining table, plus a bathroom with a shower. For Austin and me, a king-sized bed awaited in the next room, along with another little sitting area and a bigger bathroom with a lavish tub made for two. As Mr. Tom was in the kitchenette, organizing snacks, we inspected the bedroom area. Someone knocked at the door as Austin's phone rang.

"Don't you dare answer that door," Mr. Tom scolded me as I turned in that direction. "Were you born in a barn? You're an alpha, not to mention the Ivy House heir. You do not open doors."

Except...how would the door get answered when he wasn't here? Because whatever he might think, he was *certainly* not camping out on the couch.

"Bags," came Broken Sue's voice as Austin wandered toward the bedroom window to answer his phone. "Does the alpha want to get the car himself, or should I send someone to collect it?"

Mr. Tom swung the door open wide.

"Send Tristan," I said, meeting them at the door. Mr. Tom nearly knocked me over to prevent me from reaching for my bag, and I rolled my eyes as he took it. "Tristan will want to drive it, and this is the last chance he'll get to. Tell him not to wreck it."

Broken Sue nodded but didn't move away from the door. He gazed at me expectantly.

I sighed. "If you're trying to say something, I have no idea what."

"Of course you don't," Mr. Tom said as he came back to collect Austin's bag. "You can't speak *stone*."

"Aurora has asked to visit her father before you all go to dinner," said Broken Sue. "They should probably talk before this gets underway. They haven't spoken in months."

Kingsley was holding firm on the silent treatment, trying to scare Aurora into returning home. He didn't want her in a dangerous pack, which he thought we led...and in fairness, we kinda did. We were targets, after all.

Aurora clearly wanted to clear the air. She wasn't here in a pack capacity, but rather as family. She'd wanted to speak to her dad face to face, which I thought was mature of her.

"It's her dad. She can go whenever she wants," I replied.

Broken Sue nodded. "Tell Alpha Steele to call me when you're ready."

I agreed and closed the door as Austin appeared from the bedroom. "That was Kingsley," he said. "We're going to go off campus for dinner. All the other packs are here, and they have people stationed everywhere. He advised us to keep our people in their rooms."

"No." The firmness of my tone shocked me. Not allowing him to call the shots, when this was his gig, shocked me more. But sometimes, the willfulness of my gargoyle couldn't be ignored. That was what I blamed it on, anyway. "I will not sequester my people because they might be judged. Besides, Niamh is probably already in the bar, and Edgar is probably letting loose a hog-tied gnome or commandeering a garden or something, who knows? If you want to hide your shifters, that's fine, but I won't punish my people because they're different."

Austin studied me. His emotions were turbulent, and I couldn't tell what he was thinking or feeling. Finally, he said, "Fair enough. Let's shower and get ready. I can't wait to see Kingsley's face when we give him that car."

CHAPTER 16

JESSIE

"MISS, I REALLY think I should go with you," Mr. Tom told me as we exited the suite. He'd hung around as I got ready, putting my clothes away and commenting on my choices.

"We're only going to dinner, Mr. Tom. It's a family thing. You'd have to wait outside."

"I am well aware of how family dinners work, miss. I'm fine keeping a lookout."

"That won't be necessary," I said firmly. "Kingsley isn't bringing any of his people, and neither are we. I'll call if I need anything."

Mr. Tom harrumphed but didn't press me.

"It's a good thing he can't read body language, or he might've known you'd lied," Austin murmured as we headed for the stairs.

"It was a little white lie. Kingsley's only bringing a couple people, and that's for protection, not as a lookout. Our protection will be casing the whole area, not the restaurant specifically—"

"Face it, you didn't want him to embarrass you by hanging around outside in his disguise. What happened to not punishing your people because they might be judged?"

"Okay, first…" I held up a finger, then surrendered. "Fine, I'm the one who doesn't want to be judged, okay? If we're being watched by the visiting packs, then I don't want my first impression to be colored by a butler wearing an Elvis wig. Sue me."

He chuckled as we met four of the weaker shifters in the pack at the main entrance of the building. Alphas always had a team to walk them places during these things, all to show off the pack's power. No one tended to challenge at a meeting of minds.

"Not Tristan or Broken Sue?" I asked.

"The other packs don't know how to size up your people. They won't understand Tristan's power, not unless they see him in battle. I want to save the power they *will* understand for a surprise," Austin explained.

"Ah." We passed through the doors and headed along the path to Kingsley's building. Each pack had their own, and the packs together accounted for fifty percent of the reservations. "You allowed my people to wander because it wouldn't really matter."

"I allowed your people to wander because I want the only shock to be the shifter power. The weirdness of your crew will hopefully be a boiling frog situation. If the other shifters get it in doses, maybe your people won't seem so overboard tomorrow…"

"Sure, yeah. Keep telling yourself that."

He silently chuckled, looser now than he'd been earlier. I suspected it was because of his brother. Kingsley was well respected in this circle of alphas, and it probably gave Austin some assurance to reconnect beforehand.

Kingsley waited outside the door of his building with his mate, Earnessa, and his kids, Mac and Aurora. He had four shifters with them, only two of whom I remembered from his pack.

"Is he doing the same thing?" I asked in confusion.

Austin followed my gaze. "No. He…did some restructuring. They got a surge of new shifters after the battle. He's been moving things around. James, his old beta, is no longer living in that territory. He didn't take the firing well. You know what happened to Bruce."

Broken Sue had claimed his revenge. Bruce was no more.

"Jessie, good to see you again," Kingsley said, showing me a slight smile. He put out his arms for a hug, and I glanced at Earnessa with unease. "It's okay," he assured me. "She knows this is your Jane thing."

I accepted the hug, then paused to look at Earnessa again. She gave me a quirk of her red lips, almost a smile.

"Hi, Jessie." She put out her arms as well.

"Oh, yay, we're a hugging family now." I gave her a squeeze.

"C'mere," Mac said with a huge smile, wrapping me in a tight hug as soon as I'd released Earnessa. I wheezed within his embrace.

"Hello again," I said to Aurora, whose relieved expression and lack of coiled anxiety made me hug her tightly for different reasons. She must've worked things out with her dad, which had to be a relief—she'd hated being cut off from her family.

Austin was giving nods or handshakes, not accustomed to hugging, and Kingsley took the lead. "Okay, shall we—"

Austin held up a finger to his brother. "Wait. I have something for you."

A tiny line between Kingsley's eyebrows showed his confusion.

"Ha!" I pointed at his face in triumph, then ripped my hand down in mortification. *Way to go, idiot.* Draw all kinds of attention to yourself when people were surely watching out of windows or in bushes or who knew where.

"She's been learning to read body language," Aurora offered. "She's gotten worlds better at it. Kinda worse at not showing her own, though. Somehow."

Mac started laughing, but Austin took my hand. "Everyone, come with me."

Tristan waited in the parking lot with his arms at his sides and his gaze directed at a walkway to the right. His bearing suggested someone had been checking him out, and he was ready for a challenge. It wouldn't come, but he always hoped.

Kingsley swore as Mac whistled. Aurora's grin said she was enjoying this.

"Tell me that's not what I think it is," Kingsley said to Austin, stopping to stare. "Tell me that is not a Ferrari 250 Europa. Tell me this is a dream or a mirage or something."

"Nineteen fifty-four, yeah. A classic, and in great condition," Austin replied. "That car was owned by one of Momar's and the Guild's people. He helped orchestrate the attack on your territory, and now he's dead. Sebastian and Nessa are gifting it to you. Merry late Christmas. We had it shipped to a secure location here so you could see it, and we'll arrange transport to your garage. Tristan will drive it back to the secure location when we leave for dinner."

Tristan lobbed the keys to Kingsley, who snatched

them out of the air but didn't step forward. "You know I can't accept this," he said. "It's dirty. How they got it was dirty, I mean."

Austin scoffed and walked closer to the car, a fine-looking thing in navy. Probably horrible to drive, I mused. I liked my plush seats and modern suspension. Kingsley followed him, his gaze hungry.

"How that mage got it was dirty," Austin said. "That's what they do—they kill each other and steal their stuff. It's a mark of...whatever it is, I don't know. Niamh is figuring all that out. Sebastian and Nessa framed us for killing this mage."

I sucked in a breath. I *really* hated hearing that out loud.

"The magical world thinks *we* took this car," Austin continued. "But it belongs to you. By mage rules, this is yours, fair and square. Sebastian and Nessa facilitated, we'll take the heat, and you'll get compensated, however shallowly."

"Seriously, Kingsley, this is how they work," I said. "You insist I follow your rules when I'm in your territory. Well?"

"You're not a mage, you're a female sorceress gargoyle," Kingsley muttered. "Those aren't your rules, and you never really do follow mine."

"Maybe, but I'm in that world, and whatever the

mages' reasons for framing us, they were genuine in offering this to you. They thought of you specifically when they saw it. It was meant for you, earned by blood, sweat, and tears."

"Dad, just take the thing so we can go to dinner," Aurora said. "You know you're going to anyway, and I'm *starving*."

Kingsley shook his head again, circling the car. His expression was one of blind joy mixed with incredulity. "It's really hard to do the right thing when this is staring me in the face," he whispered.

"You need to stop thinking of shifter rules as the only rules in the world," I told him, peering in the windows. "They aren't. Right and wrong are defined by a society. In mage society, this is right...and I'm with Aurora. Let's eat."

"All right, all right." Kingsley grinned like a little boy, then gave Austin one of their bro-hugs with much beating on backs. "*Phew.*" He wiped a finger along his jaw before opening a door. "Thank them. I mean...you'll obviously have to explain this framing thing—that didn't get past me—but for this, thank them. It really is too much. You should've kept it for yourself."

Austin smiled, filled with joy. "After all you've done for me, and *still* do for me, this is a drop in the well. I'm chipping away at what I owe you."

Kingsley gave his brother a *look*, pleasantly exasperated, but didn't offer a rebuttal. I could tell it was hard for him to tear his eyes away from his new prize.

"C'mon." Austin slapped Kingsley's shoulder. "Everyone is hungry. Let's get this dinner underway."

✧   ✧   ✧

A FEW HOURS later, Austin and I returned to the resort, aglow with family and good times. We'd had a fun and lively conversation at a delicious Italian restaurant. I'd asked after Austin and Kingsley's mom, who hadn't come because she'd wanted to watch over the pack in Kingsley's absence, and they'd asked after Mimi, who'd stayed behind for similar reasons, wanting to manage Austin's various businesses. Time passed in a flash, with no discussion about business, per Earnessa's rules.

"I really would've liked to ask a bunch of questions about tomorrow," I told Austin as we climbed the stairs.

"Me too. But I've asked everything we need to know, and we've gone over it. He couldn't have offered any more insight, and we would've bored everyone else."

"Not Aurora. She listens to every word you guys say about business."

"Earnessa and Mac, then."

That was true.

Mr. Tom stood from the couch when we entered. "Hello, miss, sir. I trust you had a lovely evening, utterly exposed as you were without anyone to keep an eye out."

"We managed, Mr. Tom, thank you," I said. Austin barely paused before heading into the bedroom. "I should've told you not to wait up. You can—"

"Nonsense, miss. Who would pour you a glass of wine if I were off somewhere, freely going about my evening?"

"Riiight… Well, we're headed to bed, so you can head to your room. Or elsewhere—"

"Get out," Austin yelled.

I tried to keep a straight face.

"Ah. He's in one of those moods, is he?" Mr. Tom arched an eyebrow. "It's the sugar. When he consumes too much sugar, he's all over the place. I know the signs." He sniffed. "Fine." He poured me a glass of red that I didn't want and wouldn't be drinking, then a bourbon for Austin. "Don't stay up too late, miss. I know you can heal him and yourself, but you have a big day tomorrow. First impressions are everything. You'll want to be—"

"*Get out,*" Austin yelled again, and I broke down into giggles.

"Yes, well." Mr. Tom cast a sour look at the bedroom before heading for the door. "I'm glad you and not I have to deal with him. I'll bring you breakfast tomorrow at ten a.m. sharp. I have your key. Good night."

I threw the deadbolt, a habit from my Jane days, and then paused because it meant Mr. Tom would be locked out. Knowing I'd never hear the end of it, I undid the bolt. Breakfast brought to me was worth a little danger.

"Did he say he still had our key?" Austin asked as I slipped into the room.

I didn't answer him because he knew the score here. Instead, I ran my hands up his broad back and to his shoulders. "You're looser now," I murmured in a feminine purr, trailing my fingers down the back of his neck and hooking them into his collar. I pulled, stripping his shirt away.

"It's easy to have confidence when your hero believes in you," he said softly.

I smiled with the warmth in his tone. I loved how much he loved his family, how tightly they'd bridged the gap caused by their past. He thought the world of his brother, and I was glad Kingsley got to see that.

"I assume you don't mean me," I joked as I moved around to the front of him and grabbed fistfuls of his undershirt.

His eyes were deep and serious. "You are the love of my life. My heart. My eternal happiness. You are my everything, and I'd give you the world just to see you smile. But no, not my hero."

I blurted out a laugh as I bared his torso. "Well then, I guess we know where we stand."

He put a bent finger under my chin and lifted. I angled my face up to his as I walked my fingertips down his chest.

"Thank you," he said, brushing his lips against mine. "Thank you for helping me rise to this place, where I'm reaching for a noble purpose. Where I can use this rolling darkness within me for good."

He deepened the kiss as his arms came around me. His fingers found the zipper on my dress, and warm air caressed my quickly exposed back.

"Thank you," I murmured against his lips, dropping my hands to his slacks. "For joining me on this incredible journey with these very weird people."

I felt his smile against my lips. "I'll walk with you, no problem, but I will *not* take credit for the weird people. If anything, you shoved me into that, not the other way around."

His zipper whirred before I pushed down his pants. "Fair enough." I matched his smile as my dress pooled at my feet. His slacks and boxers, and then my panties, quickly followed. "I love you," I told him, and wrapped my fingers delicately around his length. He sucked in a breath and swiped his tongue through my mouth. I backed off a little and ran my teeth against his lower lip before sinking to my knees. "Let's get you good and distracted. I'm not going to heal you—I'm going to work you until you're too tired to keep going, and then I'm going to cuddle close and sleep soundly against your incredible body."

I licked him before taking him in my mouth. He went deep before I struck up a rhythm, my hand moving in time to my suction, slow at first and then faster. His fingers fisted in my hair as I looked up at him, marveling at the cut muscle and then falling into those beautiful cobalt eyes. He watched me strive, his hunger and pleasure plain. Faster and faster I went, my arousal coiling as I watched him near the edge. His body tensed, and his fists tightened...and then he released with a long, low groan.

I let him come down slowly, licking and teasing, before standing and kissing my way up his sweat-glistening chest. I took his hand and led him to the bed before pulling back the covers and directing him to lie down.

He watched me with deep, open eyes as he settled in. I crawled over him and kissed across his chest and up to his neck. There, I raked my teeth down his throat and smiled with his shiver. I pushed back until his tip dragged across my wetness, ready and aching, but I didn't sit down. He loved to hate being teased—it was the thing that worked him up the most—so I let his tip kiss my opening before sliding by. His growl was soft and his eyes feral, but he didn't rush me. He liked the anticipation.

I bent to flick my tongue across his nipple, rubbing against his building erection. I pushed up and once again let his tip slide by. His fingers tightened, and his muscles bulged. I could feel his ache through our bonds.

Smiling to myself, I teased him mercilessly, almost sitting down and then moving, rubbing and massaging by staying light and gentle. He rolled his hips toward me and away, looking for friction. Still, I made him wait, building him higher, getting him into a fever and making him pant. I scooted off and flicked my tongue across his tip, and he groaned in tortured bliss.

"Jess," he whispered, curling his hips up to me. Begging me to take him any way I would.

I flicked him again before dragging myself lightly against the tip and returning to sitting. I lined up, pretended like I was going to tease him just a bit more, then sat down.

"Fu—" He bit back the word and jolted like he'd just

grabbed a live wire.

My eyes fluttered shut with how good it felt to be filled by him. I jerked my hips as he thrust upward, the two of us crashing together. He moaned, long and low. I matched him, working toward my apex. His slide within me was forceful, the thrust creating friction that wound me tightly. I groaned, arching. I clenched around him, working faster now, harder. Nearly cresting. Almost there.

"Now, baby," he commanded, and I blasted apart. He clutched me, shuddering his climax. The waves of pleasure rolled over me, and I vibrated in the aftermath.

My breathing was ragged as I lay over him. I nestled into his neck, kissing softly, giving him a chance to come down. And then I started to tease again, this time with little nips and the grazing of my lips.

"Your plan is to kill me by way of teasing tonight, is that it?" His voice was a deep thrum in his chest.

"We shall see."

That was *exactly* my plan, and I carried it out to perfection. By the time our fun ended, he was putty in my hands. He curled around me possessively, let out a deep sigh of contentment, and fell asleep. I'd done what I could. Tomorrow, he'd have to shoulder the weight of the convocation's future.

CHAPTER 17

JESSIE

THE NEXT DAY, Broken Sue and Tristan waited for us in the living room of the suite. Aurora sat on the couch, able to inject herself into the situation because of family status. She'd chosen to hang out with us over her dad because we were, apparently, the more interesting party. I wasn't sure about *that*, but we were certainly the less organized.

Mr. Tom was in the bathroom, working around Austin to finish straightening up after taking over my makeup application. He'd also taken over my wardrobe selection, even though we'd collectively chosen the pantsuit and matching accessories in O'Briens. Clearly, he was trying to ensure he was needed at all times; I supposed he hadn't forgotten being left out of my affairs in Kingsley's territory.

I stopped in the middle of the room and pointed at Broken Sue. In the past, he'd apologized for giving me a once-over and declaring I was fit for a professional setting. It had been a habit of his as a former alpha. Now, his expertise was truly needed.

He gave me a small grin. Following Aurora's lead, he'd been allowing more expression in my presence, as they clearly thought I was beyond saving. He inclined his head. *Checks out.* Or maybe *good to go.* Hell, it could've been *close enough*, and I'd be none the wiser.

"You look great, Jessie," Aurora said, her eyes glittering. She was laughing at me. "Very boss bitch. You'll fit in perfectly."

"Well." Tristan wiggled his hand. "With your crew, I'm not sure about the fitting in part…"

I rolled my eyes at his teasing, making him laugh.

Mr. Tom came bustling out. "Now, let's see, how about some coffee? No, what am I saying—you sometimes get jittery when coffee and nerves collide. Tea? Water? A laxative?"

"You're worried about her being jittery, but the sudden urge to crap herself is okay?" Tristan asked incredulously.

Mr. Tom scoffed and waved his hand. "I meant chocolate. Austin Steele's pulses of power have me addled. Would you like a chocolate, miss?"

"No, I'm fine, thanks." I slipped on my heels.

"It's customary for alphas to go barefoot to meetings like this," Broken Sue said. "In case there's a heated debate leading into a challenge, the alpha will want to change as quickly as possible." He half turned to Aurora. "Unless things have changed?"

"Susan is correct," Aurora said, and I snickered at the name. "Alphas of this caliber rarely challenge in a professional setting like this, especially since my dad knows them very well, but it's a custom and a precaution."

"Austin told me all that." I stopped by the window with my hands clasped behind my back, looking out but not seeing anything. Spells were whizzing through my mind. "I don't need to shift to be deadly—I just need my hands. I can smear an attacker across a wall." I turned back to show how serious and a little horrified I was by that. "I can *literally* smear a person across a wall. It sounds so gross."

"Then why did you learn how?" Tristan asked with a lopsided smile. He tended to enjoy gruesome things. A big lover of Halloween, that guy. It was a wonder he didn't make friends with the dolls and gnomes.

I turned back to the window. "Honestly, each spell was more horrifying than the last, and I couldn't stop myself. It was like watching a car accident. I wanted to turn away, I didn't want to see the carnage, and yet my eyes were glued. I learned half the spell book before the nightmares started getting bad. I haven't returned to it. Yet."

I didn't see their reactions. They were probably talking among themselves without words.

"I can slice off a head." I cut my hand through the air. "Just slice it right off. It's supposed to be a clean slice, too. It takes a lot of power, so I'd really only have the one go with it. If I miss, it'd probably be curtains because I wouldn't have the energy to keep fighting."

"Why would you use all your energy on one person?" Broken Sue asked.

Tristan's answer was haunted: "In case you're up against a revenant."

I nodded, my back still to them. "Or a vampire in its prime. Or countless other magical species that I wish I didn't know about—the book gave some examples. I tried the spell on a *big* tree, and it cut about a quarter of the way. The original basandere had to carry me back to Ivy House. After she nearly stomped on me, that is, thinking I was an enemy. It drains me that much."

"What kind of species did it name?" Tristan asked, his voice guarded.

"You were probably listed." Aurora's tone held humor. She didn't care what Tristan was any more than the rest of us did.

"Watch yourself, monster," Broken Sue teased Tristan. "If you step out of line, she can kill you without batting an eye."

Tristan huffed. "She's already almost killed me, and that was by accident. If she wants me dead, I'll first ask Mr. Tom to make my favorite coffee drink, and then I'll say goodnight."

I scoffed, then turned in confusion when no one else scoffed with me. Broken Sue was nodding, like that made perfect sense, and Aurora didn't show any sign of tension—evidently, she believed them.

"What's this now?" Mr. Tom said. At least someone had sense. "You have a favorite coffee drink?" he demanded of Tristan. "And here I am making all these other things. What is it?"

Never mind.

Austin emerged from the bedroom in a black twill suit with a black silk shirt underneath. His leather dress boots were polished to a high shine, and gold-and-diamond cuff links, matching his watch, gave the black on black a stunning bling.

"Boots?" Aurora lifted an eyebrow. "Those are even harder to get off than regular shoes."

He was making a statement, then.

"I'm already painted as reckless and volatile." Austin adjusted a cuff link, dapper as all hell and so incredibly handsome. "Unpredictable. I'm wearing boots in good faith. They'll know I intend to mind my manners."

"Does my dad know?" Aurora asked.

"No. I'd intended to follow custom, but Jess's reasoning made me think harder about it. This is the right message. I should've planned this all along."

Aurora's slightly narrowed gaze swung to me. She was thinking that through. A lot of her shifter customs were being challenged in the convocation. Instead of resisting, she was analyzing and, in many cases, opening her mind to different perceptions. She was an intelligent and driven young woman. Even though I was new to the family and probably didn't have the right to be, I was so incredibly proud of her.

"Not to mention, if something kicks off, you won't have to get up from your chair." Tristan laughed. "Jessie will freeze the room or just blast them all to hell."

Austin smirked. "There *is* that. It can't hurt to show the trust I have in my mate's dangerousness."

The rest of our group waited out front. Every alpha was allowed ten people with whom to show their team's strength and power. We were exceptions. There were a lot of rumors about the convocation, and these packs wanted some assurances. Or maybe they were just curious. Regardless, we'd show up with a larger force, bringing shifters, gargoyles, and my whole crew.

Broken Sue stepped to his position in front of the line of shifters, a row to the right and waiting next to the railing on the walkway. Tristan sauntered to his spot in front of the gargoyles. Both lines were crisp, stoic, and polished.

And then there was the Ivy House delegation.

"What…" I put out my hands in utter bewilderment.

They were all over the place. Dave was standing down the walkway next to the wall, Indigo and Edgar leaned way over the railing to see the flowers below, Niamh was waiting by a maid's cart and clearly thinking about taking something… Only Hollace was where he should be, pushed out from the other lines, my crew partially in front of the others. His hands filled his pockets in his stylish cream suit, *not* the color we'd agreed upon.

"Did we not practice this?" I ground out, not supposed to show emotion but unable to help it. "Get in line!"

"Edgar, hurry, it's starting!" Indigo twisted to look at me, shoving the vampire as she did so.

"Whoa!" Edgar's feet swung into the sky as he tipped over the railing. He tried to hold on, but he was falling before he could get purchase. His nails scratched against metal, and then he dropped into the bushes and flowers below with an *oomph.*

"Oh, no. Shoot!" Indigo scrabbled over the railing after him.

"No, Indigo, save yourself!" Edgar shouted.

"Don't go after—" I began, but stopped as Indigo leapt from the second-floor walkway and into the bushes.

"It's okay, I heal fast!" she called up.

I sagged, not daring to look, or even allow myself to feel, Austin right then. What a mess he'd shackled himself to.

"Right. Great." I shook my head, at a loss.

"At least we get to be in the gargoyle line," Ulric said out of the side of his mouth to Jasper, who nodded. Tristan's fierce gaze darted that way, silencing the two.

"Okay—let's…" I waved my hands, trying to bring everyone in. "Come on. Get in line. Niamh, put that back. You don't need any more toothpaste."

"They're the best size for traveling, sure," she protested. "I could just call the front desk. This saves everyone the hassle."

"Steal on your own time." At least she hadn't brought that dirty old cooler. "Come on, get in line. Let's go." I kept waving them on, noticing the variously colored suits. The shifters and gargoyles all wore black to match Austin, with the shifters sporting blue pocket squares and gargoyles choosing purple. Perfect. My team, like in Elliot Graves's caves, were also supposed to wear black with colored pocket squares to match their magical type. Mr. Tom matched the gargoyles, like Ulric and Jasper, but they were the only ones who fit in. Hollace had his cream, Niamh was in brown, Edgar and Indigo wore different shades of green—

"Where is Cyra?" I demanded, checking my really cute, chic watch. "Come on, you guys, hurry up!" My magic blasted everyone present. "We're going to make Austin late!"

"I'm here!" Cyra ran around the corner without a stitch of clothing on her but carrying a somewhat burned red suit under her arm.

Dave fell in with his pink kilt. Bringing up the rear, not actually having been invited, came Fred. She wore a pastel-yellow pantsuit with red trim. The pants stopped at her shins, and her boots had half-inch spikes sticking out of them.

"Sorry, Jessie!" Cyra shoved Niamh out of her place, jostling Hollace. "Sorry! I thought I saw a gnome, blasted fire without thinking, and accidentally scorched part of my suit. I was trying to DIY a solution, but…"

She spread it out to show me the jacket. Holes were burned into the chest area, and I had a sneaking suspicion it would be the tips of her breasts. She didn't have an undershirt with her. The pants had been scorched down the thighs, and half a pant leg was burned clean away.

Edgar and Indigo, having righted themselves and taken the stairs back to the second floor, jogged in, each with a limp. Their limps didn't match, as they'd hurt opposite feet. Their suits were ripped in several places and stained in many more.

My eyes stung with unshed tears. Austin was always so perfect when I needed him. He was patient, put me first, and handled his end without a hitch. Yet after practicing with my team for months, I showed up like *this*?

My throat tightened, and I nodded. "Just put it on, Cyra. Mr. Tom, will you get her an undershirt? We're out of time, and I don't have anything else that will fit you. My suits—*in the correct color*—are tailored."

Mr. Tom ducked back into my suite to grab one.

"Oh, no, Hollace, I made her sad," Cyra whispered, stepping into her pants. "I feel terrible. My heart hurts, Hollace."

"I definitely think you deserve it," he replied.

"That was not a gnome, Jessie." Edgar raised his hand from his position at the end of the line. "I did not bring any gnomes on this journey. I've possibly learned my lesson. Time will tell."

"Well, it *could've* been a gnome." Indigo turned to him. "Just not one of *our* gnomes."

"Oh, yes, quite right. That's true. It could have. I can check it out—"

Finally, in utter defeat, my tears winning, I faced Austin. "I'm so sorry. I—"

He put a palm to my cheek, and amazingly, I didn't feel anger in the bonds. Or frustration. Or anything I really should have.

"I suspected something like this would happen. Maybe not so"—his gaze flicked toward the constantly moving line my crew was attempting—"flashy, but certainly not uniform. It's better the packs know what we are up front and agree to it anyway than to agree thinking we're something we're not."

"Like able to get in a straight line," Hollace murmured.

Austin tilted his head in a nod, checked his watch, and turned. "We're a bit early. Let's get moving."

"Wait." I checked my own watch. We were ten minutes late.

"Not uniform, and never on time," he amended as we started forward. "I planned ahead."

I glanced at Broken Sue. "Shove my people into place if you have to. Keep them from wandering off. You too, Tristan."

"He already is," Indigo said with a grunt. "Shoving him back doesn't yield any results, in case anyone else thinks to try."

"I could get results with a shove," Cyra said.

"You're in enough trouble," Hollace reminded her.

"This is my life," I muttered. "*Why* didn't you wear the right color?"

It felt like a whine, but the volume of my voice made it a yell. I simply couldn't help it.

"Are these not the right colors?" Niamh asked. "I was told to order brown."

"A brown pocket square," I said as we descended the stairs. Soon, I'd have to button up my personality. The other packs were probably already there. They'd want to see this mess of a crew show up. "A brown *pocket square*. Like at Elliot Graves's cave, remember? I'm not crazy, you were all there. This is not a new situation for any of you. And how did Fred get a suit so quickly? More importantly, why is she here? No offense, Fred, but you're not magical."

Mr. Tom cleared his throat, catching up to us. He handed off the undershirt to Cyra. "That might be my fault, miss. About the suit color, not about the off-center Jane tagging along without permission. It seems I misunderstood what you meant. I was very precise in ordering the correct suits and getting them tailored, as requested, so Edgar had plenty of room at the front of his pants. They come in all colors, and you'd been firm on the color scheme when I asked. I wasn't aware it was just...the square."

"But then why are *you* dressed appropriately?"

"Because that's what Ulric and Jasper said we were wearing. With the purple pocket... *Ah.* Yes, I see. I should've put two and two together. Well..." I could hear his wings flutter. "There is nothing for it. Miss, I humbly ask to be retired in disgrace."

"I'd take him up on that," Niamh said.

"I had my own suit, don't worry," Fred called up. "I've found my people!"

"That's not something to be proud of, I don't think," Ulric murmured.

"You're one to talk," Jasper said. "You two have the same hair."

"Are you color-blind?" Ulric shot back.

"What are you even doing with me?" I asked Austin, sagging once again.

He took my hand and threaded his fingers through mine. "Remember when we arrived at the town outside of Kingsley's?" he murmured, directing me to the interior of the resort. "You were trying to squish a basajaun into a van when a local asked if you wanted help. You agreed, and I realized then that we'd be showing up with a lot of dirty, decrepit trailers and motor homes instead of the sleek, matching fleet I'd reserved. I'd worried, above all, about losing style points. About not showing well to my brother and his pack."

"Yeah. Old me would've caved and resumed shoving the basajaunak into the vans."

"Yes. And old me would've been a nightmare when I didn't get my way. I realized that at the time—that I was acting like a remnant of my old self. In trying to show my brother I'd changed, I was regressing."

He hadn't told me that.

He nodded, as though hearing my thought. "The realization shocked me. Scared me, honestly. It's why I apologized. Why I backed off. And in the end?"

"They were impressed that the locals would help, and the basajaunak...were the basajaunak?"

"Yes, but also, in a moment with just the two of us before our final goodbyes, my brother complimented me on how I'd handled that situation. He'd been impressed that I'd allowed it. That I'd let you handle your side of things, even though it didn't follow custom. At the time, he couldn't believe I'd been that calm. No alpha likes to look messy on arrival like that. Our training forbids it. To do so, to look messy, makes the leadership look weak. It was only after getting to know you and your people, and seeing how you lead, and learning how incredibly effective your style of leadership is with the power amassed in your crew, that he came to respect my reactions. To him, I proved my growth as a person."

Now I teared up for a different reason. "Why didn't you tell me all of that?"

He shrugged. "I don't know. Maybe I didn't really believe it, or thought that if I voiced it, the shine and glimmer would wear away, and it would stop being true. But...well..."

"Here we are again."

"Here we are again, and this time, I'm calm. Like I said, I expected it. And what I said was true—it's better they know about your leadership now than find out as a surprise."

"Okay, but let's get serious. The colors of suits, fine. The extra person...sure. Hopefully, it means we can keep her, because from what I've heard so far, she's invaluable."

"Did she say I was invaluable?" Fred asked from the back. "Is that what she said? I'm eavesdropping as much as I can, but I'm no bionic woman."

"Yes," Mr. Tom said. "Now, *shh*. The miss doesn't like to be reminded we eavesdrop."

"*Seriously*," I said to Austin, lowering my voice a

little more. "Burn marks on the suit? Rips and stains? A line that looks like a snake slithering through the grass—no, I don't have to look back to know it. It's happening. I can feel it happening. This is on a level…"

I shook my head.

"Calm," Austin murmured, squeezing my hand. "It's what we have, and what we have is incredibly effective in battle. We might not show well in a line, but what we bring to the battlefield is plenty."

He really had grown as a person, because I just couldn't with all this. For *months* we'd practiced. Two months! How was getting in a line so damn difficult?

"Two people," Austin said as we entered a square flanked by two large buildings. Each was named and featured two double doors evenly spaced apart. Above each double door was an A or B. The doors on the building to the left stood open—clearly, the place we were headed, though you wouldn't know it from the silence. At the top of the square was a food truck serving barbecue, and off to the side was a makeshift bar. Attendants stood idly, not stoic like shifters but with nothing currently to do.

"That's what we're having for dinner?" I asked.

"No. That's what the *personnel* will have. They'll bring in more trucks as the meeting wears on. This is for the setup crew, probably. Only the alphas will be served dinner from the kitchens, after our discussion. The kitchens aren't nearly enough for a full-scale dinner for all of our crew."

"Gotcha."

Austin slowed as we neared the first set of double doors on the left, under A. He kept hold of my hand and finally stopped just before the door. Through it, I could see most of a pack lined up at a diagonal in the back corner. Standing out front was a woman with dark skin, a loose black dress, and no shoes. I bet she didn't have underwear, either. It would take very little time for her to change shape.

Of the Ivy House crew I could feel through the bond, the line was about as straight as it would probably get.

"Ready?" Austin asked.

"Two people?" I asked belatedly.

"Two extra people. I included Aurora," he replied. "I want her to see what this is like, and I want her to do damage control."

I hadn't noticed her slipping into the line.

"Damage control?" I whispered, trying not to move my lips as we entered the huge space. The partition down the middle had been pushed away, merging areas A and B.

"For you. If something unexpected happens to me,

she needs to keep you from killing everyone. She has experience jumping in front of very dangerous people. Before you ask, she volunteered for the job."

Had she been wearing a suit? Honestly, I hadn't even noticed. I had no idea what she was wearing.

In addition to the pack in the corner, nine other groups of people were spaced around the area. Kingsley was directly next to us upon entry, and the corner to our immediate right was vacant. That would be our area to show off.

It wasn't big enough.

Huge hanging curtains had been gathered in that area, and various seats and chairs were stacked. Tables lay on the ground, and boxes with numbers were somewhat haphazardly placed. Whatever had been in here last hadn't taken everything away, and it severely diminished the space we had in which to mass.

"Did you tell them how many people we had?" I whispered, barely moving my lips.

"Yes. Minus two. They're trying to assess how we handle an unforeseen hurdle. Sometimes, the old-timers do this to a newly emerging pack."

"Joke's on us. We won't handle this well at all. Here…" I released him. "You deal with your people. Show off. I'll…take mine…away."

Austin split off from me as though this had been the

plan all along. He made small movements and almost unseeable gestures. Tristan and Broken Sue understood him perfectly, directing anyone—most of the gargoyles—who didn't. They folded their lines so that they were in rows, Tristan and Broken Sue still at the front, big and strong and intimidating. Austin took position ahead of them as if they were in a synchronized dance.

The whole situation took no time at all and had been orchestrated to perfection.

I huffed. "That easy, is it?" I grumbled to myself.

This wasn't going to go smoothly for me, especially because I had no idea where my people were supposed to be.

"Should I just...guess?" I whispered to Austin.

His eyes sparkled, mirth came through the bonds, and he'd clearly lost his mind, because he didn't offer me any help.

"Aurora?" I called, but she was hidden away in one of the lines.

Ivy House bonds told me my people were uncertain. So was I.

"Have no fear, miss—I am perfectly capable of handling this matter." Mr. Tom's wings fluttered, and he was probably just about to prove why he wasn't in the gargoyle line.

"Pretend it's battle," Tristan whispered, and Austin

faintly nodded.

Battle?

I glanced around at the other alphas and their people, who were patiently waiting. Their focus was acute. They were clocking all this.

It was Kingsley's faint nod, though, that gave me the confidence I needed.

I shrugged. They'd gotten themselves into this mess. They'd reap what they sowed.

CHAPTER 18

MY MAGIC BLASTED out, filling the entire space. It was how I always prepared, as it let people know what was going on. Another blast followed, this one still felt by all but isolating a directive to my people. Their connections sparkled in my mind's eye.

I gave them firm pulses, their directions, like in battle. Brooking no argument.

"Oh, whoa," Fred said, looking around as she followed the herd. They were simply incapable of a crisp line, practice be damned. "Okay. This is next level. Is that magic?"

"Hush, Jane. We're supposed to be quiet during these," Mr. Tom told her.

"I strangely don't mind that nickname," Fred murmured. "Better than being called a dick, at any rate." To Mr. Tom she said, "Did you ever think that maybe the name Rufus would suit you better than Tom?"

"That *is* a nice name," Dave commented. Someone huffed out a laugh, but I couldn't determine who.

I gave them a whipcrack of magic to hopefully quiet the crew while walking forward with them and motioning where they should stand. Magic pumped, working on those connections, organizing them into a loose cluster. It would have to do.

Glancing back at Austin, I shrugged. People were never going to think I was the organized one. As he said, better that they knew up front rather than be surprised.

He took my hand again.

"Do not yank my wing," Mr. Tom told someone. "I know that was you."

"Sure, ye're fluttering it in me face," Niamh said. "What do ye expect me ta do?"

"Moving back would be a start," he answered pompously.

The other alphas all began forward toward the table in the center. Except for Kingsley, they wore loose, flowing clothes that would be quick and easy to take off. No one wore shoes, not them nor their people. Not even Kingsley.

Something belatedly occurred to me that I really shouldn't have forgotten about. I ripped my hand away from Austin and spun. "Wait—Cyra, did you actually blast whatever it was that you thought was a gnome?"

Austin tensed and turned back. That potentially huge problem had escaped him as well.

"Is it going to make you sad again if I say yes?" Cyra asked me, peering out from around Niamh.

"Did you set anything on fire?" I demanded.

"Oh, no, nothing like that." She smiled. "I just melted a bucket and crisped half a bush and took out a flower bed and kinda blackened the cement a little teeny bit. No one will even notice."

I stared at her with what I knew was an incredulous expression.

"Which flowers?" Edgar asked, and I noticed he'd already started to slink away from everyone else. He was probably off to find a corner to lurk in or wander over to the other packs and stand too closely. "The lovely pink ones with the leafy stems, or the—*hopefully*—work-in-progress purple ones that really aren't fit for the human eye just yet?"

"Purple ones," Cyra said after some reflection.

"Oh, good." Edgar sighed with a smile. "That's okay, then. Punishment fits the crime."

"Mr. Tom," I said, willing patience. "Could you please go check it out? If it's bad, connect with the hotel manager, and we'll work out compensation."

"Of course, miss. Right away. Happy to be of service."

"Kiss-arse," Niamh murmured.

"Niamh, keep an eye on Edgar. He's skulking away," I told her.

Everyone turned to look. Edgar froze halfway behind a curtain. He stepped back out with a simpering smile, offering no explanation.

"Everyone is definitely going to know where we stand," I told Austin as we resumed walking. "We certainly aren't hiding any of our weird."

"And you certainly didn't hide any of your power," he murmured, squeezing my hand. "Good."

"Is that Aurora I see tucked away in your lines?" Kingsley asked when we neared the table. "She wasn't on the list."

"Neither was one of Miss Ironheart's people," a woman in a flowing pink dress said.

Everyone stood behind a chair, all evenly spaced with more than an arm span between them except for two. Those were closer together and were clearly intended for Austin and me, as ours was the only group with a co-leader.

"It is Aurora, yes," Austin said as he reached out to grab the back of a chair. "She's alpha material and our family, not to mention symbolic. She was the one who stopped my attack on you all those years ago. I assume that's at the forefront of everyone's minds. Now she will act as liaison to Jess and step in the way if anyone should attack me."

"You'd let your niece try to stop someone from challenging you?" the woman in the pink dress asked in disapproval.

"No." Austin pulled out a chair and looked at me, intending for me to take it. I did, and he sat in the one next to me. "She'll stop Jess from ending the fight prematurely."

I doubted that, but it was a nice sentiment. I'd be fine with a sanctified challenge—probably—but if a surprise attack kicked off, I doubted I'd be still long enough to remember to back off.

CHAPTER 19

JESSIE

KINGSLEY SETTLED IN the chair next to Austin. The rest of the alphas watched me.

"Allow me to make the introductions." Kingsley reached for the pitcher of water and a water glass. He filled it as everyone hesitantly took their seats. They were wary of Austin, that was obvious. It seemed like they really did think he'd just randomly lose control and rush them.

"This is my brother, Austin Steele, original co-alpha of the Dusky Ridge Convocation. Beside him is Jessie Ironheart, original co-alpha of the Dusky Ridge Convocation and mistress of the fabled Ivy House, a magical house harboring the essence of a female gargoyle. She was previously a Jane, but she's been at this for over a year and has had to hit the ground running. Because of the help she and my brother provided my territory, she's now a target of the most ruthless mage we've ever seen. They're both pack friends, I support them in their endeavors, I trust them with my life and the safety of my people, and I plan to help them unify magical people into a moral establishment that benefits all."

Austin nodded in greeting, so I did the same. Kingsley then went around the group, introducing the other nine alphas, who had slowly taken their seats and were studying Austin and me with calculating expressions. None of them were original alphas, most having inherited their packs and continuing to build on them. One was a fifth-generation alpha, and I had a feeling he didn't do much more than keep the peace. Only one of them had had problems with mages in the past, and that had been nothing more than a skirmish. They'd lost a couple people, but they'd been able to run the mages off.

"First, we should probably clear up the second additional person you brought, Jessie," Kingsley said when he'd finished the introductions, "and then I think it would be wise to run through the rumors. It seems a large portion of the alphas out there believe the worst of my brother and none of the best. I'd like to clear the air."

Austin nodded. Once again, I followed suit.

"Jessie?" Kingsley prompted me.

"Oh," I said. "Sorry. She's a recent addition to my

crew and felt compelled to join us today."

"And you let her?" asked Margery, the woman in the black dress I'd seen at the doorway.

I shrugged. "She looks the part, as odd as that is. She's now on the team and getting everyone organized was just shy of chaos. You have nothing to worry about. She's a Jane. We're trying to infiltrate the mage world electronically, and we needed someone exceptional to navigate the technical side."

"She's a *Jane*?" asked Zack, the fifth-generation alpha with graying hair and sharp brown eyes.

"I really like how generous she is with compliments," Fred said from the corner. She'd plunked down on the ground to wait. Dave had joined her. "Exceptional, did you hear that?"

"Shh," someone told her.

"Yes," I answered Zack. "The magic she does with computers is all brainpower."

"I'd like an introduction to this team of yours," said an alpha named Dale, his deep voice reverberating through the space. He was only second generation, in his mid-thirties, and seemed a little more intense than the rest of them.

"Yes, let's tackle those rumors first, shall we?" Kingsley clasped his hands on the table. "Jessie, can you take us through your people, and then Austin, you can talk about your betas."

"Yeah, sure," I replied. We really could've done this before I'd gone through the effort of filing them all away. I rose and headed for my people, my heels clicking against the floor as I crossed half the distance. "Come on, everyone." I motioned them on, then turned to face the table. "You saw Mr. Tom. He's a gargoyle. I have two others on my team," I said, and pointed at Ulric and Jasper.

They didn't ask why Mr. Tom had been left out of the gargoyle line, for which I was thankful, because no one had told me.

"Dave, the basajaun." I put my hand on his arm when he stopped beside me. A few alphas' gazes flicked to Austin.

"So, you don't have a team of basajaunak?" asked one of the male alphas, a guy with blond hair and a small ponytail. I'd already forgotten his name.

"She is family," Dave told them with a growl. He didn't seem to like being questioned. "When she needs her family, they come to her aid."

I rubbed his hairy arm. "Yes, we have a team, but Dave is the only one on my house council. It's a magical bond forged by the house. I have space for thirteen people, and there are only a couple seats left open. So, while the other basajaunak are on the team, they don't have the house bond, if that makes sense. Dave's mother, the leader of their group, has joined the convocation. We have yet to meet the elders. We just…haven't had time. We have a lot to do and no time to do it all."

No one else asked questions, so I moved on to Hollace.

"Can he show us his form?" someone asked.

"No," he replied. "There isn't enough space in here." I looked around and then up. "Yeah, we'd have to push chairs and everything out of the way, get rid of those speakers… He can shift somewhere outside. In the parking lot, maybe."

"His form is large and somewhat spectacular," Kingsley said.

"*Spectacular*, atta boy!" Fred leaned forward to see Hollace and put her fist in the air.

"Cyra?" I rubbed my eyes, and then cursed, remembering I had on makeup. "Why didn't you put on the undershirt we got for you?"

She held it in her hand. Her nipples showed through her burned jacket. "I didn't want to get soot on it. Should I ditch the jacket and just wear the shirt?"

"Free the breasts," Niamh said, and Fred put up her fist again.

"Right. Fine. This is our phoenix, if you hadn't already guessed," I said. "If you want to see her other form, she can do that when Hollace does. She can use fire in this form, but this isn't a good place. She'd ruin the floor and furniture. And the rest of her clothes."

I went through everyone else. No one asked any questions or commented when I had to retrieve Edgar from the far corner, where he'd slipped in behind the shifters of the other pack. Given that two startled when I called over to him, they hadn't even realized he'd been there. They clearly weren't great at sensing presences. Mages would have it easy around them.

My crew went back to their spots while Broken Sue and Tristan came forward, a wall of muscle. They stood tall with their gazes almost straight ahead, as if they owned the room.

For most of these alphas, that would be *very* close to a challenge. Kingsley's group had all bristled when they met Broken Sue, and had remained on edge. They hadn't known how to read Tristan. This room had no such problems, however. Some of the alphas visibly tensed. The others glanced at Kingsley, who inclined his head, agreeing with something.

As if knowing I couldn't read the room, Kingsley leaned my way and lowered his voice. "I told them that Austin's betas posture as though they are alphas, and he doesn't call them down. They thought I was exaggerating."

"About the posture *and* the power," Margery said. "They have the power of alphas. At least, that shifter does."

"They both do," Austin said.

"The Austin Steele I've heard about all these years would never allow someone that close to challenging," Zack murmured to a short man with a bald head. Kevin, I thought his name was.

"Make no mistake," Austin said in a growl, "if they *were* close to challenging, I'd handle it. My beast would push me hard. I *am* that Austin Steele you've heard of. They aren't close, however. They know their positions, as do I. Our hierarchy is firmly in place. There is not a question of my dominance, and so I'm not worried about how they posture. Neither am I worried about my mate's team, packed with power and seemingly in constant chaos. What we've cultivated works. In battle, it works. Kingsley can attest to that."

"I can." Kingsley nodded. "I taught Austin everything I know, and he's taken it to the next level. He thinks he's the same Austin Steele from the rumors, but he isn't. He isn't the hotheaded kid from my territory. He's grown into his might, and he's trying to do noble things with it. So, let's talk about those rumors, shall we? As you can see, my claims about the people he has on his team are true. The phoenix, the basajaun—

they're here."

The alphas inclined their heads. "I'd still like a demonstration of some of their magics," one of them said.

"You'll have it," Kingsley replied. "Austin and Jessie's team is stacked with power. Their whole territory is stacked with power and battle-ready. It's not a territory of restful inhabitants, like I have. Like *you* have." He looked at them pointedly. "You know my daughter. She lives there now, and she can attest to those claims at a later date. But let's talk about Austin."

Austin settled back in his chair and draped his hand over the back of mine. He ran his thumb against my shoulder, and I knew he wasn't looking forward to this.

"He's obviously powerful," Kevin said. "He also obviously has a firm handle on his people."

"He does," Kingsley said. "Shifters and gargoyles."

"Not the basajaunak?" Margery asked.

"The basajaunak…" Austin thought for a moment. "Their leader, Dave's mom, is in the convocation, as we mentioned. She follows my or Jessie's battle directions and organizes her basajaunak accordingly. In Dave's mom's absence, they answer to Jessie. The convocation is in segments. Jessie handles the people we have over there. She and Tristan command the gargoyles and other fliers. I handle the ground crew, turning certain aspects over to Brochan or my other top personnel. I oversee the whole to create a cohesive unit while Jessie combats any magic wielders. Dealing with mages and all these other magical types is a balancing act, one that's always moving and changing. We have a unique situation we're trying to manage, which was why we were able to handle the battle in Kingsley's territory."

"With mage help, right?" Zack asked.

"Our mages...went their own way," I said with a heavy heart. "For now. It's part of the reason we need Fred. Nessa is better than us at technology. We had to find her, and soon, we're going to bring them in. They're misguided in their thinking, and I'm about out of patience."

The uncomfortable feeling I'd had regarding their situation coiled in my gut, like I was running out of time. Like something was gravely wrong, and soon it would all blow up.

I shook it off. I'd need to get with Niamh and come up with a plan.

"We need them," I said, the assurance of that statement ringing in my voice. "*I* need them. I'm not enough to combat Momar. Not even close. I'm strong, but I'm not experienced. I don't know the culture, the rules. I don't know where to focus my magical learning or even how to test-drive the new, intense, and extremely dangerous spells. While I also need to find, meet, and unify other mages, like Austin is trying to do with shifters, they are our core group. Without them, we're vulnerable."

My heart sped up as I said that, knowing it deep in my bones. Without Sebastian and Nessa, we would fail. Without us, one or both of them would die. I wasn't a seer, but my gut feeling was so strong, I would never dare question it.

Without thinking, I turned in my chair. "Niamh, you're not needed here. Take Fred and get back to work. I want to meet to discuss everything later tonight."

"Sound." Niamh pushed to standing and gestured for Fred to follow her.

"On it!" Fred called, and followed her out.

Austin twirled a lock of my hair around his fingers, and I turned back to the table at large. "Sorry about that," I said. "We just have a lot of irons in the fire right now, and we often need to divide and conquer."

"Thank you for that display of leadership." Margery clasped her hands in her lap. "I'd wondered how you could possibly control the power you've amassed. It seems that when the situation calls for it, you step up."

"She's very easygoing," Austin said, "until she isn't. It's how our co-leadership works so well. She lets me handle things most of the time—or Mr. Tom, or another of her people—and steps in when she needs to."

"And you." The tall man squinted. "You seem to be easygoing where it concerns her. I never in my life would've thought Austin Baraza could share power. You've always had potential, but you were so…wild. Unpredictable. No balance whatsoever, and incapable of true leadership."

"I was a kid," Austin said, his tone almost bored. "I was spinning out of control until I finally challenged my brother. It was a dark time in my life, and I caused a dark time for my family. I realize that. I cannot apologize enough for it, and I cannot go back and change it. It scarred me to the point that I never imagined myself stepping into an alpha role. It was Jess who changed my mind. I'd already grown up, but she gave me the courage and stability I needed to reach for my potential. I'm still reaching. I'm here today because I'm not that spoiled kid anymore. *Because* I have changed and continue to evolve. There's a need for unity, and I, with Jess's help, can work toward acquiring it. Our goal is to provide a safe haven for all magical people from corrupt organizations like the Mages Guild. From destructive tyrants like Momar. It's why I established O'Briens in the first place, and why I want to spread that ideology further."

He fell silent for a moment. Everyone was still as

they took that in.

"However," he went on, "I am every bit as wild as that kid back in the day. I'm even more powerful now. More destructive, if I have reason to be. I made Kingsley's territory nervous with my fighting prowess. With my darkness. Do not think, for one minute, that I'm a nice man. I'm reasonable, and I'm open, and I will do right by my people at all costs, but I'm just as vicious as I always was."

I put my hand on his thigh, and he covered it with the hand not braced on my chair.

"I can attest to that," Kingsley said somberly.

"Just so we're clear," I said into the following silence, "I'm no picnic in a battle setting either. I get a bit wild myself. As does my crew. Don't get me started on the basajaunak."

"In the battle for my territory, I was glad for it," Kingsley said. "In the months to come, when Momar regroups and comes for his vengeance, I'll be relying on it."

"Austin, Jessie..." Kevin leaned forward. "What is this convocation? What do you have in mind?"

CHAPTER 20

JESSIE

I SIGHED WEARILY as I dragged myself to the main lobby to meet Niamh and Fred at the hotel bar. The meeting had run on for hours, Austin hashing out his plans for a company-like organization, with a CEO and board of directors and voting parameters for a ruling body. It wasn't entirely ironed out yet. He'd wanted Kingsley's help with the best approach, and the meeting had acted like a round table of sorts to do just that.

Everyone was interested. They'd been on board with the original attempt to unify, though they were nervous about Austin being the organization's head. They wanted some assurance he really was a changed man, and they wanted to see him in action.

Apparently, they had a way to do just that. Margery had gotten word that a nearby pack was in trouble: a ruthless sort of character had challenged for power and killed the governing body. He'd become a terror to his people. He wouldn't let pack members leave if he could help it, and the body count of those trying to push back was growing. The couple who had escaped were begging for help.

The alphas had agreed to let Austin and me handle it. They'd be watching, ready to step in if needed, seemed to expect they would have to, and probably planned to say, "I told you so." They'd even offered us some of their people to fill out our ranks, which Austin politely declined. We didn't need them.

They thought it was bravado. One of them had even smirked.

Shifters seemed to hold grudges—that was what I was noticing, anyway. Or maybe they'd just never heard anything good about Austin until recently. He wasn't the boastful type, and for the longest time after leaving Kingsley's pack, he'd lain low. They'd heard his name, that he'd wiped out whole hunting parties and others besides, but it had seemed like tall tales. That, or it had cemented the "wild" persona they'd stuck him with.

My annoyance with their attitudes was on a high simmer.

Still, they weren't outright telling him "no." They were giving him a chance to prove himself. I'd held my frustration in check solely for that reason, though I wasn't far from calling them idiots to their faces. When the shoe fit...

When I entered the bar, Niamh was nowhere to be found, but Fred sat at the end corner, still in her yellow suit. Her laptop was open in front of her, and a tablet sat beside it with the stylus resting on top. She didn't glance up as I sat kitty-corner to her.

The bartender stopped in front of me. "Hi there. Do you need to see a menu?"

"No. Can I have a Cosmo, please? Thanks." I ran my hand down my face, probably smearing what was left of my makeup.

"Oh, hey!" Fred glanced up at the sound of my voice and beamed. "How was the meeting? Tired, huh? You look tired."

"Very, yes. Where's Niamh?"

"Her room. I weaseled my way through a hard-to-crack firewall and got a bunch of info about that Momar dude. His current operations, more specifically. She said she couldn't think with the chippy bartender always smiling at her, so she went back to hide out for a while. She does that, I've noticed."

She had these last couple months, it was true. Niamh had been on her porch a lot more lately, pondering, working things out. Then she might disappear for a couple days, wanting to take care of something in person. Mr. Tom said it was how pucas worked when they were dialed in and that I should leave her to it. He was pleased that she was *finally* being useful rather than wasting bread for dry sandwiches and drinking the town dry.

Given I had so much to do myself, and I had to trust my team to do their part, I left her to it. She'd been on this earth a lot longer than I had, and her whole existence up until O'Briens had been dedicated to an elaborate game of chess. Or so I'd been told. She had experience that would hopefully benefit us all.

I nodded and thanked the bartender when he brought me my drink.

"Do you need anything?" I asked Fred.

She looked around at her setup. "Oh. Um…yes. I didn't realize my drink was gone. Just a coffee, please. Three sugars. Thanks." With that, she bent back to her computer, and her fingers danced across the keyboard.

I nodded to the bartender and pulled up a game on my phone.

"Did you know about these things?" Fred indicated the electronic notepad before writing something. "I didn't. They're the best freaking thing on this earth, I'm tellin' ya. I mean, I knew they existed—I don't live under a rock—but I've never tried one until now. I've been missing out."

She finished her note and went back to her computer. Her silence resumed. The soft murmur of conversation ebbed and flowed around us, interrupted by the click of keys. After a while, her typing stopped, and she leaned forward, closer to the screen. She made another note, then shook her head and started to shake, slowly bubbling into laughter.

"I have a crush, bro!" She leaned back again, hands back at the keyboard. "If the Captain had more coding knowledge, she'd be unstoppable. Her tactics are so fresh. Her evasive maneuvers are ingenious."

"The Captain..." My heart skipped. "You mean Nessa?"

"Yeah. Get this: she has this shack in the middle of nowhere. I thought she'd mostly gone off the grid, using that shack of equipment at odd times. But no! It was a decoy. She installed a program to seem like it's active, but it really just messes around on the dark web a bit and doesn't cover much ground. No, she's out using random IP addresses and different accounts and aliases." Fred held up her hand. "But she's checked into her other accounts here and there. She didn't hide her breadcrumbs well enough. I'm on her trail."

"You know where she is?"

"I'm nearly positive, yeah, and I'm double-checking now. Once I'm sure, we can figure out what they're up to." Her smile broadened. "This is so fun. I feel like I'm rupturing something, it's so fun! It's like this enormous, complex puzzle, and we only get hints at a time. This Momar person seems like a spider. We're just in the outer web now, but he skitters here and there, then hides out of sight. He'll be a tricky one."

She continued muttering to herself as she worked her keyboard, her focus zeroing in again on her screen. I let her be as her coffee arrived and paid the tab.

"Just...save your receipts, okay?" I told her, only finishing half my drink before pushing it away. There was no point in my being here if Niamh wasn't. Besides, I'd gotten enough information from Fred for the time being. They were still working on things, and we didn't have anything concrete yet. "We'll reimburse your expenses."

"Meh." She waved me away, her gaze not leaving the screen. "There's no point in paperwork for a few coffees and a truckload of sugar."

"Okay, well...the offer's there."

"Thanks." She gave me a smile before going back to her task.

She was certainly diligent. A hard worker. Also, clearly great at her job. Niamh had made a good call with Fred. We were that much closer to closing the gap between us and our missing mages.

My heart ached to see them again. My gut said I'd better hurry up and make that happen.

✦ ✦ ✦

AUSTIN

"HER CREW IS incredibly messy," Kingsley said, resting in his suite's living room with his feet up on the coffee table. He held a scotch and closed his eyes as he leaned his head back. It had been a long afternoon. "I didn't warn the others before the meeting."

Austin gritted his teeth against a surge of anger. Kingsley wasn't trying to be mean-spirited toward Jess—he was stating the truth. Austin knew he was right. Had always known and had never been able to do anything about it. He'd stopped trying.

"They've been practicing lining up for a couple months," Austin said, watching the fading light dance across the brown liquid in his glass. The suite was quiet. Mac was playing golf, and Earnessa was at the spa.

Kingsley laughed quietly. "Huh."

"Yeah. In practice, they actually looked mostly okay. Passable. Then, today…it just went all to shit." Austin joined his brother in laughing. "Spectacularly. I've never seen anything like it. It's like when she tries to push order onto them, they become that much harder to control."

Kingsley took a deep breath. "The thing is…" He shook his head. "It's not a deal breaker. I'd worried it might be. Did you see Jessie's reaction when someone asked what would happen if her crew turned on her?"

"I felt her tense. Her feelings through the bonds were confusion."

"It was this…" Kingsley started laughing again. "This *that is the stupidest question I've ever heard* expression teamed with absolute confusion, yeah. I figured I better interject before she came right out and called someone an idiot. Though by then, everyone knew there'd be no challenges. It was a solid move to wear what you did. Her as well. It immediately put people at ease." He paused. "A little more at ease, anyway."

"That was the point. I know the rumors that surround me. I'm exactly as wild as people fear."

"Nah. You're a controlled wild."

"To you. You're my brother—you've seen my absolute worst. What you see now is a far step above that, but it isn't far enough to make the alphas in there today comfortable."

"They're entrenched, generational alphas without any strife. They don't understand the sort of issues that your territory and your mate face. I didn't either, and I'd been to your territory."

"Exactly. And seventy-five percent of the big-time alphas in this country are generational alphas. Maybe just second generation for some of them, who might be more modernized in their way of thinking, but Armendale is an eighth. His territory has done things the same way for literal generations. Why? Because it works. In the world they think they're living in, it works."

Kingsley released a slow breath before taking a sip of his scotch. "Armendale, yeah. He's what stopped my momentum the last time. He wanted to do things the *right* way. His words."

"And that's challenging for dominance?"

"Yes. Even though this isn't a traditional pack setup, and I didn't want anything to do with the leadership of his pack, those were his terms."

"You couldn't take him, and he knew that."

"Exactly. Since you almost certainly can, he'll probably have a different *right* way. The end result will be the same. I doubt he'll join, and he'll try to make sure no one else does, either."

Armendale wasn't as strong as they came—a legendary alpha called Yazanth Golden Fang had that honor—but he was one of them. He had power, money, and a lot of connections. And ever since Yazanth was exiled from his pack five or so years ago, presumed dead, Armendale had become something of the king of alpha network—at least, *he* thought so. His influence could be far reaching, and he would not like an upstart with a bad rep, like Austin, trying to climb up onto his perch.

Austin had purposely stayed away from the alpha rumor mill in his past, knowing how heavily he was featured in it, but he'd had to get caught up for this. Armendale was stuck in his ways and felt justified in that because he had a strong, prosperous pack—a peaceful pack that hadn't hit a bump in the road in generations. He had wealth and privilege, and no one was stupid enough to challenge his authority.

Well…*almost* no one.

"Yes, I can take him," Austin said. "I can make him say uncle. And I will, just to prove a point. But do you know what he'll say once I do?"

"That you aren't the right stuff? That my territory isn't as big or properly set up as his and what befell me wouldn't work on him? That he would have no trouble swatting down mages?"

"All of the above, yeah." Austin took a sip of his drink. "He knew you wouldn't challenge him, so he didn't need any more excuses. It's not about the *right* way, it's about the easy way, and he's never had it hard in his life."

"Until he meets you."

"Until that day, yes. And Jess. She doesn't react well to people digging in their heels and pretending danger doesn't exist. And if his people kick up to protect him, my people will make sure they stay out of it. Regardless, he won't want to hear our plans or join unless he can lead us, and since he's never had to build anything, he'd worry about failure. He's a no-go. We won't have his support."

"Except his voice is the loudest in the alpha network, and his views are rarely disputed. If he puts the thumb down to you, the rest will follow."

"The rest? You think the people at the meeting will change their minds?"

"Not them. The people here trust me. They might not have totally believed me about you, but they had enough of an open mind to meet you and hear you out. I don't have that kind of sway with many others. It's why it all fell apart last time."

Austin curled his fingers into a fist and then released them slowly. "It won't fall apart this time. It *can't*. You don't have any idea of the stuff Niamh is finding with Fred's help. Momar isn't just some random mage who's managed to amass power and now holds it by a thread. He purposefully climbed to where he is, he built an empire, and now he is chipping away at the Mages Guild. He's aiming for total control, and the shifters are his number-one enemy. If someone doesn't stand in the way, he'll wipe us all out. He failed last time because he wasn't counting on Jess and didn't know about Sebastian, but he's incredibly smart, cunning, and methodical. Next time, he'll have a different plan, and we might not be so lucky. Jess will be standing in his way, and I'll be standing beside her, but we won't be enough. This won't be a battle the shifters can pretend doesn't exist. I'll make them see that."

"Lucky?" Kingsley huffed. "You think Jessie sacrificing herself was a stroke of luck?"

"I think it was lucky she had the option. It was lucky that it took them so long to erect that spell. Just a bit longer, and she wouldn't have made it. None of us would have. We didn't see it coming. Even now, the ball is in his court. He holds all the power because he holds all the knowledge. We don't have a foothold in the mage world, but he has a damn good idea of how shifters work."

Kingsley nodded slowly, his eyes analyzing Austin. "And how will you get Armendale to come around?"

"Screw Armendale." Austin's power surged through the room, and he didn't bother tamping it down. He didn't have to apologize to Kingsley, not after they'd talked it out. "He'll be a statement. People are going to doubt my power, Jess's magic, and our abilities until we prove our might. We're seeing it right now with this errand your friends have us going on tomorrow. I don't have time to travel around the country doing small chores to prove our worth. Armendale is how we prove it. And if he slights me, I'll prove it viciously."

Kingsley's eyes widened, still analyzing. He was a methodical thinker. He took what *was* and altered it just enough to create what *needed to be.* Austin was the brawn, Kingsley the brain. They needed to play to their strengths for this to work.

Austin changed the subject to something he'd realized that day. "You steered that meeting well, from the moment we walked in to the second you wrapped it up."

Kingsley took his time taking a sip. Though he seemed reluctant to switch topics, he finally relented. "I figured I'd better. Your crew and hers are a lot to take. You have an extreme amount of power in your setup—not just those betas, all of them—and she has more. It doesn't help that when you or she gets incensed, your beasts sparkle through your eyes manically. It was making people nervous."

"I will always make people nervous. I saw the evidence of that in your territory, and that was once my home. I can work with gargoyles and mate a gargoyle because I'm a battle species, just like them. I *am* wild, Kingsley. That'll never go away. I'll never be properly housebroken, not to people like Armendale."

"What are you saying?" He was back to analyzing.

"I'm saying that right now, I'm what's needed. I'm the determination, fire, and muscle that will unify everyone. I have the power and the drive and a damn good reason: to protect my mate. I'll force a path where there currently isn't one. I will create a safe haven because that is, apparently, in my nature. But if we should ever be lucky enough to see peace…I'll become obsolete."

A crease formed between Kingsley's brows. "I'm not following."

"I won't be what's needed. I'm the battle commander. I'm the steel that Momar will crash against. But once he's destroyed and we have some semblance of a fair governing body represented by all magical species…I'll step aside. I'll let you tap in and do what you do best—lead a peaceful, organized faction where everyone thrives. This time when I step away, though, I won't leave the organization in ruins. I'll do it the right way."

Disbelief warred with pride and respect in Kingsley's expression. "What about Jessie? Does she get any say in this?"

"She wants what I want—to be magical without the danger. She literally battled her way into magic, and she'll battle her way out. And then she wants to rest. I stepped up so that I could stand beside her, and I can't wait to step down to stay at her side. This is your vision, Kingsley. I see the necessity of it, and I'll help you achieve it, like you have helped me achieve all that I am, but I won't hang on to it. I didn't want your pack, and I don't want this. It's yours. I'll force you to take it."

His Adam's apple bobbed. He was clearly lost for words. Just like he would've stepped aside if Austin had wanted his pack, Austin knew he'd planned to step aside in this. Had already. He wanted what was best for the people. Somehow, he'd never realized *he* was what was best for the people.

"Now," Austin continued into the silence, "I can see you want to argue or get sentimental or who knows what, but I need to know what I'm walking into tomorrow. I assume you know the details…"

This time, Kingsley didn't speak for a full minute before he finally relented on the topic change. And then they got on with the job, together.

CHAPTER 21

JESSIE

I STEPPED INTO the crisp morning air, which would've been downright frigid and unbearable if I didn't have magic shielding me from the worst of it. I was trying to save my energy for what would surely turn into a battle for a territory.

"It's as cold as a witch's tit out here," Ulric said, meeting me in front of my suite.

"I never understood that expression," I said as Jasper joined us, and then Dave and Cyra. Indigo and Edgar came next, followed by a trickle of the rest of them. Today, they were early. Yesterday, when it was important, they were late. It was like they didn't want to do things the expected way.

"Witch's tit." Jasper pointed at the sky. Ulric and I looked up. Nothing but pale blue. "Like...they fly on their brooms, and it's cold, so their tits would be cold."

"Huh." I nodded. I could see that.

"Okay, but what about a witch's nose?" Ulric countered.

"It's a swear." Jasper frowned at Ulric. "You don't swear using *nose*. 'It's as cold as a witch's nose out here!'" He lifted his eyebrows. "Not the same punch."

"What about warlock's balls?" Ulric asked.

"In the stories, do warlocks fly brooms?" Jasper paused, but when Ulric didn't supply him with an answer, he shrugged. "Well, even if they do, their balls are probably the warmest part about them in that scenario. Also smashed. Now, 'it's as uncomfortable as a smashed dick' might work, but then you lose the witch and warlock scenario. Or wizard. Or whatever."

"Flying brooms aren't actually a thing, right?" I asked as Austin stepped out of our suite in a dress shirt and trousers. I wore a similar outfit. This was a professional situation, and it was thought we should dress the part, even though it was almost certain that we'd end up fighting. A muumuu made a lot more sense.

"Not that I know of," Jasper said.

"Neither are witches or wands," Ulric replied as Austin started walking. "Dicks and Janes got that part of magic wrong."

"Wait, sir!" Mr. Tom hurried out of the suite with a breakfast burrito wrapped in foil. "You forgot the other half of your breakfast. You can't be fighting and killing on a half-empty stomach. Here—"

Austin slowed, cocked his head in annoyance, and put out his hand. Mr. Tom filled it with the burrito.

"What do you say?" I grinned at him.

"Thank you," Austin growled, giving me a *look* before starting forward again.

"Manners. Lovely." Mr. Tom sniffed. "Now, miss, do you require more coffee for the drive?"

"No, I'm fine." I hurried to keep up with Austin as Mr. Tom headed back to the suite, where he'd left a whole basket filled with treats for the group.

"I should probably be more nervous," I murmured as we took the stairs and met the others out by the building's main door. Tristan and Broken Sue had everyone in formation, a larger crew than we'd brought to the meeting yesterday. Basajaunak waited in the trees, no more than a handful. Traveling with a large force was difficult, and so we'd brought as many as we could comfortably handle. We hoped we wouldn't need them.

"Why?" Austin asked.

"I'm always nervous before a potential battle."

He directed people to the vans, and Tristan and Broken Sue took over.

"You don't have enough information to be nervous yet, on purpose." Austin glanced back at my people still waiting by the door. "I'll fill you in on the ride. Why aren't they coming?"

I stalled and turned, putting up my hand to block the glare of the late morning sun. Immediately, it was clear. "Where's Niamh?" I asked.

"I got it." Ulric pulled out his phone.

"Also, why aren't you guys with the gargoyles?"

It was Jasper who answered: "We're with you today. Remember the subset of training we're doing now?"

Right, right. My team within the larger team of fliers. Essentially, the people who would help me stick to the plan.

"Jessie." Niamh walked in from the right, Fred in tow. Her steps were hurried and her eyes tight, not usual for her. Fred's expression was closed in solemn worry.

"What's wrong?" I asked immediately.

"Momar's people know where Sebastian and Nessa are," Niamh said without preamble. "We spent the morning making sure. Nessa had some tagalongs, as Fred calls them, on their setup. Spies, in other words. Fred bucked them off, but that just changed their spying from computer to in-person. They've kept their distance, but they're there. They're documenting schedules, activities, dwellings—they're gearing up for an extraction. Sebastian is powerful, but they have more people."

Shadows pooled and coiled as Tristan joined us. His arms flared out from his sides, and his power thrummed. I put a hand on his arm to keep him calm—or maybe keep myself calm, because I was suddenly blanketed in a cold sweat.

"Where are they?" I asked.

"Kansas, two states away."

"That spider is meticulous," Fred said, and there was no hint of her humor or color in her tone. She realized the seriousness of this. "Momar, I mean. If it were up to the ground crew, as they're calling them, they would've gone in and grabbed the mages weeks ago. The spider is nailing down all the many details so nothing will go wrong."

"Jessie, I think he knows that Sebastian and Nessa are Elliot Graves and the Captain, and that they were the ones helping us." Niamh put her hands to her hips. "I can't be sure, now, but it wouldn't be too hard to deduce, like. They weren't active leading up to and during the time at Kingsley's, when some unknown and powerful mage was helping ye behind the scenes. A mage with a special interest in ye. An ingenious mage, one that knew the dark web so well that they could hide the weapons purchase. And then ye showed up to collect. They have the two mages that escaped the caves—or *had*. They're probably dead now. They knew

Elliot was moonlighting on ye. And then the deaths they framed us for—that looked like their handiwork, not ours. I noticed right away. If Momar is as good as he seems, he would've noticed too. It's all there if ye piece together the details."

My blood ran cold. "But…" Elliot and the Captain had gone dark when I was getting training from Sebastian, but then they'd immediately shown up on the map when I went to Sebastian's caves.

"Kinsella," I drew out. I would've killed him, not knowing it would get me in trouble with the Mages Guild, but he'd disappeared.

Disappeared, and then turned up on Elliot Graves's kill list.

I hadn't known who was behind Elliot Graves at that point, and then so much had happened. I hadn't properly backtracked to think about the ramifications. Elliot Graves had been dark all those years…until he showed up with an interest in me and did me a favor by taking out my enemies.

"The Anal Repository never would've made those connections," Niamh told me, using the name she called the Mages Guild. "Their game is in extorting and throwing their weight around. They want easy money. Momar is a different sort of animal. A much more dangerous one." She snapped her fingers at Mr. Tom.

"Come here, ya *eejit*. Can't ye see there's a change in plan? We need to get the plane here as soon as we can, boy. We need to get those mages out of there."

"How much time?" I asked Niamh.

"We don't know, and that's the honest truth. There were messages of the extraction crew going dark, but Fred was able to get their locations, though we're not sure how valid that intel is. They appear to be moving into the area, but not necessarily into position. We want to get moving."

It felt like my brain was rapidly firing. It had always taken us a few days to sort out private jet travel, what with the various planes, pilots, and tiny airports. There wasn't a magical strip in this area, and we needed a magical pilot and certain size plane for the basajaunak. I didn't dare leave them here. If we showed up to grab the mages while Momar's people were attempting the exaction, we'd need the extra hands.

But there was no way we could leave *right now* to handle this. The earliest would likely be in the evening, but more probably the next morning or even the day after.

"Can you get a message to the mages?" I asked.

"I've left a message on the encrypted phone," Fred said, "and through their setup in the woods, but we don't know how often they check those. The IPs they use seem to be cafés and other random locations. Going off-grid means they aren't easily reachable."

"Damn it." I dug my nails into my sides.

I took a deep breath and let it out slowly. Austin waited to the side, and Broken Sue stood in front of an open van door. They would leave right now to get the mages, not bothering to prove anything to the collection of alphas.

But we had no transportation. That was the sum total of what we needed to plan. Get there, bust in, and either force the mages to come home with us or fight them out of the enemy's grasp. Until we had planes, however, we could do nothing but wait. Doing one thing at a time was a luxury we hadn't had for a while now.

"Dang it. Mr. Tom, get on that transportation. Niamh, you and Fred find out more information, or help Mr. Tom. The rest of us are going to take care of a bad alpha while you handle that. Call if you have something, but don't interrupt us if you don't. The very *moment* we have a way to get to Nessa and Sebastian quickly, we're taking it. Okay?"

"Right, so." Niamh motioned for Fred to start walking back the way they'd come.

Mr. Tom held out the basket to Edgar.

"No, not to—" I started.

"I got it." Ulric ran that way, intercepting the basket just as Edgar's fingers brushed the edges. "Sorry, Edgar, but you get really weird about food."

"Oh, that's okay," Edgar said. "No one seems to eat my offerings anyway."

"He just told you why," Jasper said.

I started toward the vans. My power blasted out, a call to arms. "Load up." I made a circle in the air with my finger, belatedly noticing Kingsley and some of the other alphas down the way, watching. I pointed at them. "We're doing this to prove to you that we can handle ourselves in battle. Better get there on time, because we can't dally. We have other people to save."

Austin didn't need to bark orders. Everyone filed in quickly, with the basajaunak in the large cargo vans at the back of the convoy.

"How hard is this going to be?" I asked Austin as he climbed into the van. Tristan sat in the driver's seat.

"Kingsley doesn't think we'll have a problem. With you in this mood, that is almost certainly true. We'll knock this out and figure out what needs to happen for Nessa and Sebastian, okay?"

I looked out the window. The saving grace was that I knew the extraction team wouldn't kill the mages. They'd want information, and for that, the mages would need to be kept alive. Sebastian had undergone torture before, and Nessa was tough. Even if we didn't get there first, we could still save them.

Still, I'd really rather we got there first.

CHAPTER 22
TRISTAN

"**L**ISTEN TO ME closely," Alpha Steele told Jessie as we neared the homestead, a beaten-down place with small dwellings, dirty streets, and very few people out and about. It almost looked like a ghost town. "Watch your six at all times. If someone comes at you, that constitutes a challenge. The outcome is at your discretion, but in a situation like this, you kill. The people in charge have made life miserable for the pack members. They've committed atrocities because no one could stop them. If they're spared, they could, and probably will, move on and do it again."

"No problem," she answered.

"You don't have to make it flashy, but you can if it gets the job done. Do not heal."

"Got it."

Alpha Steele had filled her and Tristan in on how one of these things typically worked. Essentially, they waltzed in, threw their weight around, challenged, killed the baddies, and tried to help facilitate a new leadership. That, or help them move on.

Not today.

They wouldn't have time for cleanup. Nessa and Sebastian needed them. Tristan understood Jessie's deciding to help these people with the time they would be idle anyway, but the other alphas were in tow, and *they* could help these people pick up the pieces. They shouldn't have waited to help in the first place.

Jessie's magic created a solid drumbeat of urgency in Tristan's middle. The connections were active, and through her, he could feel everyone's basic location. She had her finger on the pulse. The enemy had no idea what was on their doorstep. Their worst nightmare was about to see them into the afterlife. The alphas tagging along would get to see what it was like when a mage entered a shifter fight.

"I might make a spectacle," Jessie said in a small voice laced with worry and anger. In the rearview mirror, Tristan could just see her fingernails clawing into her knee.

"Then you make a spectacle," Alpha Steele replied, and tingles crawled along Tristan's spine. Alpha Steele had not only given Jessie the green light to go hard, but he also clearly intended to go hard himself.

Brochan would go scorched earth. He had a history of not helping when he thought he should have, but he'd been lost and defeated during that time, unsure of his own existence. He'd damn well prove he intended to help now.

The larger street wound through town and stopped at what must've passed for their central hub. A brown patch of dead grass supported a kids' play area that didn't look like it had seen kids in a long time. A broken tire swing hung from an abandoned house down the way, and the row of businesses in what passed for the main strip seemed in disrepair and were mostly shuttered.

"Park, or stop in the middle of the street?" Tristan asked Alpha Steele.

"Middle. Block it up."

He stopped the van and exited. The others did as well. A surge of magic washed across Tristan and kept going. It would cover the town.

Come out and meet your fate.

Another shiver washed over him, and urgency ate at his core. He didn't want to be here. He wanted to be airborne, flying toward Natasha. She needed him and he wasn't there. But his wings would take too long, and he couldn't go alone. Their enemy was organized and highly effective. Tristan wouldn't be enough to combat even lower-tier mages, not if they brought numbers. Against a mage as powerful and cunning as Elliot Graves, they'd *definitely* bring numbers.

He gritted his teeth as they walked out in all directions from the van. Another peal of magic thundered forth. With Jessie, they didn't need to go knocking on doors.

Alpha Steele led the way to the square of dead grass, giving them some space. The basajaunak didn't climb out.

Tristan learned why when Brochan caught up to him. "I didn't want to scare our new friends away."

Fair.

Their people pushed to the sides in organized lines. Tristan stood in front of the gargoyles, Brochan in front of the shifters. The other alphas from the meeting stayed in their vehicles, watching. They probably thought along the same lines as Brochan.

Another peal of thunderous magic: *COME HERE!*

Alpha Steele waited in the middle of the space, and Jessie came over to wait next to Tristan. She wasn't afraid. Tristan could feel her anticipation through the connection—she was giving Alpha Steele the limelight. They were a damn good team, each happy to help the other show off.

"If they get one look at us and try to run, you get

airborne and bring them back," she said in a low tone.

The ragtag Ivy House crew ambled forward, filling in the space between the shifters and gargoyles. They hadn't had a chance to shift last night to show the visiting packs—everyone had been too tired. They would do it soon.

Or maybe that had been the plan all along.

With the next magical wave, movement caught Tristan's eye. A shiny Corvette stopped at the end of a side street, the way blocked by the procession of vans. Other vehicles stopped behind it. The enforcers.

They exited their vehicles, alpha first and then the others, no one in sync. Bulky forms walked in a haphazard line with their arms flared and a padding of fat on their person. They weren't in their best shape. Even from here, Tristan could tell they would be no match for Austin Steele. Not even Brochan. Hell, half the shifters here could take the approaching alpha.

The alpha crossed between parked vans, looking them over. His gaze ran down the line to the head, where there wasn't a shiny sports car to scream *status* and *money*. The man, only in his late twenties and clearly too dumb to know what awaited him, sneered. His enforcers were of a similar age, and only a couple showed sudden wariness.

"What's all this, then?" The alpha stepped onto the

grass and looked everyone over. His gaze lingered on Brochan and he entirely dismissed the gargoyles and other magical types. Jessie might not have been there at all. His people spread out behind him, half the force of Alpha Steele's people. Finally, the resident alpha met Alpha Steele's gaze. The newcomer's muscles flexed, and his jaw clenched. He was very expressive for a shifter and downright comical for an alpha. He hadn't had good training.

"This is the end of the line for you and your enforcers," Alpha Steele said, his voice hard and authoritative.

"Look," Jessie whispered.

Tristan followed her gaze. People peeked out from around buildings, clearly frightened and cautious. They had their phones out, filming. That was what they needed for the shifter side of things—someone like Patty. They needed someone facilitating gossip.

"That right?" The resident alpha spat to the side, not taking his eyes off Alpha Steele. "On whose authority?"

"Mine." It was more of a growl than a word.

"Well, see, you can't challenge me." He sucked at his teeth. "You gotta have some sort of official capacity to come in here and throw your weight around."

"Is that what you're doing here? Creating rules that make no sense?" Alpha Steele didn't move, didn't even twitch a muscle, but suddenly, the resident alpha jerked as though slapped. Alpha Steele must've let his beast peek out of the darkness. "You've been plaguing these people long enough. It ends today. You can challenge me officially, or you can run. Either way, you will die. Choose."

"Gracious," Jessie murmured. Heat soaked her tone—her gargoyle liked that threat. Tristan knew how she felt. He wanted to be in the action.

The resident alpha huffed. "We've got an imbalance of power here, and I didn't challenge you. You've gotta allow me to choose another."

"You're a cancer to the world of shifters," Alpha Steele said in a rough voice. "A disgrace to our magical type. I don't *gotta* do anything. Made-up rules won't help you with me." He undid his buttons. "Neither will real ones. Or don't you know who I am? I'm Austin Steele, and I'm here to tuck you into your grave."

The resident alpha smirked, but his eyes appeared cagey in a hurry. "Steele? Never heard of ya," he said—obviously a lie. A big one. Fear soaked into the lines of his body. His panicked gaze flicked right, to what was probably his beta. That shifter had been in the middle of their line, but he seemed to have the most power besides the alpha. The beta inclined his head slightly and touched a flat area in his pocket. Someone else in line couldn't keep himself from glancing off toward the buildings of the town.

"Heads up," Tristan whispered to Jessie. "Incoming."

"Yeah. Even I could—Oh, no."

The "incoming" wasn't what Tristan had been expecting, which was the rest of their force running to ambush. Instead, it was five people shoving children in front of them. Two kept their hands wrapped around the backs of little necks. All the adults held knives, and suddenly Tristan couldn't see anything but red. Red everywhere, pulsing at the edges of his vision, tightening his chest, curling his hands into fists. If he had his way, these shifters would die painfully for this horror. For using innocence as a shield.

Gruesomely.

A pulse of magic swept the area. Jessie was calling in the basajaunak.

She put a hand on Tristan's forearm. "I won't let the children be harmed. Be easy, Tristan. We don't want any sudden movements here." Her expression and voice were utterly calm. "Keep the gargoyles in check."

"What…" The resident alpha was trying to look around in confusion while not taking his eyes off Alpha Steele. He shook it off. "Just remember who it was who said they didn't like rules." One of his guys pulled away from their haphazard line, taking out his phone, and presumably started filming. "You don't have rules, then neither do I. We have a nice, quiet little setup here. We don't need any outsiders coming in. Keep to your business, leave here without trouble, and we'll have no reason to spill the kiddies' blood."

Jessie walked toward a frozen and seething Alpha Steele, her movements syrupy slow and graceful. The wind fluttered her hair. She wore a kind smile as she addressed the resident alpha.

"Hello." She crossed in front of Alpha Steele, trailing her hand behind, and took one of his. He shook. Clearly, he was doing everything in his power to keep his beast at bay, but it was a struggle. He, like Tristan, like the inferno on the other side that was Brochan, wanted to smear this vermin from the earth.

The resident alpha's expression closed in confusion.

"I'm the co-ruler. Alpha." She shrugged with a big smile. "Whatever." She leaned against Alpha Steele, looping her arm around his. "I'm his mate, so please have a care how you speak to me. You must know what happens to an alpha if his mate is threatened. He won't be able to help himself, and all our viewers at home will blame you and not him. How about we try to settle this peacefully?"

Basajaunak crawled across the street, low to the ground. They darted into the bushes or against the trees growing from the dirt squares breaking up the sidewalk. Once they were near any sort of natural element, they disappeared. Very clever.

"How about this?" The resident alpha scowled at her in annoyance and confusion. "How about you get back into your crappy vans and see yourselves out of here? The people here are doing just fine. We don't need any outsiders." He paused for a moment. "What the hell *are* you, anyway?"

She shrugged one shoulder. "A mom."

She spun away from Alpha Steele as a peal of thunderous magic rang out around her. *Attack.*

A jet of magic sliced across the five newcomers and their hostages. Tristan had a moment of abject terror that she'd hit the children, but then the people standing behind them shook. Their knives fell from limp hands. She was disarming them. She'd figured out how to do it without messing with the animal portion of a shifter.

The enforcers shuddered in fear and confusion, watching the knives drop from fingers they no longer controlled.

A basajaunak surged forward from behind one of them, seemingly appearing out of thin air. Then another. One of the enforcers reached for a kid, but another basajaunak was there immediately. A vicious crack said his neck snapped.

Jessie ignored the resident alpha and shoved out her hands at the shifters nearest her. In a moment, it was like someone had lost control of a paint blaster. Red sprayed everywhere—across the ground, jetting into the air, and then smearing into a sort of paste on an invisible wall. Bones turned into pulp. An eye somehow rolled away.

Tristan could handle a lot, and had, but the suddenness of all that, and the extreme nature, made his stomach roil.

She didn't stop, only turned and fired another jet of magic. And another. Skin was ripped apart. Limbs were severed. A man was torn in half, and then each half exploded like a piñata, parts blowing out or collapsing or who knew what.

Brochan stood there, stunned, like Tristan. Like most of their people…except for Aurora. She burst into her animal and loped across the grass for the beta, who had dropped his phone and started running. He caught sight of the up-and-coming alpha tiger at his back and morphed into a mangy wolf. She was on him in an instant, clawing at his back and ripping into his fur.

A giant roar startled Tristan. Alpha Steele stood on his hind legs in his great polar bear form. In front of him, cowering, was a largish black bear with matted fur and no hope in hell. Alpha Steele gave no quarter and was on him in a flash, punishing him for all he'd done. For daring to bring out children. For daring to breathe.

Tristan finally shook himself out of an embarrassing stupor.

"No."

It took him a moment to realize that command had come from Edgar, who was currently standing very close to his side.

"No, no, Uncle Trish," the vampire murmured. "We must not interrupt the miss when she is practicing. I wish I would've brought my helmet and padding. This situation clearly calls for it. She's really on a roll."

And so she was, having trapped the other shifters in a magical bubble to keep them from running and systematically trying one horribly grisly spell after another. Blood spatter hit him, and he didn't know what part of a body it had come from. Or which body. Or why he was suddenly having trouble with his stomach when he had surely done worse in his lifetime.

Right?

Nessa really should've been here to see this. It would lay to rest all her misgivings about her own darkness. She could never hold a candle to this.

Alpha Steele finished ripping the resident alpha apart before he launched forward to help his mate. She let him into her magical cage, leaving the enforcers trapped with a monster. She finished off a spell that had a shifter strangling himself, the least gruesome of them all but somehow the hardest to watch, before magic pumped into the field.

Boom. Boom. Boom.

It came out in gushes, hard and heavy. It wasn't meant for her people—it was meant for the watchers in the cars. The alphas wanting to see what Jessie and Alpha Steele could really do.

Boom. Boom. Boom.

If they hadn't already been staring with slack jaws at the field, they would now. The magic made it so.

Jessie stripped quickly, and the feeling through the connections told them all to do the same.

No, not all of them. Just the fliers. The spectacles. Those a shifter was unfamiliar with.

The directives came quickly, pulses of magic through the sky and through the connections, just like they had in Kingsley's territory. Like in a genuine battle.

Tristan let out a mighty roar before he shot into the sky. Once there, he hovered and issued the call for the other gargoyles, working his hardest to ensure the vibration worked into the bones of the alphas in the cars. It would blast for miles.

Gargoyles rose all around him, followed by the beautiful luminescence of Jessie with her streaks of pinkish purple. Her magic rained down on the field below, a call for flight. A command to organize and get moving.

Cyra streaked fire before spewing it down on the car Kingsley and some of the other alphas inhabited.

Tristan was moving at the same time Jessie was, only he was much faster. He grabbed her around the middle and darted toward the car as Hollace took flight. Jessie pulled the fire away with magic before pounding the observing alphas with a spell that dinged off the metal. It couldn't get through—it was just for effect.

Hopefully that wasn't a rental car, and if so, hopefully they'd gotten insurance.

Lightning crackled from Hollace, and thunder boomed.

Jessie pointed, and Tristan felt what she needed. She wanted to fly over the town and ensure that everyone was safe, that there wasn't anyone else they needed to take care of.

He swooped low, not far from the roofs, then slowed his pace and tossed her away so that she could work on her own. She did, dropping lower still and peering in windows and waving as she flew by. Her magic now was swells of peace and comfort, compassion and welcome. She was trying to set the town at ease.

K.F. BREENE

People came out of their houses and looked up in wonder. More than a few took out their phones to film the action. A great many headed toward the hub of town.

She met them there, changing back into her human form and accepting a muumuu from Ulric. Tristan landed and stepped aside to let Jessie work. She was the model of grace and kindness, hugging the children she'd helped, speaking to families and hearing their woes. Indigo was there as well, a physical healer in battle, but an emotional healer after the fact. She walked among the townspeople, touching arms or grabbing hands and chatting.

Jessie and her people were showing why she'd sparked such loyalty in her territory—fierce in battle, compassionate in peace. If Jessie felt the urgency to leave, she didn't show it. She did, however, always have her phone in her hand, retrieved from the van. She was on call, and she didn't forget it.

"I should...burn all this, right?" Cyra stopped beside Tristan, her gaze on his junk. He hadn't received a muumuu yet, as Ulric had gotten busy helping a boy find his parents.

"No, please don't burn my dick off. I'm rather partial to it. Also, it's rude to stare at other people's private areas."

"It's not very private right now." She grinned up at him. "It's a little distracting because it's quite big. The gargoyles agree that your size isn't preferable because then your partners don't want you to stick it in their rump."

He blinked at her for a moment. "That's my burden to bear, I guess."

"Yeah." She nodded, then pointed at the messy playground. "The blood and goo and stuff—I should burn all that, right? These people probably don't want to clean it up."

"Give me a moment. I'll check with the alphas."

"You might put on a muumuu so you're not as distracting. People might fear for their rumps."

It was clear she wasn't a sexual being, which invited so many questions about how phoenixes existed through the ages...and also made him want to laugh manically. She was so genuine in her absurdity.

He grabbed a muumuu.

Jessie and Alpha Steele stood with Kingsley and a couple of the other alphas. The rest were clustered by the somewhat discolored car.

"Very"—Margery, one of the more powerful alphas, swallowed hard—"eye-opening."

"She's just one mage," Alpha Steele told her. "*One.* And she could do all that."

"From a distance," Kingsley said. "Now, imagine hundreds of them, spaced all around your territory with trained combat professionals besides. You just saw what Jessie and Austin's team are capable of, and yet it was almost curtains for us. Think that through next time someone says mages pose no threat for an alpha of their stature or a pack of their size."

Kingsley put out his hand to direct Jessie and Alpha Steele away. Margery and Kevin, left standing behind, looked at each other warily. It was, Tristan presumed, one thing to hear about it and another to actually see it. Although, in fairness, he had never seen that level of horror from any other mage. He bet Sebastian hadn't, either. Ivy House had some seriously hardcore spell books. Others like it had probably been outlawed somewhere through the ages, and burned.

Kingsley lowered his voice. Brochan stepped up, his body language saying he was looking for directions, like Tristan was. Since none of the alphas tensed, telling them to move on, they both hung around.

"That was…" Kingsley swallowed hard and gave Jessie a poignant look. "I didn't realize I was squeamish until today."

"Yeah." She checked her phone screen. "Those spells aren't something I can use all the time. They take a lot of energy to pull off. I didn't want to scare the townspeople or anything, so I didn't intend on practicing, but then they...played dirty." She shrugged. "I reacted."

His jaw clenched. "You did, yes. It was ingenious how you handled that. The soft touch for Austin to keep him in line while working yourself closer so your spell would be effective. I explained how you can connect with your team. How you were able to call in the basajaunak when you needed them. That's what you were doing, right? All that?"

"Yes. There was a lot going on. Everyone was keyed up. I was trying to time everything so those kids stayed safe." She shook her head. "As safe as possible, at any rate."

"I was about ready to detonate," Alpha Steele said gruffly. "It took every ounce of control I possessed to keep from exploding into my beast."

Kingsley inclined his head. "You showed well. Those in my car could see your battle for control. Margery almost got out when we saw their hostages. I told her not to aggravate matters, that you'd handle it." He put his hand on Jessie's shoulder. "You showed *extremely* well. You can't keep your people in a line while walking, but when it really counts, your level of precision and battle acumen is unparalleled. The way you handled everyone, including checking in with the people afterward..." He nodded proudly. "You've proven every single claim I've laid at your feet, and you've done it spectacularly. Your gargoyles have as well, especially your monster." His eyes sparkled for Tristan, his version of a full-blown smile. "Brochan, however, didn't get to do nearly as much as he would've liked, I think."

Brochan's shoulders hitched, and he turned just slightly. *Not relevant...*

Kingsley glanced over at Aurora, who was clad in a purple muumuu and talking to the townspeople. Brochan hadn't been relevant because Aurora had handled matters.

"Yes, she's always been great at anticipation," Kingsley said.

"She beat me to it." Brochan cocked his head. *Fair play to her.*

"She said..." Kingsley shifted his weight. *Uncomfortable.* "She mentioned, Jessie, that you worked her out of her beast in a challenge. Not forced her out, as usually has to happen, but coaxed her out."

"Yeah." Jessie checked her phone screen again. Still nothing. "I had to learn that myself. It helps when someone guides you. I had Austin, and she has both of us."

He looked at Alpha Steele. "I didn't realize she had

that much of Dad in her."

"I didn't either," his brother replied. "I also didn't realize it was a problem until Jessie gave her a teaching moment in front of all her peers. Amazingly, it just made Aurora look more badass."

"Jessie has a gift." Kingsley winked at her. "Controlled chaos. I cannot *wait* to say 'I told you so' to the other alphas. I'll see you back at the hotel."

With that, he turned and strode away, any looseness of manner quickly returning to his stoic alpha façade.

"It speaks highly of you two that he treats you as equals," Alpha Steele told Brochan and Tristan. "Now, let's get all this cleared away. The others have already agreed to set this place to rights and offer the help these people need. We'll head back."

Tristan asked Jessie about Cyra's fire—about burning all the blood and goo so the townspeople didn't need to clean up.

"Yeah, probably should. Damn it, why no news?" She handed her phone off to Tristan. "Hold that, will ya? She's going to go too extreme, and I'm going to have my hands full trying to keep the whole place from burning down."

CHAPTER 23

SEBASTIAN

NESSA WAS PROBABLY asleep.

Sebastian sat on the couch in the living room in near darkness, watching a muted cooking show Nessa had left on. The hour hand on the wall clock had slowly worked its way past two. A critter scurried in the bushes outside the window, stopping in its foraging. After a moment, it slowly worked its way down the wall, not unlike the movement of that hour hand.

There were a lot of critters this near the woods. When they first settled here, it had put him on edge. He'd constantly checked the windows, trying to figure out what was lurking out there. He'd sent spells out the door looking for prowlers. He'd always come up empty, only finding animals, and so his anxiety had mostly subsided.

You've got a tagalong.

A spy. Someone hanging around without Nessa being aware. That meant a level of personnel the Guild had never employed. It meant a new, harder sort of game. One Nessa was barely fit for.

Being off-grid was hard, but it was safer.

Another critter scurried on the other side of the house, this one larger. Too large?

He looked that way, but what would he see? There was only a sliver of a moon tonight, and it was mostly obscured by clouds. The streetlamp on this run-down corner of nowhere was fifty yards away and sported one of those incredibly ineffective LED lights. It glowed, but the light barely reached the ground.

He waited for a moment, rewarded with more scurrying. Large, but following the sound patterns of a normal critter. Nothing to worry about.

He tapped his fingers against his knee. Nessa was definitely asleep. She'd gone to bed nearly two hours ago. These days, she didn't tend to stay asleep, but she could usually conk out pretty quickly.

The minute hand clicked a few more notches. He finally stood and quietly walked into the kitchen. Among the papers in the corner was the pushed aside but not-at-all-forgotten encrypted phone. They had to stay off the grid to avoid detection, and so they couldn't use it. Besides, Niamh had changed the message style, now delivering incoming texts to their social media accounts or other message centers. Jessie had mostly gone quiet.

For reasons he couldn't explain, the breath caught in his chest. His hands shook so badly, he had to stop reaching for the phone. He squeezed his eyes tightly and braced against the counter, struggling to control his breathing, to work his way out from under the sudden panic attack. He hadn't gotten one of these since his sister's health had started failing.

Not for the first time, and certainly not for the last, he wondered if they were doing the right thing. Times had changed, drastically. They had a new enemy now. A much savvier, more intelligent, more controlled enemy. Their old tricks weren't working as well, and back then, they'd had guidance from his sister's visions. Now they didn't have any cheat sheets, and he wondered if they were actually good enough to get to the goal line. He wasn't so sure.

A tear slipped from his eye. He wiped it away, straightening up and regaining composure.

"Harden up, Sebastian," he murmured. His sister had said that to him when she was slipping away. "Harden up. There's always a rainbow if you look hard enough."

He reached for the phone. He didn't care if Jessie and her crew knew where he and Nessa were. He didn't care if Tristan sent Nessa those gorgeous purple flowers or books to help her learn. He welcomed it, in fact. Her sassy little smile said she rather liked the game, as annoyed as it made her. She liked being the object of the predator's focus.

Sebastian liked being useful, liked coming up with that broach for Cyra or a new serum to help Edgar cheat in his flower shows. If only he had a magical way to help that vampire with his doily obsession…

"I wonder how his killer flowers are going," Sebastian mused as he pushed the button on the archaic phone and waited for it to start up.

The screen flashed. The line inched across…and then it went dark.

"Dang," he muttered. No battery.

He pulled open the nearest drawer. Notepads, pens, scissors—Nessa liked order. She didn't seem to understand that a junk drawer was supposed to be messy.

The next drawer had wound-up, perfectly arranged electronics cords. He grabbed the one he needed as a *snap* outside caught his attention. The cord unfurled as he turned that way and listened. Nothing disturbed the silence. The critters had found something to eat…or they hadn't and had taken off.

He plugged the cord into the socket and turned the phone around as a strange feeling caught in his chest. It felt like...a release, kind of. His panic attack finally subsiding?

He frowned as he pushed the connector into the phone and set it gently on the counter. The symbol for charging lit the screen. In a moment, he should be able to turn it on.

The feeling in his chest happened again, stronger this time. It was then that the silence of the night snagged his attention. Not the stillness—that often happened when the critters had all wandered away. No, the *silence*. No owls calling to each other from opposite sides of the house. No shrill cry of a coyote or the chirping or trilling of various kinds of frogs from the nearby creek.

His small hairs stood on end, and he straightened, absently pushing the button to start the phone while his mind went back in time. Did he remember silence in the middle of the night?

Near dawn, yes. There was a period where the night creatures went to bed and the day animals hadn't yet roused. He often went to the porch with a cup of coffee to enjoy the first rays of the sun. In those times, it felt like he was the only one awake in the world.

The phone started to life, but his ears strained to hear the sounds outside. He looked at the nearest window, its blinds pulled. That feeling went off in his chest again.

His wards! Someone was dismantling his wards in a way he'd never felt before. The magic didn't alert him, but the person—or persons—wasn't strong enough to completely hide the effects of deconstructing his spell. If he'd been asleep, he never would've noticed.

The phone's screen flared to life. One new message popped up. He'd barely gotten a glimpse of the warning before he was spinning for the hallway.

One foot hit the ground, and then everything happened at once. Glass shattered in three of the windows in the living room, caught by the blinds and showering a small section of the floor. More glass broke at the back of the house—the bedrooms.

Nessa!

He put on a burst of speed. His socks slid against the polished wood floor as he tried to turn the corner. Ripping sounded behind him as his shoulder rammed into the hallway entrance corner. The blinds were coming down.

Magic flared all around him, shot from the windows. It blackened the wall near his face and flew into the hallway by his side. More glass shattered, and he realized people had surrounded the house. They'd brought a hell of an arsenal. Momar really wanted Elliot Graves. If Sebastian and Nessa were caught, they'd be mercilessly tortured for information.

Heart in his throat, knowing he had to somehow get them out of here, he turned to throw up a defense, and a shot hit his barrier.

Nessa screamed from behind her closed door.

His feet pounded the wood. A flare of light caught his notice out of the corner of his eye, and a shot of magic zipped behind him as he ran past the bathroom.

Nearly at his room, he constructed another magical barrier. A black boot stepped out from the shadows, followed by a big body and a face in a ski mask.

A club swung around before he could further raise his hands. The hard wood struck his head as Nessa screamed again.

Blackness rushed in.

✧ ✧ ✧

NESSA

TERROR SQUEEZED HER heart as a knee was braced on the center of her back. Her hands were ripped behind her before she could reach her knife. A zip tie secured her wrists, and rough hands grabbed her shoulders to pull her upper body off the ground. A bag was yanked down over her head and a string pulled tight to keep it there.

Her breathing accelerated as adrenaline flooded her

body. Shouting and thumps came from the hallway, the sounds of feet running and then someone hitting the floor.

Her bedroom door didn't burst open as Sebastian came to save her. Instead, all she heard was boots scraping the ground. The thumps must have been Sebastian.

Panic froze her as two people jerked her to her feet, one on each arm. They walked her forward, stopping at the door to open it.

Someone in the hallway grunted. Something slid along the ground, and then everyone was moving. They'd picked Sebastian up. He was limp, knocked out. Not walking.

Oh, God.

She reached for her magic. Not the mage kind, which she couldn't do without her hands, but the energy kind. The kind Tristan had helped her realize and wanted her to learn. It was coercion magic very few people possessed, a mood-altering talent that, unlike a spell, was mostly undetectable. If she were powerful and experienced enough, she could bend people to her will.

It seeped into her, battling the adrenaline. She'd never practiced in heightened circumstances. It wasn't a magic that could be turned on and off, fired at will. It had to live inside the wielder, always there, used with finesse lest the enemy notice the foreign emotional sensation and rail against it.

She didn't have much finesse now, and she sure didn't have the presence of mind to work through her terror.

Her energy swirled around her, heating her in that way it did. Tingling through her body. Reaching for the people holding her arms. Feeling around the room for others.

Her heart sank. The room was full of them, one carrying Sebastian and the rest hurrying for the front door. Even if her escorts released her, the others would grab her. If they dropped her, still more were on hand. Eventually, they would realize what she was doing, even if they didn't know how, and they'd knock her out.

She pulled the robust part of her energy closer and only left fingers of magic floating. She'd at least keep tabs on the enemy.

Cold air gushed in from the front door, and Nessa shivered. All she wore was an oversized T-shirt and panties. She hadn't dressed for the occasion because she'd put her faith in Sebastian's wards and their style of living. *Stupid.*

The air grew colder until she could tell they were outside. Her bare feet hit the frigid cement of the porch. She felt her way down the steps but was too slow, and her captives dragged her forward. Her toes and the tops of her feet scratched against the walkway, tearing her skin. She tried to get her feet under her again, but the people holding her didn't slow, nor did they lift her that little bit to help. They were content to drag her like an animal carcass.

The frostbitten grass of the lawn was a welcome relief. They cut across, went right, and then crossed the street. Branches scraped across the top of her hood. The crunch of boots echoed through the wilderness in front of her. She was the last in line, and her handlers were the slowest.

Water gurgling through the rocks announced the creek. Freezing water doused her feet and licked her ankles, then calves, as they waded through. At least their boots would fill with the icy water. They could share in her misery.

Murmurs filtered back to her, but she couldn't make out the words. The groups split. Sebastian was carried left with most of the enemy, while she and her two captors went right. Sebastian was the dangerous prize. Once he was properly secured, he could be plied for information, then reprogrammed and used. She was merely a source of information. They'd torture it out of her and then discard her like trash.

At least he had time. They'd handle him with some

care. If she could get out of this mess, she could call Ivy House and beg them to save him. They'd have the ability, assuming they could find the holding facilities.

If she could get out of this.

Tears leaking from her eyes, worried she'd never see Sebastian again, she reached for her magic.

CHAPTER 24

NESSA

S HE DIDN'T HAVE time to be subtle. Couldn't be in this situation. She wrapped her energy around the two holding her and asserted all her *will*.

They reacted differently, one jerking in surprise and the other immediately letting go of her arm. Some people were more stubborn than others. She pushed, her energy flowering out now, keeping solid pressure on the weaker-willed one and doing a little more coaxing on Stubborn Guy.

"What are you doing?" Stubborn Guy asked, slowing. His fingers spasmed on her arm. He wasn't talking to her, but the other guy.

"We don't need her," Weak Willed replied, full of conviction. "She's nothing."

"We're...supposed to..." Stubborn Guy sounded confused, his voice wispy. Her magic continued to press on him. "But...we're..."

"Come on." Weak Willed moved away. "We did what we came here to do. Let's go."

"But…" The fingers slackened, as though Stubborn Guy wasn't quite sure why he'd been holding her in the first place. "Yeah…"

He didn't sound completely convinced. He pulled his hand away, but he didn't move.

A little distance, a little logic, and he'd realize he'd messed up. Nessa had to take the chance while she had it. She doubted she'd get another one, not when they rendezvoused with the holding team.

She changed the message and shoved her will at them as she hurried away.

"Useless," Weak Willed said, still convinced. "We shouldn't have bothered to grab her in the first place. She'll just die—"

Stubborn Guy swore. "We're supposed to bring her in, you idiot! She's put a spell on us."

Damn it!

Nessa kept her magic circling while she ran. But she couldn't see! She'd gone for walks in this area, followed the creek, checked exit plans, but they all involved her eyes. She hadn't accounted for darkness, a bag over her head, and her hands tied behind her back.

Her foot hit a rock, and she pitched forward. Footsteps ran after her. She hit a bed of frozen ground and sparse leaves before rolling. Her hood loosened a bit, but not enough to come off. Someone swore, and the other one grunted—were they fighting through their convictions? She couldn't be sure. Her magic was weakening. She hadn't built up a lot of endurance yet.

More footsteps, closer. Stubborn Guy had won out.

"No, please," she said. It never hurt to beg. "Please, I can pay. I can pay you."

Large hands grabbed her upper arms and lifted her to her feet. Her back hit a hard chest before the configuration of the arms changed. One slid along her back, and the other scooped under her knees.

"*Shh*, Natasha, I've got you."

That whiskey-rough voice loosened every muscle in her body. A sob choked her, and she twisted in his arms, pushing her face tighter into his shoulder.

"It's okay, I've got you," he cooed, starting to jog. He turned this way and that as branches brushed across, shielding her from the worst of it as he pushed farther into the trees. His familiar smell enveloped her, amber and woody with a hint of chocolate on his breath. "It's going to be okay. I've got you, little angel. I won't let anything happen to you."

Sobs of relief and lingering fear for Sebastian shook her body. She kept her whimpers as quiet as possible so he could work. His footfalls barely made a sound. Hell, she'd barely heard him take down her captors. They surely hadn't seen it coming.

He stopped and then bent. "Stand here, little angel. I need to shift, and then I'm going to fly you out of here, okay? I had to fly ahead of the others. We need to meet up with them and see what's next. Curse me, baby, you're freezing. It's okay. I'll try to envelop you as much as possible. Just hang on."

She didn't care about the cold. She didn't care if frostbite took a toe. He'd come for her. They'd all come, somehow knowing this would happen without her knowing it herself. She'd been so careful.

She'd been outgunned.

The sound of boulders moving was his shifting, and then the hood was ripped off her head by the huge gargoyle-monster towering over her. His touch was gentle for a creature so large and powerful as he turned her. A finger slipped between her wrists delicately before a vicious yank sliced the zip tie away with a claw. His muscular arms came around her again, and then they were airborne.

✧ ✧ ✧

JESSIE

TRISTAN FLUNG ME toward the group of mages carrying

Sebastian to a row of three vans. They only had about ten feet to go. Tristan took off with a burst of speed, spying a couple other mages going in the opposite direction with what must've been Nessa. Our other gargoyles, carrying the shifters and their speed no match for Tristan's, were on their way, going as fast as they could. I needed to stall until they got here.

I swooped down at the ten or so people, a spell at the ready. They'd probably be powerful, having to deal with a mage like Sebastian. Barely in range and I let fly, wanting to get the jump on them before they put up their defenses. My spell hit the two people at the rear, thankfully walking close together. Part of it cracked into one of their shoulders, severing a limb. The other hit farther down—the same effect, if less of the limb.

They screamed, knocked sideways. Being mages, they didn't try to keep fighting. Instead, they wrapped magic around themselves and crumpled to the ground, rolling and twisting within their pain.

The other mages turned in my direction, but they didn't look up. These mages must not have been at Kingsley's and weren't used to fliers. That, or they were slow to think of the possibility when on strictly mage business.

I hit another one with a lot of power, close now. It cut through him. He barely had time to scream before he hit the ground. My wings beat quickly, making far too much sound. I wasn't good at gliding like the male gargoyles.

Spells jetted through the night sky, right for me. I banked, wrapping myself in a protective layer, and fired one of my own. It missed, striking the ground. A spell hit my shield, and then two more. The magic singed my defensive layer, definitely powerful.

I banked again, shooting another spell and then dodging one of theirs. A second spell struck me, though, then a third, hammering at my defenses. I fired, thought of a blistering spell that didn't need as much power, and fired again. Another spell went down, but there were still six more mages. One hustled Sebastian to the van while the others shot spell after intense spell, slamming into me.

My stomach tightened as I dove and then cut right, firing as fast as I could. The flight path helped—they were not used to a moving target—but not enough. Their spells cut chunks out of my defensive layer now. Magic burrowed past and slashed at my tough skin. I took a moment to reapply a stronger defensive shield, giving them that moment to fill my world with jets of magic.

Breathing heavy now, I climbed for distance, still firing. I had more power. At a distance, I could still do damage where theirs wouldn't be so great. It took more energy, though.

I fired, thought of a simpler and easier spell, and fired again. Their spells still reached me, not digging through my defenses but still sapping my energy and therefore my strength. I fluttered in the air, and they rushed for their vans, leaving their fallen behind.

If they took off, I wouldn't be able to keep up. Not without Tristan or someone flying me.

Damn it, where *was* Tristan?

My heart sped up as I worried he might be in trouble, or that he couldn't get Nessa. Or that Nessa was already lost.

Choking back fear, I dove again, firing at the mages pausing to get into their vans. They returned fire. One door closed. A mage fell, but another got in. I wasn't strong enough to blast through metal, and I couldn't see them within the glass at this angle.

Closer still, as I decided what to do, the sound of wings filled my world. Snarls and roars preceded shifters running toward the vans, led by Austin. The gargoyles must've dropped them off before rushing to me. Someone grabbed me and the others surrounded me.

Help had come.

✧   ✧   ✧

SEBASTIAN

HE CAME TO with a crick in his neck, then picked up his head and winced at the stiffness of his body. His hands had been zip-tied behind him and his elbows secured with rope to the sides of a wooden chair. His feet were likewise tied up.

The holding cell was as he might expect, a ten-by-ten space made of cinder blocks, cold and dank. Blood spatter coated a few of the walls, and large, dark stains spread out over the ground. This cell had seen a lot of use.

He wondered if it was Momar's or the Guild's.

He wondered if they would trade Nessa for Jessie. Was this what inevitably led to his betrayal of Ivy House?

It had been a vision of his, half-cocked and distorted, as they always were. A feeling more than anything. A dreamscape. He'd gotten a slice of the seer gene that ran in his family; he had visions occasionally, and they always came true, often with a lot of bloodshed. By now, he'd learned to just go with them, to find the quickest path and somehow make it work.

Momar would give a great deal to have Jessie and Austin delivered to him. Jessie, they'd repurpose, probably, even though she was an animal by their standards. They wouldn't want to waste her awesome power—assuming Ivy House would stand for it and not kill the compromised heir itself.

Austin, they'd torture. They'd show his broken body to the shifter world and heft his head on a spike while systematically taking out the rest of his kind.

Sebastian would get repurposed as well, of course. They wouldn't waste him any more than they would Jessie.

Jessie and Austin, however, would have a chance to break out. Slim at the moment—Sebastian had intended to build them a bigger force—but they were resourceful and powerful. Determined. If anyone could beat Momar, they could. Serving them up to Momar with himself was the only way to directly get them an audience. Those were the rumors all over the mage world, and that was the distorted, strange vision he'd been sucked into.

In order for Jessie to get her chance at striking the elusive mastermind of the mage world, she'd have to be a captive, and Austin and Sebastian with her. She'd have to be betrayed.

He'd have to be the one to do it.

They would win and rightly kill him, or Momar would. Either way, it would be Sebastian's end.

Was *this* his end?

No, not yet. First, there would be pain. *Great* pain. Elliot Graves had caused this magical outfit a lot of effort and humiliation, and they'd want to get their shot at hurting him. At breaking him.

Minutes passed into hours. He kept count in his head. Keeping time when there was no sun, no day and night, staved off insanity, he'd heard. Even if it didn't, it had helped the last time he was in one of these types of cells.

Somewhere, water dripped. It rhythmically splatted on the floor.

Belatedly, he realized there were no spells draped in front of him. He didn't think there were any coating the walls, either. The sheen he'd expected wasn't present.

They couldn't be so stupid as to think he couldn't do magic without his hands, could they?

In another hour or so—his count surely wasn't accurate—he heard something metallic. A shining metal disk on the teal-painted door spun in time with the grating sound. The door opened slowly, and someone prepared to come in.

He shot magic before he could see the face.

It hit off a shield and was absorbed into a female body. He'd never seen that happen before. What spell was that?

And then he felt faint.

"It soaks down into me and then filters through the connections to my army," Jessie said as she walked in. Redness lined her eyes, and disappointment creased her features. "It takes the magic from the enemy attack and fortifies my shields on my people with it. Ingenious, isn't it? I found it in one of the Ivy House books."

"Jessie," he said on a release of breath, sagging in his chair. "Why…"

He didn't know what to think. How to feel. Their environment registered: the lack of spells, the tension in her shoulders, and the regret in her eyes. She'd been pulling away. She'd been betrayed.

The strength went out of him. "Please, Jessie, don't torture me. I deserve it, but please—it'll strip away my feelings for you. You'll deaden me if you do this. I'll tell you whatever you need to know, and you can kill me after. Please, though, spare Nessa. She's only involved in all this out of love for me and my sister. She never wanted any of this for me or for herself. Blame me, not her. She's of no value to you."

He was babbling. He'd never babbled with a captor, but he felt like babbling still. Begging.

Niamh walked in with a plain wooden chair. The legs were painted red in the exact way the Guild did it. He remembered that vividly because when the chair appeared, the pain started.

"What..." He looked around again. All of these stains couldn't have been from the cells Austin had prepared. They couldn't have been done by Jessie's people. Some of them were surely older than the length of time she'd had magic. They couldn't be another shifter's, either. Their type didn't torture—they killed you face to face. Gargoyles, too, with plenty of warning besides.

"Is this...a Guild holding cell?" he whispered, his mind spinning and dread spiraling.

Niamh smirked, then tsked as she left again. The door closed behind her but didn't lock. That, at least, wasn't Guild protocol. They locked in the questioner just in case the subject got loose.

The red wooden legs dragged across the concrete floor. "Yes," said Jessie.

She placed the chair close to him and sat. He drank in her face. It hadn't been long since he'd seen her last, but it felt like ages.

"This is exactly how you would've ended up had we not gotten to you in time." She clasped her hands in her lap. "Nessa would've been taken to a different place. A horrible place, by the sound of it. Not that this one is good."

"How..." His voice was pleading. "Why..." He

cleared his throat and realized his face was wet from crying. "How'd you find me? Nessa hasn't been able to find their holding cells."

"How?" She quirked an eyebrow. "By paying an exorbitant amount of money for a private jet in the middle of the night, getting flown to your wilderness location at breakneck speed by Tristan from an airstrip we weren't supposed to use, and letting him grab Nessa while I took on a team of mages by myself, waiting for the rest of the gargoyles. I'm in a *huge* fight with my mate over this. He's livid that I got Tristan to take me ahead to then fight on my own until help arrived. *Livid*. Banging it out isn't going to work for this one. The rest of the crew got carried by gargoyles, except the basajaunak, because they were too big and would slow everyone down. They're pissed they missed the fight, and they're now talking about training regimens to increase their speed and endurance so they can be at least as fast as gargoyles."

"But…" Sebastian couldn't stop crying. He couldn't even understand how happy he was to see her, a joy that permeated every cell of his body. "How'd you get *here*?"

"Oh, *here*?" Now her eyebrows settled low in anger. "We had an impromptu *fact-finding* session in the woods. That's what I'm calling it, because 'torturing the enemy to punish them and also get information' isn't something I want to say very often. But my crew is, like...a nightmare incarnate, and this is apparently how mages work—*for now*—and so I'm trying to harden myself to it. Niamh let Edgar help her make a fucking exhibit out of the leader. An *exhibit*, Sebastian, like an art installation. Out of a body. What's next? A blanket made of human hair? If I gave them half a chance, they probably would. They're not normal. How gruesome must it have been back in the old days?" She shuddered. "For the record, I hate all of this, even though my gargoyle seems to revel in it. And also for the record, I let it happen because Austin said I had to. That Niamh needed to deliver the right message. Given he is *so mad* at me, which I blame you for, I didn't argue."

Magic flared through the room, pounding Sebastian with Jessie's frustration and pain and fear and worry. He'd caused all that, and while it hurt and he was sorry, the fact that she cared this much about him made him sob.

He'd missed her so much. He hadn't realized how much he loved her and the others. *Needed* them, even Edgar.

"So," she continued, "we got all the details of this place, including setup and magic and defenses. We pretended to be the extraction team with stolen clothes, and they let us in. Then we grabbed them, forced them into their little cells, and now..." Her lips tightened. "I chose to see you. I don't want to know what the rest of my team is up to."

"Fact-finding," Sebastian helped.

Her beautifully expressive eyes narrowed, then softened, and a sheen filmed them. "Why, Sebastian? Why didn't you confide in us rather than setting us up? I let you go so that you could regain your feet, but instead, you pushed forward without enough knowledge. Hiding yourself from us. *Not* hiding yourself from the enemy. You put yourself in needless danger while making the wrong choices for us." Tears welled in her eyes. "I'm disappointed in you two. You've broken my heart."

Nail, meet coffin.

He lowered his head, overcome with emotion. Maybe the torture would've been better. It would've stopped him hurting instead of making it so much worse.

She stood, then pulled a knife from the back pocket of her jeans and cut his bonds. "We tied you up at my request. I wanted you to have a moment to think about your choices and where your line of thinking got you. You needed this lesson, Sebastian."

He didn't argue with her. She was right, after all.

"You're coming home with us. Well..." She wiggled her hand. "First, you have to go back to the shifter meeting with us because we have to tie things up. Oh, and then we have to—You're going to stay with us now, that's what I mean. If it has to be a kidnapping, so be it. We're doing this together from now on. Your choice in the matter has been forfeited."

He nodded mutely. She was right there, too. "I'm sorry," he said, dropping his freed hands to his lap. "I'm sorry for all of it."

She hugged him from the side. "I know." She knelt in front of him then, her glistening eyes serious. "We're going to talk all of this out. No more secrets. Nessa won't say a word without you present, which I've let go for now. When we have a moment, I want to hear everything, do you understand? *Everything*. We can't stay alive if we only know half the story."

He nodded again and, as they stood, hugged her tightly. "You can take me to her," Sebastian said. "She's keeping secrets for my benefit. It's time she stops being caught in the middle of all of this. Her well-being has been a casualty. It's time she starts making her own choices, and time I retire to a magical entrepreneur."

Jessie chuckled low. "Oh, no, you're not retiring. Not by a long shot. Elliot Graves is just about to be upgraded."

CHAPTER 25

NESSA

THE HOTEL ROOM was simple, with a king-sized bed, a small desk built into the corner, a few ugly paintings, a couple of uglier lamps, and a hard chair by the wall. Her bathroom was small, with just a shower, sink, and a couple of drawers. Her computer sat on the desk with her phone beside it. It wasn't much different than the countless other hotels and rentals she'd been staying in, except for one thing.

She braced her hand on the wall.

Ulric and Jasper were sharing the room on the other side. Jessie, Niamh, Edgar—they all had rooms or suites within this block, merely a saunter away. They'd welcomed Nessa and Sebastian back in, even after what the mages had done. After framing them, pushing them into the line of fire, and telling them of Sebastian's vision. After telling them, point blank, that Nessa and Sebastian had always planned to betray Jessie and

Austin, to their possible demise.

Jessie, the dear heart that she was, hadn't even blinked.

"At least we have a cheat sheet for getting in front of Momar." She'd looked at Niamh. "We need a *lot* more information before we make that vision a reality. Austin and I will work on the shifters and gargoyles, but you need to get me meetings with mages. Work with Sebastian, Nessa, and Fred to find the right ones, slip into their messages or whatever, and get me an audience. I can't have that hole in my arsenal, and we have no idea how long it'll take Momar to make a move against me. After today, though, we can guarantee he will."

Yes, they could. And now, Nessa was part of a team rather than a duo. She was included in a family instead of being in the remnants of one.

She didn't deserve the second chance, she knew that. Sebastian thought the same. But neither of them would voice that reality. Hell, Sebastian hadn't been able to. He'd finally found the emotion he'd walled up all those years ago. Jessie walking into that interrogation room had shaken something loose in him, and maybe now he could heal.

Maybe, miracle of miracles, she could too.

A soft knock sounded at the door. She pulled her

hand away from the wall and readied herself to put on a smile. "Come in!"

When she saw who it was, she didn't bother. She never fooled him with the fake sunshine. He saw through her pasted-on exterior to the puddle of self-loathing and regret that gurgled beneath. Before, that annoyed her—scared her, even. Now, it was a relief. She still felt raw and vulnerable after the meeting with Jessie this morning.

Tristan's glowing amber gaze held hers for a moment, and then it traced the air between them.

"You can see my energy," she surmised. She'd remembered him doing that in Kingsley's territory. It had taken the books, practice, and seeing it herself to connect the dots.

"Yes."

"Do you have this magic, too? The ability to alter a person's will?"

He carried in her suitcase, taken from the rental house. They'd had to return and get their stuff, all of it fitting into the back of a rental truck Mr. Tom had procured. It hadn't taken long to remove everything they'd been carrying around from place to place.

"No. I can see the effects of your magical energy, that's it." He set the suitcase down by the bed before going over to the closet. He grabbed the luggage stand

and placed the suitcase on top, but he didn't unzip her bag, preserving her privacy.

She swallowed. "I have a lot to thank you for."

He closed the closet door before leaning against the corner of the wall, then studied her for a time before saying, "No, you don't."

Emotion bubbled up. "You saved my life."

"That was a pleasure first. A duty second. And an 'I told you so' third." He smirked. "The last negates your need to say thank you."

She bit her lip as tears came to her eyes. "You and Niamh showed me that I'm not the biggest monster in this outfit. Not by far. I would balk before doing the things you and she did. That Edgar got really into. His...*display* turned my stomach."

Tristan grimaced. "Yeah. That vampire." He released a breath. "Thank God Niamh stopped him before he tried to hollow out the eye sockets and implant the testicles. Like...*what?*"

His bewilderment made her smile.

"The things I did were always out of necessity," she said. "I got good at them because I had to. We had to survive. I never felt like I had a choice." She crossed her arms over her chest, her emotions so damn raw from this morning's meeting. She felt so vulnerable. It was hard to button it all up.

"I told you—you don't need to do stuff like that, not anymore. I'll handle it. Niamh will. Edgar would love to. You can *choose* the life you want now, Natasha. You're in danger, so you have to stick with us, but you don't have to get your hands dirty. You don't have to do the things that you despise yourself for."

A tear overflowed and trailed down her cheek. "I know," she whispered. "It feels like I've been cut loose, but not pushed away. It's like…I no longer have chains tying me down. I no longer have to solely shoulder the burden of Sebastian's fate." Another tear fell. "B-but…" She wiped her cheeks. "What if I'm given a choice and decide I don't want the white picket fence? What if I don't mind taunting an enemy with a knife to his balls? What sort of person does that make me?"

His grin was wicked. "Magical. As you said, you aren't the biggest monster on this team."

She studied him: his loose, easy confidence, his infallible swagger. For once, his eyes didn't turn guarded. His walls and defenses didn't come up while she assessed him. It was like he was allowing her to take a good look. Trusting her when usually he didn't trust anyone.

"I owe you thanks for something else, too." She licked her lips.

His gaze rooted to her mouth. "I don't want thanks.

I want to make you beg."

Heat infused her cheeks, her body. She rolled her eyes, hearing the humor in his voice. She didn't mistake the hunger in his eyes, though. What would it be like to take him up on that? To feel his powerful body pressing her into the mattress?

She cleared her throat. "The energy magic. The books. I've been practicing."

"Good."

"You directed me toward a magic that could essentially control you."

"One hopes you'll eventually be that good, but right now, I think I'm much too hardheaded."

"But…you know what I mean. You willingly helped me with a magic that could render you vulnerable to me if I so chose."

It was his turn to study her. "And?"

"And…" She shrugged. "You don't seem like a guy who allows people to make you feel vulnerable."

The silence stretched this time as he surveyed her. "You've made me feel vulnerable since the first moment I laid eyes on you. The effect you have on me is so strong, I thought you were a sprite. I'm not worried about you trying to control me any more than you're worried I'll kill you and turn you inside out." His eyes sparkled with humor. "You have a good heart, Natasha.

When you love, you love completely. You won't do me wrong with that magic, just like you wouldn't do Sebastian wrong. Or Jessie. If you want to use it to make me fall to my knees and worship between your thighs…it won't take much energy. I'll already do that gladly."

He winked and pushed away from the wall. "Get some sleep. It's been a long night and a longer morning. We're all tired."

He turned to go, and she had the sudden desire to pull him back to her. To paste him to her side as a shield in case nightmares should come. In case she heard sounds and thought the enemy was closing in on her again. With that gargoyle-monster standing in the way, nothing would get to her, not even her ghosts.

But she didn't reach out for him and instead took a deep breath. She was just tired. Raw and tired. She was trying to latch on to him like a security blanket, and she needed to put on her big-girl pants.

He slowed as he neared the door. After he pulled it open, he paused. Instead of continuing through, he closed the door again and turned back, his eyes glowing brightly.

She didn't speak as he started her way. Butterflies filled her stomach as she watched the smooth grace of the large predator. The battle-hardened monster. Crap, but he was handsome.

He stopped in front of her, incredibly close. His hands came up slowly to brace the sides of her face, and his thumbs moved across the wet tracks on her cheeks.

"How many times do I have to tell you?" he murmured, and then bent. His soft lips touched down on one of the tear tracks, then the other. "If you need something…ask. I can do more than torture people for you."

His lips grazed across hers, and her eyes fluttered closed. Her core tightened, throbbing. Her heart felt ragged. She didn't want eroticism—she wanted to be taken care of for once. Protected, especially after nearly succumbing to an extraction.

"I don't want to—"

"Shh," he whispered. The zipper of her hoodie made a whirring noise as he pulled it down, revealing a babydoll T she'd grabbed from the house as they were quickly packing. He hooked his thumbs into the top of her leggings and pushed them down her thighs and to the floor.

Tristan straightened, his gaze tingling against her lips. His breath fell around her as he undid the buttons on his shirt. Nessa watched his large, strong hands as they parted the fabric and then worked it off and over his wings. His delicious, muscular chest was exposed to her, and while she didn't want anything sexual, she couldn't help but reach out to slide her palm across his washboard stomach.

He tugged at his jeans, and the material gave way from around the button. The rest followed shortly after, and he bent to push the denim down his muscular thighs. He stepped free of shoes, socks, and pants, and his large bulge strained at his boxer briefs.

"Tristan," she said with uncertainty, a thrill speeding up her heart. If she'd been in a different mood, she would've gotten off on his taking control. Doing what he wanted, her wishes be damned. She hadn't realized she'd be into that.

She had a feeling, with this monster, that she'd be into a whole lot she didn't realize. She suspected he'd open up a new world to her, but she worried he'd also open her heart, something she wasn't ready for yet. Maybe ever.

"Shh," he said again, his fingers gliding across her cheeks, dry now, and up to her hair. He ran his touch over her to the ponytail holder before tugging it free. Her hair fell down around her face in messy waves.

He bent to her, his lips inches away from hers. His breath smelled like chocolate, and his body surely tasted like sin. She closed her eyes again, waiting for his kiss.

But the air felt disturbed, and she sensed movement.

Fabric rustled. His hand touched low on her hip. With a nudge, she stepped to the side, backing up to the bed. She frowned, opening her eyes.

He pulled back the covers before crawling in and pulling her down with him. She complied, conflicted: hot and shivering in anticipation, core begging for him, head not wanting this but liking the treatment all the same.

"Come here," he commanded, settling her back on the bed. She was helpless to say no.

He turned her away from him, settled his wings, and then curled around her body protectively. One arm pushed under her and wrapped around her torso. With the other, he pulled the covers over them before bending to envelop her. She was wrapped in his big body.

"What…" She sighed in satisfaction within his warmth. "But I thought…"

"I can see your energy, little deathwatch angel. I know what you need. Sleep, now. I've got you. I won't let anything get to you."

Emotion bubbled over, and she cried within his arms, needing the release. After a moment, as her breathing slowed, she blurted, "But why do you always smell like chocolate?" then laughed through her tears.

"Chocolate is one of my two great weaknesses and greatest pleasures."

"What's the other?"

He didn't respond, and she was too tired to ask again. It took no time at all to fall into a comfortable, deep, dreamless sleep.

CHAPTER 26

JESSIE

THE KNOCK AT the interior door was a little more forceful than was absolutely necessary. Austin moaned and snuggled into me, breathing in my scent before settling again.

"Miss, we've been requested to attend the other alphas," Mr. Tom called in. "Kingsley is out here, giving me an impatient sort of scowl while refusing the coffee I'm happy to provide him."

"Is it too late to quit?" Austin mumbled against my hair.

"Come in," I called.

The door swung open to admit Mr. Tom with two steaming mugs in his hand. "Good morning, miss, sir. It's a lovely day if you don't mind the horrible chill and boring hotel landscaping. I trust you're not at all rested after the amount of exertion we've been forced to do with very little rest in between. Alas, Kingsley seems to think his schedule is the only one that matters."

He set my coffee on the nightstand before walking around the bed to deposit Austin's.

"This is why I try to get out of the room by the time he comes in," Austin grumbled, still not rolling away.

Mr. Tom wasn't wrong. After staying up all night and well into the morning, we'd talked with Nessa and Sebastian on the way back and continued once we'd returned here. By the time we'd eaten, showered, and gotten to bed, it was late afternoon, and we'd been up for an obscene number of hours.

The red letters on the clock radio read 9:58. That was a normal time for getting up, assuming one night of sleep was enough. It hadn't been. I'd have to heal the whole team.

"He doesn't have any other chores for us, I hope." I pulled the bedsheet with me as I sat up and reached for the coffee.

"Even if he does, we're not doing them." Austin rolled to his back and scrubbed his hands down his face.

"Can I bring you breakfast in bed, miss, or would you rather get up and face the surly alpha darkening the living room?" Mr. Tom waited patiently for an answer. I knew Kingsley could hear all of this. Mr. Tom's comments had probably been what soured his mood in the first place.

"No, thanks, Mr. Tom," I answered. "I'll get up after I finish this cup of coffee. Keep 'em coming, though. I'm going to need the caffeine."

Austin finally sat up, resting his forearms on his bent knees. "That was close last night. It might've gone a lot differently if we hadn't arrived when we did. Niamh and Fred figured it out in the nick of time. Hell, Mr. Tom secured us transportation in the nick of time."

I didn't like thinking of how close the mages had come to being captured. If we hadn't hired Fred, we never would've known they'd been taken in. We never would've thought to look for a detention center, or whatever that had been. Even if we had, Niamh and Tristan wouldn't have been good enough to find it. The mages would've been lost to us.

No. That wasn't true. Sebastian would've tried to make a deal to bring us in and let Nessa go. We would've faced Momar before we were ready, and we surely would've died. It had been a close call for all of us.

I broke out in a cold sweat. "I'm not ready to think about any of that yet. We have a lot of work to do."

"We also have some things to talk about, you and me." Austin watched me with fierce eyes as I exited the bed.

My stomach wiggled in unease. He meant my going

after Sebastian without him, putting myself in harm's way without proper backup or regard for my safety.

His anger was on simmer because we hadn't had time to properly hash this out, and worse, it was justified. I'd been stupid trying to battle that many mages on my own. They'd nearly taken me down by the time reinforcements showed up. If they'd been any stronger, or used to fighting someone in the air, or hadn't been surprise-attacked, I would've taken serious damage or accidentally gotten killed.

"I know," I muttered, heading into the bathroom.

After I'd washed my face and put on jeans and a T-shirt, I met the others in the suite's living room. Austin was finishing a breakfast bagel, while Kingsley had finally relented and taken some coffee.

Their chatter died down when I entered.

"And here we are." Mr. Tom turned from the preparation area with another cup of coffee. "This will be just the thing. Maybe a nip of healing might help as well, miss. I don't have any cucumber for those puffy eyes."

"What's the plan?" I asked Austin and Kingsley, ignoring Mr. Tom and my puffy eyes. I wanted to work out how much energy Indigo had before I wasted any on appearances.

"Kevin has been called back to his pack, and the

others agree it's a fine time to wrap things up. They've seen all they need to see." Kingsley watched me steadily. "There's something I wanted to discuss before we head to the meeting."

"Oh, please don't tell me you're mad at me too." I'd always had a guilty conscience, and I hated being in trouble.

His slight frown was relieving...well, until Austin's mood darkened. Kingsley noticed and quickly moved things along, for which I was grateful. "You and Austin showed your battle prowess. You backed up my claims. You also proved how much you care about those you fight beside and about team members in trouble. All in all, you proved that there could be no better commanders of a unified army. The other alphas solidly agree with that."

I sipped my coffee. That was great news. We'd have to keep proving it to new people, obviously, and there was bound to be some hothead alpha who thought they could do it better, but this was a good first step.

"They also believe me when I say you won't try to take over their people. You will command when it's needed, then leave the packs without further disturbing them."

"I don't know what that means," I said.

"He means that we won't try to recruit their people

for our territory," Austin explained. "We also won't try to claim alpha status over them and their people."

"You won't try to put yourself above us," Kingsley added. "They saw Austin's indifference at how Brochan and Tristan postured as a good sign. It also helped that none of my pack went back with you when you left." He paused. "Except Aurora, but that's a family matter. That doesn't count."

"That wasn't our fault either," I reminded him.

A crease formed between his brows. "Yes," he drew out. "I'd love to have a talk with those mages…"

"That all sounds good, then," I said quickly. "They're right—we know our way around a battle, we won't steal people, and we do care about lives."

"There is one problem." Kingsley set down his mug. "You made them nervous the other day."

"Ah." I grimaced. "Yeah, sorry about that. I did go a little overboard. But honestly, they needed to see what a mage can do."

"It's not just you." Kingsley braced his ankle on his knee. "Austin has said it himself—he's wild. He has a lot of control, which they were pleased to see, but he's still…"

"Vicious," Austin supplied. "Ruthless. Barely housebroken."

"*Wild* really did sum it up just fine." I waved it

away. "Fine, we're vicious and wild. So, what does that mean for them joining us? They don't want to because we make them nervous?"

"We spoke yesterday, and all but Margery were still on the fence. That battle was a lot to take in from people who've mostly known peace their whole lives." Kingsley's gaze beat into me. "I passed on what Austin had mentioned to me in private as a *possibility* of a way to ease their misgivings. But as he spoke for you at that time, I would like to hear your thoughts on the matter."

Nervousness ate at me again. There was that danged guilty conscience. "What?"

Kingsley's frown was subtle. I was probably advertising my (hopefully baseless) guilt. He looked at Austin to continue.

Austin didn't hesitate. "I told them that after we defeat Momar, tear down the Guild, and unify magical people into a fair governing system, represented by all, Kingsley would be the best person to move forward with the organization. This is his brainchild, and he's perfectly suited to handle it. We'd step down when our vicious and wild talents become obsolete."

"Oh. Well, yeah. Wasn't that always the plan?" I gave Austin a confused expression. "I was just in it to create a sanctuary for people. We can, which means we should, right? You promised that once we did, we could finally have our own peace."

Kingsley's eyebrows lifted. He huffed out a laugh and shook his head. "You two are perfectly suited for each other, do you know that? If I believed in fate, I'd think it had a hand in all this."

"Seriously, though, that was always the plan," I said. "It was for me, at any rate."

"That makes things worlds easier, then." Kingsley finished his coffee and glanced at the time. "Mr. Tom, I think I'll have one of those bagels, if you have one handy."

"If you'd just had it in the first place," Mr. Tom said, "you wouldn't have been so unbearably grumpy while waiting for the miss to peel herself from her much-needed slumber."

"Is it really worth it with all the backtalk?" Kingsley murmured to me. "It's settled, then. You will be the original alphas of the convocation. There will be those who won't believe you'll step down, and those who won't want you to, but we'll cross that bridge when we come to it."

"We need to put someone in charge of creating and maintaining a database of the shifter packs." Austin looked at me. "Is that something Nessa or Fred can handle?"

"Is Fred short for something?" Kingsley asked in dismay.

"No. She chose that name, much like Mr. Tom chose his." I shrugged. "At some point, you just learn to roll with it."

"I've always wanted to be a Tom," Mr. Tom murmured as he prepared Kingsley's bagel.

Kingsley looked like he was sorry he'd asked. He took a deep breath. "Aurora wants to return home with you guys. It's been made clear to me that she's an adult, and I have no say in the matter. With the mages back, though, she's not sure of her living situation. I've—"

I held up my hand. "I'm not sure anyone should live in the mages' house. If they learn Sebastian's real name, which probably won't be hard, they'll track him there. It's not safe. We'll figure something else out."

Kingsley didn't agree right away, probably nervous for Aurora's safety. I couldn't really tell because he wasn't giving anything away. To me, at any rate. Finally, however, he nodded. "Okay." He paused. "I get to keep the car, right?"

I spat with my unexpected laughter. "Sorry!" I wiped my face. "Yes, he wanted you to have that. That's yours."

Kingsley grinned. "Good. It's a thing of beauty."

"So that's good, then." I lifted my eyebrows at Austin. "These are experienced alphas with big packs, right? This is a good start for the convocation."

"Very." He inclined his head. "It'll go a long way to instill confidence and lend some credit to my reformed nature. Maybe one of these days, I won't be so fun to talk-trash and speculate about."

"Oh, I doubt that." Kingsley grinned at him, but his smile quickly dwindled. "When are you going to go after Armendale?"

Austin leaned into the cushion and put his arm along the back of the couch. "Not yet. I want to hit a couple of the bigger, surlier alphas first. I want a few of the unhinged original alphas that make people nervous. Like me."

Kingsley studied him for a long beat. "Is that wise?"

"We need viciousness, Kingsley. We need adaptability and open minds. If I can dominate, they'll respect my position. They'll fit best with the gargoyles in battle. I've heard of a few serious power players living a somewhat untamed life, and I've heard about some rogues who don't want the responsibility of their own pack, but that no alphas will take in because they're too powerful."

"I've heard of some of those, yes. That's a dangerous move. You'll have to keep control of them."

"I'll keep control, and I'll provide a home for those who otherwise can't find a place to settle."

"Aiming high is one thing, but just make sure you

don't become reckless and get yourself or your mate killed."

I grimaced as anger swirled through the bonds. Kingsley had unknowingly reminded Austin of the night before.

"Anyway. Cool." I gave them a thumbs-up and stood. "I'll just go see if my people can form a line. I'm not expecting great things, but you never know."

"Are you going to hit those after this?" Kingsley asked Austin as I put my mug in the sink.

"No. We have some gargoyle business to tie up first…"

I let myself out of the suite and, shivering with the cold, quickly wrapped myself in magical warmth before sending out a burst of magic to get people moving. They didn't hurry. I didn't blame them, and I didn't push.

Downstairs, just outside the building's small sitting area, I found Nessa on a bench with a to-go coffee cup in hand. She wore warm clothes, mittens, and a fuzzy beanie. Her gaze was far away as she looked out over a slice of parking lot and the green beyond.

"Hey," I said, shoving my hands into my pockets.

She glanced up with a big smile. "Hey." Her brow scrunched before her lips pulled to the side. "Still tired, huh?"

"Yeah. One of us didn't get to sleep half a night before being accosted."

"True." She grimaced and sipped her coffee. "I know I'm not supposed to apologize again for—"

"Then don't. I'm glad you're back."

She bobbed her head. "I'm glad to be back. Really glad."

I squinted at her. "Why do you look so fresh? Did Indigo heal you?"

"No, I just slept really well. Better than I have in a *long* time."

I grunted and looked away. I would really have liked to go back to sleep just then.

Ulric yawned as he joined us, followed by Jasper. Some of the basajaunak drifted over, sticking to the greener areas. Edgar skulked in with Indigo in tow, each clutching a bouquet of what they thought of as the ugly flowers.

"Hello, Shadow." Edgar sat onto the bench beside Nessa. "It's great to see the back of you."

"Missed that one," Ulric murmured. Jasper grunted.

She smiled at Edgar and patted his knee. "It's good to be back. I'm excited to see the new developments in your killer flower experiment."

I pretended not to notice Edgar glancing at me furtively. "More about that later," he said out of the side of his mouth.

I made a mental note to check into it. It sounded like he was hiding something.

The rest of the crew showed up, moving slowly but showing smiles and giving encouragement to Nessa.

"Oh—is that her?" Fred's smile had some serious wattage. She came through the doors after Niamh, holding her laptop and wearing a muumuu over a strange sort of skeleton shirt and legging set. "Nessa?"

"Yes?" Nessa pushed to standing.

"Hi." Fred stuck out her hand, and Nessa took it hesitantly. "I'm Fred. I've been cyber-stalking you for Niamh. Let me just say, your instincts are incredible. *In-*credible! It's not often I'm stumped, and you made me really think a couple times. I love it! If you had more know-how on the tech side of things, you'd be unstoppable." She bobbed half her body in that weird nod she did. "I can help you with that, if you want. I mean, it sounds like we'll be working together, but I can show you a few things right off the bat. You'll pick 'em up, no problem."

Nessa laughed. "You definitely fit in here."

"Thanks!" Fred did that body nod again. "Yeah, I think I've found my people!"

"Me too," Nessa said with glassy eyes.

"Fred, hey." I put my hand on her shoulder. "I wanted to say thank you on behalf of all of us. If you hadn't joined our team, we wouldn't have been able to grab the mages, and we'd ultimately have gone down a dangerous road because of that. You very likely saved all of our lives. I'll obviously give you a big bonus, but...thank you."

Fred's mouth dropped open. She looked around at the others, who were all nodding. "Whoa. That's heavy." Her eyes rounded. "This magical stuff is intense. But, you know, I just followed Niamh's directions. She was the maestro. But thanks, yeah. That's pretty surreal to hear."

"Speaking of...where *is* Niamh?" I asked, cluing in to her location. Ah—she was in the building's sitting area, just inside the lobby doors. She probably didn't want to brave the chill. "And Sebastian?"

"Sebastian is sorting his potions and notes," Nessa said. "He wanted to pack them a little better for travel."

Mr. Tom bustled through the door of the building with a deep frown. "That insufferable woman is sitting in there with that god-awful cooler. Could we look any more unprofessional?" He scoffed. "Miss, the alphas are coming down now and expect your line to be pristine. Kingsley's words. I think that's some sort of joke, but it's hard to tell with such bland, straight-faced humor."

Honestly, I couldn't be bothered. Instead, I went into the building to see if Niamh had anything with which to make a mimosa. We were all back together again. It was time to celebrate before danger once again reared its ugly head.

EPILOGUE
TRISTAN

TRISTAN'S TEAM OF powerful guardians colored the crisp blue sky. Mountains rose up to either side of them, creating a sort of channel that fliers had to use or else be subjected to the unpredictable winds higher up. A couple miles in front, nestled into a large, mostly flat slope between two ridges, rested the Gimerel cairn.

The cairn had been established ages ago for its defensive capabilities. The winds were too turbulent to drop down from directly above them, and only one road wound up along cliffs and tunnels to reach the town. To access this remote place, a flier would have to take the route Jessie's crew currently flew. *Slowly* flew.

So damn slowly.

He had to carry Jessie off and on to give her tiny wings a break.

This speed of an advance would make it look like they were incredibly confident in their team's prowess.

Robust guardian teams did this for smaller cairns and production facilities. It was a gargoyle's version of "being fair."

But that wasn't why Tristan had advised this tactic. He wanted to keep Nelson's eyes on the sky. He and his people probably had their binoculars out right now, determining who was advancing and looking at Tristan's flight pattern. Guardians would be organizing, while garhettes scurried around, dressing up or dressing down, depending on whether they wanted to be grabbed by an attacking guardian—that is, if they wanted a speed-dating situation that started with a "kidnapping" and ended with the garhette choosing either to stay with the attacking cairn or to free herself (usually violently) and head home. It was a tradition that existed to allow garhettes to get the hell out of their towns without having to break off engagements or make excuses or sneak out in the middle of the night. Odd, but there it was.

With the cairn in a flurry of activity, all watching Jessie's team advance, they'd miss Alpha Steele's team working their way up the mountain. Jessie didn't run a cairn—she co-led a convocation. It was important that *all* their team get to participate. Jessie and Alpha Steele were just about to show the gargoyles how effective magical unity could be.

Jessie tilted a tiny bit to the right, her telltale sign that she was starting to tire but would try to stick it out. Tristan swooped down and grabbed her around the waist. She pulled her wings in and slumped in his hold. The female of the species wasn't made for extended flight. She couldn't even soar properly.

He wondered why they'd evolved like that. Nature baking in a single weakness, perhaps? They didn't seem to have any others.

Jessie pointed, her claw gleaming in the noon sun. "Cooo."

He wasn't sure what she was trying to say. Cool, maybe?

Two weaknesses, then.

Scores of little dwellings surrounded the large stone fortress of Gimerel's main hub. It *was* a cool sight, he had to admit. Formidable, even. Ancient. But dank as all hell. Its bowels weren't exactly pleasant. He'd always hated to spend much time there.

The structure rose three stories into the air, backed against a cliff face. Gothic spires topped two of its towers, host to several lookout windows. Once upon a time, the structure had showcased the pride and joy of Gimerel, a multi-gem bracelet with decent artistry. A statement of wealth for their cairn.

That bracelet was nothing compared to the necklace

and earrings Jessie and Alpha Steele had created with larger gems and impeccable workmanship. Alpha Steele's jeweler had outdone himself, having clearly marveled at the size and quality of precious gems scattered around Ivy House and made something that would shine. Nelson would lose his shit when he saw them. All the wind would go out of his sails when he inevitably compared his wealth to Jessie's...which was the point.

One of the points, anyway.

Nelson still sneered about his lost raid against Ivy House. He'd spun the story to make himself look better. He hadn't left his bracelet behind because of Jessie's team, oh no. He certainly hadn't lost to Jessie herself, an upstart who'd gotten her magic from a house. A Jane. Someone who wasn't fit for gargoyle culture. No, he'd lost solely because of the house. The *house* had trapped him, not Jessie. Without the house, she was nothing.

Today, if everything went according to plan, Jessie would bitch-slap that tired rhetoric. Deniers of her power would be silenced. She wasn't just going to own the leader of Gimerel, one of the most prestigious of all the cairns—she was going to embarrass the hell out of him. *She* would, not the house.

Tristan was giddy with anticipation.

The white vans worked up the side of the mountain.

Alpha Steele and the crew were halfway there. Time to kick things in gear.

Tristan sped up. He wanted to get the timing perfect.

His people spread out around him, a new strategy he'd devised after the battle at Kingsley's. During that skirmish, his people had too easily been scattered. The team turned into individuals, and *that* had turned into far too many deaths.

Now he had pods. Each pod had a team leader and a second, like a mini pack. Instead of scattering individually, they'd scatter in teams. Each pod looked after their other members. This mock battle would be a trial run.

Tristan watched Austin's convoy climb, slowing in some places but not stopping. Tristan had always kept watchers on that road, despite Nelson saying there was no point. And at the time, there hadn't been, honestly. Now there was. Nelson and his new lead enforcer would learn the hard way.

Bodies ran around the grounds, people getting in position. From the distance, he couldn't see any organization.

Come on, come on, Tristan thought impatiently, holding himself back from putting on a burst of speed. He couldn't wait to show Nelson what he'd lost. Nelson's disdain hadn't stopped at Jessie. He'd told everyone about Tristan's muddy history, discounting Tristan's prowess and shrugging off all he'd done for the Gimerel cairn. Nelson was working hard to keep Jessie's and Tristan's statuses as low as possible.

Tristan increased his speed, cutting the distance. Watching Austin. Feeling Jessie's anticipation build through their connection.

Over the cairn, guardians rose into the sky. They spread out over their homestead, using the flight pattern Tristan had devised. Their airborne numbers would top Jessie's.

It wouldn't matter, not even a little. Tristan had learned from Alpha Steele and the shifters, and his strategies and planning had grown in leaps and bounds. He'd come a long way in a short time. Gimerel would feel their wrath.

His heart thudded. Jessie's magic matched it, the drumbeat of war. She fed it through the connections, invigorating them all. Getting them on the same page.

Alpha Steele was nearly to the last tunnel. There, they'd exit their vehicles, shift, and head up the rest of the way in beast form.

Guardians beat their wings above their fortress. At the top, a lone figure walked out onto a wide landing.

Nelson.

He'd watch the battle from his stoop, the way he

always did. He'd probably assume a smug expression as he did so, assured of his victory. He had no idea what he was about to face.

Here we go, Tristan thought, pushing himself to attack speed. Austin's motor brigade stopped. They exited quickly, hyper-organized.

Jessie braced herself within Tristan's grasp. She didn't wiggle to free herself yet. They were still too far away.

Thunder rolled through the sky. It drifted all around them as the great thunderbird flying above the guardians sounded his readiness. Cyra was next to him, probably a streak of fire. Below the guardians were Jessie's immediate crew, Jasper, Ulric, Niamh, and Mr. Tom.

Another peal of thunder reverberated across the valley. Jessie's magic pounded them with anticipation.

The big polar bear emerged from the other side of the tunnel, moving at a measured pace. His shifters followed. Basajaunak ran last. Their purpose would be to scare the absolute hell out of anyone on the ground while the guardians battled above.

Closer now. Nearly above them. Jessie's magic swelled, and the power in it stung his eyes.

She'd grown by leaps and bounds as well. When she'd confronted Gimerel's raid, she'd had training wheels. Now, she was a force to be reckoned with. She had more experience, more determination, and fewer reservations about ruthlessness. She'd found her darkness and learned to bask in it the gargoyle way.

He strained, wanting to fly faster. Wanting to slam into the enemy with everything he had. But he held himself back. They had a spectacle to provide first. The battle would come next.

Tandor Holling flew at the front of the Gimerel guardians. *Huh.* He wouldn't have been Tristan's first pick for the lead enforcer position. He could be ruthless, but he got frazzled much too easily.

Tristan would spin his head around today.

Nelson stood stoically, his hands spread along the stone banister. Tristan could just make out his expression: annoyance. It took him a moment to understand why.

Garhettes crowded the square, stood along the sidewalks, and populated the lanes. They looked at the skies, ignoring their guardians and focusing on who was coming. All ages were present, from those just barely old enough to be on their own to females well advanced in their years. Some wore slinky dresses with made-up faces, customary for finding mates, but others wore pants, long sleeves, and sturdy boots, standing in a way that said they wanted to fight. They didn't have weapons, though. They wanted to be taken, and then they wanted to be armed. They were looking for jobs, not mates.

A rush of pride filled Tristan unexpectedly. All the garhettes from Kingsley's had gone home, back to their lives. It seemed they'd liked the taste of battle, and then they'd told their friends. They were a battle species, after all. They'd been held back because they didn't have wings. But the battle at Kingsley's had proven wings weren't necessary to kick some ass, and now the garhettes wanted an opportunity that Gimerel wasn't providing.

Jessie absolutely would. Gargoyles weren't like shifters: if the raiding cairn could take their opponent's people, they did so gleefully. He'd rob this cairn blind of personnel.

The guardians above the cairn spread out, ready for impact. Tristan drove right at their heart as thunder rolled around them and fire streaked through the sky.

Jessie's power throbbed once, twice, and then her spell tore loose from her outstretched hands. A great wind rose up from near the slope, tossing the clothes and hair of the garhettes before gaining force and slamming into the guardians above. The elemental magic shoved them hard and high, scattering their patterns and tossing some into the turbulent updrafts above. Fire took over, billowing and blasting them, sending them careening into the sides of the mountains or down toward the distant ground.

Her strength and power were incredible. Eye-opening. The garhettes' mouths dropped open, and Nelson took steps away from the stone banister.

Tristan put on a burst of speed.

More spells ripped loose, more explosions aimed at the air next to the guardians so Jessie wouldn't do any real damage. They'd get a thrill, a shock, and they might think she'd missed at first, but soon, it would be obvious she was clearing them out of her way. She didn't need to fight with tooth and claw. The damage she could do from a distance was plenty to win this battle.

Nearly to the cairn, and the guardians were all over the place. Not one had been able to hold their position.

Garhettes looked up at her, dazed and smiling. More than a few put their hands up like children, wanting to be taken with her.

Jessie wiggled, and Tristan flung her toward the gentle slope and the cairn. She caught herself and flew until she was on level with Nelson, twenty feet separating them in the air. Her roar sent a thrill through Tristan's heart, and then she fired off spells, slapping Nelson with magic.

He spun to find cover, trying to duck into the fortress, only to hit a magical wall. A tumult of spells peppered him, shoving him this way and that. He screamed, terror ringing in his voice. Pain.

Magic wafted from Jessie to the town, barely reaching Tristan. Humor, it felt like. Mocking, maybe. Basically, she was letting the cairn know she was toying with Nelson.

That alone would be enough to thoroughly embarrass the cairn leader, which was the point of this raid—make a mockery of him. Jessie and her people wouldn't steal anything. They wouldn't destroy a production cairn. Why would they? Gimerel didn't have anything of value to offer her and Alpha Steele.

No, Jessie would fight her way into his fortress just because she could. And she'd leave a treasure fit for a gargoyle queen, all while her guardians and shifters took Gimerel to task. Her team was superior, as was her leadership, and she'd prove it.

Let Nelson try to spin *that*.

Austin's crew paused in their advance, waiting for Tristan's signal—all except for Sebastian and Nessa, who had already reached the edge of the slope and were sneaking closer to Jessie. Both had taken an invisibility potion and would furnish Jessie with power so she could get the size and strength needed for her spell. The weird mage had learned a few things from Kingsley's battle, too, and they were trying it out here.

The dome glittered into existence. It formed base points on the natural rock face and ground before arching into the sky over the fortress. Jessie slipped into it and turned.

Tristan's wings vibrated the air as Alpha Steele's people exploded into the township. They roared their attack as they spread out in perfect precision. Alpha Steele ran toward Jessie, scattering people before him with screams and shouts. Garhettes dove out of the way. Non-guardian gargoyles looked out windows or peeked through doors to see what was happening, and then ducked back into safety.

Jessie waited for her mate. No one approached her or charged. Nelson stayed trapped on his landing, backed against the wall, staring down with a slack jaw. He'd no doubt want to file grievances for this, but Tristan had planned this attack so that everything was by the book. If those grievances were filed, Tristan would instruct Jessie on how to tear them all down. She had knowledge on her side this time—knowledge and might.

Alpha Steele reached her side, stepped behind her as she faced the rest of the cairn, and roared. His people matched him, followed by the gargoyles in the sky. Tristan snapped out his wings, thrummed them, and prepared for battle.

✧ ✧ ✧

NESSA

"I REALLY THINK I should've gone with them." Nessa watched the dome solidify before Jessie and Austin turned for the castle-type building against the sheer cliff face. The fortress, someone had called it.

The magical dome turned an angry red, and then glossy. That meant it was locked into place. No one could go in—they could only come out. It wasn't as dangerous as the one in Kingsley's territory. That was, apparently, very important for this mock battle...thing. She still didn't really understand the point besides gargoyles being bored.

Jessie started into the fortress with Austin at her back. The guards she'd meet would be nothing she couldn't handle. Tristan had advised that she go in alone, and then he'd shut up promptly when Austin lost his shit. He had gotten so scary, Sebastian started shaking. That alpha would not allow his mate to walk into danger alone ever again.

Nessa's gaze rose. Tristan's huge gargoyle form hung stationary in the sky. The enemy guardians were still trying to get their bearings, some caught in updrafts and others scrambling to organize around a leader without half of Tristan's presence.

"Tristan said it's best for all gossip to be organic," Sebastian said.

She nodded, remembering. It made sense. This way, it wouldn't seem like a publicity stunt. It would seem like one leader proving dominance over another, like in a usual raid, but with a huge twist.

Patty had agreed with Tristan, even though she *had* wanted to see it in person. The story would just be too juicy not to share. Imagine not stealing something, but rather going through all this trouble to give a gift?

No one had ever done anything like this. No one had the money or power *to* do something like this. Jessie couldn't be faulted because she'd risked her reputation and status to give something back, bolstering the cairn and improving its wealth. This was a classy move...even though a large portion of it was directly mocking the cairn leadership.

Meanwhile, Tristan would show Nelson what he was really capable of. That, with better leadership, Tristan could shine as brightly as the sun.

She stared up at his beautiful gargoyle form, a metallic teal that burned blue when he moved.

I've got you. I won't let anyone get to you.

His arms had held her so tightly, thoroughly chasing away all her nightmares. She couldn't remember ever sleeping so soundly, could never forget how it felt to wake up next to that hard body, his delicious smell, the throbbing length pushed against her backside—

She shivered.

"You okay?" Sebastian asked, looking in concern at what she knew was her flushed face.

"Yeah." She shook it off. "Yup. Just waiting for the show to start."

She hadn't gotten a chance to turn over. She still didn't know if she would've. He'd roused, kissed her shoulder, and excused himself from her room.

"I'll give you a chance to put your walls back up, little angel," he'd said, winking. "When I win you over, it won't be because you need me to. It'll be because you couldn't resist wanting me to."

With that, he'd sauntered out. The gargoyle-monster liked to play games.

Joke was on him. He'd passed up his chance. She *had* put her walls back up and steeled herself, filing away all the mushy rawness that the day before had wrung out of her. She'd strapped on her armor and was ready for battle. He liked to play games? Great. So did she.

"I would've loved to see the setup in that fortress," Nessa murmured as a basajaun roared, running by. Three garhettes screamed and dove out of his way. They rolled to a stop and turned to look, their eyes wide.

Even from behind, Nessa could see the basajaun heaving with laughter. He was probably thinking, *Did you see their faces?!*

Tristan's gargoyles flew around him as if they were one entity. The effect was almost like a patchwork blanket moving across the sky.

"Wow," Sebastian whispered. "He's gotten better at commanding those gargoyles."

He had. A *lot* better.

The enemy guardians looked like a mess of fliers, flapping their wings at various distances apart, at various heights, clustered in some areas and too spread out in others. The leader flew in front of them, tense where Tristan looked utterly composed and confident.

"This cairn has bigger guardians," Sebastian said. "I mean, not all of them, but there are a lot more of the bigger gargoyles in this cairn compared to ours."

"Yeah, not to mention more guardians in general. For this battle, anyway." Nessa chewed her lip, suddenly nervous. "He needs to win. This all falls apart if he doesn't."

The enemy guardians were all together now. Their leader snapped his wings, then darted forward. His people started behind him haphazardly.

Tristan snapped his wings in turn, but his people matched his advance, perfectly synchronized and holding their pattern. They were clearly much more disciplined, even though they weren't as prestigious as the Gimerel cairn guardians.

"Tristan is showing that he's a *much* better commander," Sebastian whispered, watching the sky. Everyone on the ground was doing the same, the basajaunak and shifters having stopped trying to intimidate so they could look up.

"But will his people be enough?" Nessa picked at her nail. They certainly looked like the underdogs, not as large, as Sebastian had noticed. Not as robust or strong in flight. Not as numerous.

The two groups closed the distance. Gargoyles growled or roared. Hands came out to grapple. At the last moment, Tristan's gargoyles changed pattern. Small groups separated, some going high and some low. Tristan plowed through at the same level, knocking people away like a bowling ball headed for a strike.

The enemy startled, pausing in confusion at the change. Tristan's people took advantage. The groups who went high dove down now. They singled out one or two and swarmed, tearing the enemy out of the sky in short order, not killing, per the rules, just maiming. As the rest of the enemy recovered, the groups who'd gone low sped upward and punched through enemy clusters, breaking up any group effort and scattering enemy formations. Those at the back of Tristan's formation sped forward, further bursting the enemy's organization apart. As they did, they picked off guardians, reducing their numbers. It was like the inside of a washing machine, surging and twisting.

The enemy scattered, and any pretense of planning vanished.

That was what Tristan had been going for.

He thrummed his wings, giving a command. Then the real battle started. His people attacked viciously, groups going after the largest and strongest enemy gargoyles first. It was nothing like the battle at Ivy House, where there had seemed to be gargoyles everywhere, utter chaos. This was organized and systematic, Tristan maneuvering his people with obvious accuracy.

"Holy crap." Sebastian gave Nessa a toothy grin. "His gargoyles are *sensational*. He's leveled up, big time."

He certainly had. He was doing the convocation and Ivy House proud.

Cyra and Hollace didn't participate. Hollace pulled up high, into the updrafts that had given the enemy gargoyles a real problem. His great wings fluttered and rolled with the turbulence, but the winds didn't bring him down or send him careening away. Cyra dove around him and fought the gales. Fire flew every which way.

"Look." Nessa pointed them out to Sebastian. "They're playing."

"They're letting Tristan beat the cairn on his own. That way, Nelson can't say Tristan cheated and used legendary creatures to take down Gimerel guardians. Smart."

"Yeah." But even that seemed to open eyes. Garhettes were pointing, and people came out of their homes or the shops to look. "Are they marveling because Hollace and Cyra are very cool creatures or because they're strong fliers?"

Sebastian shook his head. He didn't know.

Niamh was nowhere to be found. Probably soaring below, or maybe back at the van and her cooler. She wasn't one to sit around empty-handed.

The enemy started to fall, the equivalent of limping in the sky. They sank out of the battle and struggled to their home slope. Once there, the basajaunak grabbed them and put them into a group before standing over them and roaring. Shifters walked through the crowds again, back to intimidating.

It turned out the garhettes *liked* intimidating creatures. They trailed after the shifters with sparkling eyes and hopeful smiles. Tristan had explained about the fake kidnapping thing—garhettes usually liked to play hard to get. These didn't. They were all but begging to be taken.

Only the biggest and strongest of the enemy guardians were left, including their leader. They tried to regroup, struggling to get back to each other. Tristan's team was there, though, blocking their way. Separate and conquer. He handled them expertly.

"I have *never* seen one of these go so quickly," one garhette said to another as they wandered closer. They didn't feel Nessa's and Sebastian's presences. Their heavily lined eyes were trained on the sky, and slinky dresses hugged their curves. Each was beautiful and clearly wanting a ride out of there. "Nelson never should've let Tristan go. It hurt our whole cairn."

"For many reasons," the second purred as she fixed the bust of her dress, pushing her cleavage up and out.

"He's hardly had any losses. They're working together better than any cairn that's ever attacked. He doesn't even have as good of guardians, and he's dominated this battle!"

"Maybe next, he'll dominate me."

The first huffed at her friend. "You tried that, remember? He didn't date you any longer than he dated anyone else. He doesn't settle down. He's always been very clear about that."

"You're just jealous because he never went after you."

"*I* never went after *him*. I don't chase, and neither does he."

"Well"—the second shrugged—"he didn't used to settle down, maybe, but now he has a cairn that respects him. Nelson always made him feel temporary because of his past or whatever. But I hear the female doesn't care about that. If he feels some security and permanence, he'll be looking. We got along well, he and I."

"He got along well with everyone. There wasn't one person he pined after or worshipped. He was too busy thinking about himself and playing his games. I'm telling you, you're wasting your time on that gargoyle. He's the playboy who never takes things too seriously. Wouldn't you rather have someone you can count on?"

The second waved that away. "I can count on myself. There aren't any garhettes in his cairn, or whatever they call it. Not that he wants, anyway. He's probably going to take this opportunity to snag one of his kind." She adjusted her hair. "Hell, even if it's just for a while, I'll take it," she murmured as an afterthought. "He was always the best of the bunch. I had *fun* with him."

A strange, uncomfortable feeling tightened Nessa's stomach. She glanced at the women, wondering what had triggered it. It couldn't be calling Tristan a playboy—he was, and had no reservations about his antics. He didn't boast or hide them or care much at all, honestly. Very few gargoyles did. She liked that about them, the openness. They didn't slut-shame or call women down for behavior they themselves enjoyed. It was liberating.

Jealousy? Laughable. The thought barely crossed her mind before she discounted it. She *truly* didn't care about him with other women. It was surface level for him, and she shared the same philosophy. They were a little too similar in that way. In *many* ways, she had to own.

Wouldn't you rather have someone you can count on?

Her stomach tightened again, and she dragged her lip through her teeth before looking away. She had counted on him that other night. Greatly. A part of her wanted to count on him still. Wanted someone strong and mean and familiar with the shadows in order to guard her in a way she hadn't dared let anyone. She wanted someone to handle the beasties for her, like he'd always promised. Maybe someone to grant her a safe haven so she could work on herself, so she could maybe heal a little.

That wasn't his jam, though. She knew that. Hell, these women knew that. Their whole cairn did, it sounded like. He liked to play games, to stay aloof, and to keep his secrets.

But maybe…

She picked at her nail again.

Maybe it was time she put herself out there. Not for guys like him, who didn't trust and didn't want to, but for someone else who might not balk at what she was and what she'd done.

Or maybe she was feeling sappy after coming home. After realizing that Jessie and Austin and the Ivy House crew felt like family, and she wanted to belong with them in a way she had never dared to belong with anyone but Sebastian and his sister.

Hell, she didn't know. This was all getting much too complicated.

"Anyway," she whispered, even though this invisibility spell also had soundproofing qualities. She shook her head and stared at the fortress. She could feel Sebastian looking at her. "What?"

He didn't respond, and when she glanced his way, his eyes were deep and sorrowful and troubled. She knew that look.

"Stop." She rolled her eyes and turned away again. "The past is in the past. We have a team now, and we're going to be okay."

"I know."

"Right. Well then, stop looking at me like that."

"But are *you* going to be okay?"

Jessie and Austin stepped out of the fortress in their human forms, nude and hand in hand.

"Wait…" One of the garhettes who'd been talking paused for a moment. "Wait, didn't she go in with a satchel? I saw that, didn't I?"

"I don't know, but she doesn't have anything now. Neither of them does."

The first garhette took a few steps that way, hands on her hips. The gargoyles above circled, forgotten by most of those on the ground for now. "It doesn't look like she took anything."

The other stepped forward to stay at her side. "You're *sure* she had—"

Another garhette jogged over with a crooked smile. This one wore sturdy clothes. "She had a bag going in there, did you see that?" She mimed something around her middle. "It was orange with black writing. Did you see it?"

"Yes! But now she doesn't have anything at all. Did she put something in there?"

"What would—"

"Come on." Sebastian plucked at Nessa's sleeve before standing. "Let's get to the road."

Another couple of garhettes hurried over as Sebastian and Nessa edged around them.

Jessie waved her hand and tore down the dome. She

turned then, once again giving Nelson her attention. Her voice boomed, enhanced by magic. "I'm sure you'll be tempted to file every grievance you can think of, but I have knowledge on my side now. I'll fight every single one, but hear this—I'll fight them on principle alone. I will fight them so that you don't have a leg to stand on. Rest assured, I don't care one bit about status in a community that looks to you for guidance. A community that wipes out the status of a gargoyle who's put in fifteen years of excellence because you don't approve of his origins. Your opinions don't rule me, and they don't rule Tristan. Your derision is nothing more than the ramblings of an old, out-of-touch gargoyle. I've proven here today that I can fight, that I *will* fight, and that my team is excellent in battle. We used but a portion of our people, and that was plenty." She waved her hand, and the sheen of magic trapping him in vanished. "Get a good look, Nelson, because this is as close as I will *ever* come to working with you. I have nothing against your cairn, just you specifically. Our door is open if any of Tristan's old team want to work with him again"—she turned and swept her gaze across the township—"and if any garhettes want to see how it feels to have their blood sing. Battle isn't just for men. I think I'm proof of that, no?"

She walked forward with her head held high and a

confident bearing. Austin remained at her side, his power pumping and his gaze fierce.

Shifters fell in with the precision they were known for—with the precision Tristan had shown above.

Basajaunak looked around for a moment, not following. "We get to kidnap now, right?" one of them said to another.

"I think that's just for the gargoyles," the other replied hesitantly.

One of the garhettes in sturdy clothes slowly raised her hand. "I mean...you know...for the fighting..."

The scene burst into mayhem. Basajaunak raced this way and that, male and female alike, grabbing up the garhettes who obviously wanted to join their ranks. They bore down on those ladies with teeth and snarls and their fur puffed out on their huge bodies.

Many of the garhettes screamed. Some ran, while others just clenched their fists and squeezed their eyes shut, stiff as boards. The basajaunak caught them and threw them over wide shoulders—that, or carried them under an arm. One held two garhettes, dangling them by their ankles.

"Right, but how are we going to get them all to the camp?" Jessie asked in confusion as she walked through the melee. "The additional transportation won't reach us until tomorrow. Should I fly back? Or rather, be flown back? I'm exhausted. I won't make it far."

"No, you can ride with me. We'll figure out space," Austin said, barely heard above the pandemonium as he reached Nessa and Sebastian. "The basajaunak will probably be fine to run. For them, it isn't too far."

"Here." Sebastian held out the potion that would turn them visible again to Nessa. She swallowed it down as gargoyles dove and swooped. These didn't only grab the battle-ready garhettes—some grabbed the ladies in dresses and one a man in a suit.

Nessa stepped aside as her potion wore off, not wanting a jogging basajaunak, caught up in the fun, to accidentally trample her. The shifters passed, a few nodding at her as they did so. At the end of their line, she started forward, only to hear the heavy beat of huge wings.

She startled, looking up. Tristan descended in a rush of power and strength, his arms out. She twisted to get out of the way, but he was too fast. He grabbed her around the middle and hoisted her up, gentle for a creature of his size. He gathered her close in a tight hold and blasted into the air.

Other gargoyles were already up there. The captives in their arms kicked and punched and twisted. They were all obviously idiots. Did they *want* to fall?

She thought about wrapping her arms and legs

around him in a death grip. That would give her some assurance of safety. Instead, she relaxed into his arms and let him have control, like she had that other night.

He cradled her against his chest, one massive arm around her shoulders and the other at the back of her legs. His hold was firm and strong, and the last of her worry bled away.

"*Goo-od,*" he said, and she smiled with the praise, then laughed. But it was a fun game. One she would be the victor of. She did love to win. Self-discovery could wait.

✧　✧　✧

PETER

"Pete, you hurt?"

Peter shook uncontrollably as he crouched behind a stone outcropping at the base of the fortress. This area badly needed to be refurbished, but fifteen minutes ago, he'd been glad for it. It had given him something to hide behind when that monstrous beast descended on him and something sharp and painful smacked him side-ways.

He looked up at his friend John, the other senior guard selected to monitor the cairn's most prestigious collection of wealth—mostly jewels and gold, in this case. Any textiles would be ruined in the dank surroundings of this area, a place no one really wanted to guard for long.

"I...I don't know," he answered, patting himself. No blood, no holes in his uniform. No evidence of what had caused the pain. He said as much.

"Magic, bro." John hoisted him up with rounded eyes in a somewhat comical expression. He didn't take much seriously. It's why he'd failed to become a guardian. "She zapped me good. I went ass over end. Badass, though, right?" He tsked. "That female gargoyle is something. All that magic, bro?" He nodded. "Badass. I wish we had one."

Peter wasn't sure he did. Training with her would hurt more.

"I was more worried about that...bear thing," Peter admitted as he gave himself another once-over. "What was that? A polar bear, right? One of those shifters? It happened so fast, I didn't get a good look."

"A polar bear, yeah." John passed Peter by, aiming for the entrance of the small room at the back. "Pretty hardcore. If I hadn't been flung, I might've pissed myself, yeah?" He chuckled. "Ah, they weren't trying to hurt us. They never do in these things. Just scare us."

"It w-worked," Peter stammered.

"Nah." John let out his breath in a whoosh as he entered the room. "Nelson is going to be pissed they got through, though."

"It's not like we c-could stop them," Peter said, following.

"True enough—" John tensed and leaned forward in a rush. "What in the hell?"

The glass case had been left atop the stone pedestal in the center of the room. Instead of it being empty or broken, it actually had *more* in it than when the day started. The dangly earrings, the newest addition from their production cairn, had been pushed to the corner. In the middle...

Peter rubbed his eyes and looked again as John grinned and said, "No way, bro!"

Their bracelet was back! The bracelet from their production cairn that the female gargoyle had unlawfully taken, and that Tristan hadn't forced her to give back, was returned to the case!

That wasn't all. Displayed beside it were two new pieces: a large and intricate necklace with a bunch of fat and well-cut gems and a pair of earrings that put their latest creation to absolute shame. In fact, they put the bracelet to shame too.

"Bro..." John whispered, snapping photos with his phone. He wasn't supposed to have that when he was on duty for one of these things—he was supposed to use the landlines. Not that he ever cared. He opened his text app and entered in a bunch of people.

"Wait, maybe we should wait for Nelson," Peter said hesitantly.

"Why?" John loaded up the pictures and hit send before showing Peter his widened eyes in that comical expression. "She *busted* in here, beat all our people to do it, and put the bracelet back!" He hopped up and down, pointing at the additional pieces. "And those? Are you kidding me right now?" He bent with his fist to his mouth. "She didn't need our bracelet at all. I heard she just left it on the table near the couch, out for anyone to take. She just *left* it there. I didn't believe it, but if she's got *this* kinda stuff floatin' around...and she breaks in here to hand it back?" He laughed with glee. "Maybe we need a job with her. How much money do you think she has? I mean...she picked up Tristan, right? He was Nelson's pride and—"

"What's going on in here?" Nelson demanded as he strode in.

With a sleight of hand that really should've landed John with a thief job, he tucked his phone into his pocket as he and Peter quickly backed out of the way.

"What is this?" Nelson leaned over the glass case. He tensed before stepping even closer, looking down in disbelief. His angry flush turned into pale, incredulous shock. He rounded on them. "Tell *no one*! Do you hear me? Tell no one about this."

"But sir, they're going to know." John gave a hesitant shrug. "She came in with stuff, but she didn't leave with anything. I mean…see? There's her bag…thing." He pointed at the item on the floor.

"Tell *no one*," Nelson fumed, spit flying. He snapped his finger toward the door. "Get out!"

Peter and John wasted no time. When they heard footsteps running down the corridor, the guardians probably rushing to see what was taken, the two ducked out of the way and hid until the coast was clear.

"You didn't tell him about the pictures," Peter whispered as they hurried up the steps.

"No, are you kidding? I don't want to have an *accident*, know what I'm saying? Nelson didn't seem to be in his right mind." John swallowed. "I think…" He licked his lips. "I think it might be time to get out of here. I'm tired of this detail, anyway. One of the smaller cairns will take me, I bet. I bet a garhette will even be interested. We hardly raid anymore. I need fresh blood."

Or someone who hadn't heard all his stories and jokes ten times over, Peter mused.

"Or maybe…" Peter scratched his head. "What about that female gargoyle? I heard once that she treats her cairn like a safe haven. I didn't believe it, but…well, some of the other stuff seems true. She *is* really powerful, and she clearly does have a bunch of money. Maybe she'll take us."

"*Us?*"

"Well…yeah. I saw the whole thing. He can claim those pictures are manipulated or whatever and get rid of the evidence." He paused. "I'm part of the evidence. *We* are."

"Come on!" John tugged at his arm. "If we hurry, we can catch the fliers, or at least see where they land. There are only a few places they can set up a camp within the allowed distance."

Peter started to jog with him. "What about the pictures?"

"I'll tell everyone in this cairn to keep their mouths shut."

"*This* cairn?"

"Yeah, bro. They don't want to be silenced any more than we do. If they don't say anything, no one will know about them knowing, follow me?"

"What other cairns did you send it to?"

"I gotta group of guys I see every year from a few different cairns. Look, who cares? It doesn't matter. Nelson can't mess with them, and we're gonna be gone. Hurry up, we gotta get out of here."

Nelson didn't used to be like this. He didn't used to be so…dirty in his dealings. The older he got, the more extremely he seemed to react. It probably was a good time to go. Besides, Peter liked the way that female worked. This was a pretty funny stunt. It surely flung dirt in ol' Nelson's eye. And she had Tristan. Everyone always said that gargoyle was the best they'd ever had. Nelson was dumb for letting him go. They seemed like the better team, if he had to choose, and it seemed he did.

Except, when they got out of the fortress, it quickly became apparent that containing the story would be impossible. People were already looking at their phones, pointing, smiling, and laughing.

"I *told you* she went in with a bag and came out empty-handed," someone was saying.

"Did you see it?" a garhette who usually never gave John or Peter the time of day asked as they passed by.

John slowed, stars in his eyes.

"Did you see what she left?" the garhette repeated. She showed the picture on her phone. It must've already been forwarded. Damage control was nonexistent.

"Yes!" John opened his mouth, spread his hands, and made an *oh my God* expression. "The necklace? The earrings?" He half spun around. A group of people hurried over to hear. "Out. Of. This. *World!* I about fell over, didn't I, Pete? It made that bracelet look like nothing."

"So, it was real?" she pushed.

"Come on, man." Peter yanked at John. "We don't want to get caught having sent the pictures."

"Yeah, it was real, all right. I've guarded that bracelet for years. It was *definitely* our bracelet. The other jewelry, though? I'm no expert, but it was *fine* workmanship, and it was worth *a lot*. Even if it was fake—which it definitely wasn't—she didn't have to bring anything at all. Usually, people take things, not give them."

"Come on!" Peter yanked at him again.

"I gotta go," John told the group, looking back at the fortress. "Nelson's going to try to cover it up, bet you anything. He told us to get out. He meant business. I don't need an accident, know what I'm saying? I know people who've gotten those in the past. They didn't move on to other cairns—they moved into unmarked graves. Not for me, thank you very much!"

"Dude, shut *up*!" Peter yanked at him yet again. They had no proof. It was almost certainly true—the rumors said it was true, and they'd lost some friends they hadn't been able to find again—but there was no proof. Hearing it from John, the bystanders would think there was.

Regardless, that female gargoyle had made a helluva statement here today. The story of it would echo throughout the gargoyle community. If it was intended to be political, she'd probably just granted herself the upper hand with her show of generosity. Their plan had been well designed. Nelson had his work cut out for him to come out on top of this one, and Peter wanted to be long gone during the fallout.

THE END.

ABOUT THE AUTHOR

K.F. Breene is a Wall Street Journal, USA Today, Washington Post, Amazon Most Sold Charts and #1 Kindle Store bestselling author of paranormal romance, urban fantasy and fantasy novels. With millions of books sold, when she's not penning stories about magic and what goes bump in the night, she's sipping wine and planning shenanigans. She lives in Northern California with her husband, two children, and out of work treadmill.

Sign up for her newsletter to hear about the latest news and receive free bonus content.

www.kfbreene.com

www.ingramcontent.com/pod-product-compliance
Ingram Content Group UK Ltd.
Pitfield, Milton Keynes, MK11 3LW, UK
UKHW041106021025
8186UKWH00042B/494